Rescuing Kassie

Rescuing Kassie

Delta Force Heroes

Book 5

By Susan Stoker

Table of Contents

Chapter One

To: Graham
From: Kassie
Subject: Hi

Hi Graham. My name is Kassie. I saw your profile on the Matches-R-Us website and thought you looked interesting. I'd love to talk.

~Kassie

To: Graham
From: Kassie
Subject: It's me again

Hi Graham. It's me, Kassie (again). I messaged you last week, but never heard back. I thought I'd try again in case my message got lost in the midst of the hundreds of other messages you get on a weekly basis. *grin*

How about if I tell you a little about me? Maybe if you know me better you might consider writing back. I've lived in Austin my entire life. I have a sister who is a senior in high school. She and my parents live in the Barton Creek area, which is just west of Austin (in case you didn't know). I'm thirty and am the manager at the retail clothing store, JCPenney. I'm not tall or short. Just in between at 5'6".

Darn. I tried to think of something more interesting about me...but couldn't.

Anyway, it looks like you were fishing in your profile picture. I've been fishing, but didn't catch a darn thing. But I liked the boat ride. :)

Anyway, that's me. I hope to hear from you.

~Kassie

To: Graham
From: Kassie
Subject: I'm a shapeshifting werewolf...

...who is about to go into my mating lust...

grin

Okay, that's a lie (duh), but you probably have lots and lots of emails with boring subjects like "hi" and "you're cute."

I figure since you haven't answered my other two you aren't interested, but I thought I'd try one more time in case you had a psycho ex hacking into your profile and deleting all your messages.

Anyway, I have nothing else to convince you to give me a chance.

I'm nobody special. I'm not rich. I'm not beautiful. I'm not super smart and I don't have an exciting job. I just thought that you looked like the kind of man who was like me. Boring and normal.

Shit, I didn't mean boring like *boring*, but...I'll just shut up now before I dig myself in deeper. lol

Now that I've probably insulted you and you're rolling your eyes wondering why in the heck I messaged you, and why you're even still reading this, I'll leave you alone.

I hope you find what you're looking for from this website. Good luck.

~Kassie

To: Kassie
From: Graham
Subject: Re: I'm a shapeshifting werewolf...

Now you have my attention. *grin*

The reason I haven't messaged you back is because I don't check this profile very often. To be honest, I only signed up for Matches-R-Us because my buddies kinda egged me into it. I usually don't even reply to any messages I get. I should delete my profile, but for some reason, I haven't.

So why am I writing you back? Because you made me laugh. Out loud. One of the things I appreciate most in a woman is a sense of humor.

As you know, my name is Graham. I like to fish. I'm about six feet tall and I'm thirty-two. I'm in the Army and live near Fort Hood.

I can't say that anyone has called me boring before…but I like that description. :) I'm just a man doing his duty for his country who likes to hang out with his friends and have an occasional beer.

So why are you looking for a guy on a dating website? From what I can see from your profile picture, you're pretty and don't look like a big hairy shapeshifting werewolf. lol

I look forward to chatting with you more.

~Graham

To: Graham
From: Kassie
Subject: Looks can be deceiving

I don't look like a big hairy werewolf in my profile picture because I'm in my human form…silly. *grin*

But seriously, to be honest, the picture is about four years old, although I pretty much look the same as I did back then. Plain brown hair, hazel eyes, not fat, but not skinny either. I hate to work out, and I'm assuming since you're in the Army, you don't. I've just never seen the point, since I hate it. I do try to be healthy though…you know…park in the spaces at the back of the lot, take the stairs when I can, things like that. But the gym? No.

What do you do for the Army? What's your MOS? (Aren't you impressed that I know that acronym? Don't be too impressed though…I Googled "Army acronyms" and that one came up. Ha!) I once dated a guy who was in the Army, and if I'm being honest, he was too gung-ho for me. I hope you're not one of those men who says "hooah" all the time.

My ex used to grunt it when he...well, you know. *gag*

You should know, I'm much more entertaining online than I am in person. I'm an introvert for the most part...and yes, I know it's weird that I'm a manager but I don't like being around people. I *can* be, but if I had a choice, I'd stay home. All I'm saying is that you shouldn't get used to me being funny. I clam up around people I don't know and I'm the kind of person who figures out the perfect comeback about two hours too late. (Did you see that *Seinfeld* episode? OMG, hilarious when George Costanza did that... "The jerk store called and they're running out of you!" HAHAHAHAHAHA)

Okay, it wasn't that funny, but that's totally me. And my sense of humor is decidedly warped. If we ever met in person, I'd probably offend you and three out of four people we were standing around.

I'd love to hear more about you. Parents? Siblings? When you sit around and drink beer with your friends do you drink a couple, or an entire twelve-pack? I'm interested in whatever you want to tell me!

I gotta go, the moon is full and I'm feeling the need to shift. *grin*

~Kassie

To: Kassie
From: Graham
Subject: It's not safe...

It's not safe to park in the back of a lot. I think it's great that you want to get a few extra steps in, but you shouldn't put yourself at risk to get them. Especially if you're working retail. I assume you sometimes work when it's dark? Do me a favor, and get your extra steps some other way. :)

As far as what I do, I can't say a lot about my job...you know, OPSEC and all... (Since you Googled acronyms, you should know what that means. :)) But I can tell you that I'm a 21B.

And believe me, the last thing I'd *ever* say if I was with a woman would be hooah...if you know what I mean. :)

There's nothing wrong with being an introvert. And I'm not just saying that. I'm well past the days where I want to hang out in a bar or club. Sitting at home and enjoying a good dinner, conversation, and maybe a movie or television show sounds like a perfect way to spend a night. But no worries, I can hold my own in public situations, so you can just hang back and observe.

And I bet you're hilarious in person...you just don't think you are. Anyone who can quote George Costanza is seriously cool in my eyes. And now I don't have to worry about offending you with *my* sarcastic streak. So yay!

Like you, I have a little sister. Her name is Jade. She's only two years younger than me. She currently lives in Chapel Hill, and teaches at the University of North Carolina. She got all the brains in the family. *grin*

And no worries, Kass, I like a good brew every now and then, but I am in no way close to being an alcoholic. I take too much pride in being in shape to do that to myself. The soldiers I work with rely on me to be able to have their six just as I do them. But good for you for asking.

So, do you have to wait for the moon to be full to shift, or can you do it at will?

Later, Graham

To: Graham
From: Kassie
Subject: Are you one of those guys…

…who buys his woman a gun and makes her take self-defense lessons to make sure she's "safe?" Don't you know that we're much more likely to be in a car accident than held up at gunpoint or assaulted? But…I get your point. When I have to close the store, I always park under a light and have security escort me to my car. And, before you tell me that I can't trust the security guards because they're usually underpaid and could actually assault me, I already know that. I always call one of my friends before we leave and she stays on the line until I get into my car and the doors are locked.

Actually, talking with you is probably the most "unsafe" thing I've done in a long time. You could be a sixty-three-year-old serial killer who has trolled the Internet for pictures of good looking men to use on your profile to lure women into his clutches. And yes, I know the reverse could also be true…but lucky for you, it's not. I really am Kassie Anderson. Thirty years old. And I live in the Austin area. Although I've thought about moving. Sometimes you just need to get away from your past…you know? Know anyone who has an apartment for rent up your way? Just kidding…sorta.

But thanks for being worried about my safety.

So, you're a combat engineer huh? (You have to be im-

7

pressed at my Googling skills now! *grin*) Mines, bridges, and stuff. Sounds…boring. lol (Sorry, that was mean.) Seriously, you must be pretty smart then. Probably too smart for me. (And I don't believe your sister got all the brains in the family, so whatever.)

You're a guy…can you clear something up for me? Why in the world do men feel it necessary to send pictures of their dicks to women online? I don't get it. Do they think I'm going to open up their messages and be like "OMG, what a huge dick! I must message him back now and demand to meet in a back alley so I can get up close and personal with it." I mean seriously, if I'm being honest, penises are just weird looking as it is. Hanging down, flapping around, why in the world would a guy think it's okay (or sexy, or cool) to send a picture of his dick to a woman he's never met or talked to?

Now, I get the reverse is probably not gross to guys. If all of a sudden women started sending pictures of their boobs to random men, I'm pretty sure they'd be all for it. Like, "Oh yeah, I got three more tit pictures today! Hooah." (See what I did there? *giggle*)

Anyway, maybe you can explain it to me, because I just don't get it. (And that is along the same lines of a guy whistling at a woman on the street. Does he think the woman is going to be all flattered and walk up and ask him out? It just doesn't make sense to me.)

And on that note, I've probably overstepped whatever boundaries we're supposed to have on here. There's probably a Matches-R-Us employee monitoring our messages and I'll log in tomorrow and find out that I've been kicked off the site for bringing up the "dick pic" issue. :)

I hope you had a good day today. Mine was fine. Dealt

with assholes all day who blamed me for their credit cards being declined, and insisted that the clothes they wanted to buy were actually on the fifty-percent-off rack and not the ten-percent one...when it was obvious they just peeled the sticker off a shirt and stuck it on the one they wanted to buy. (Told you my life was boring.)

I don't think I've said it yet, but thank you for your service to our country. I know sometimes people don't like to hear that, but wanted to say it anyway. Thank you.

~Kassie

To: Kassie
From: Graham
Subject: No. Just no.

I have no idea why men would think sending pictures of their junk is cool. Or sexy. Or that a woman they didn't know would want to even see that shit. With that said...I don't think I'd want to see pictures of random boobs, but feel free to send yours...

KIDDING! :) I'm not a perv. I admit that I've scrolled through Tumblr a few times and seen my share of nakedness, but in today's digital world, everything can be monitored. Texts, emails, phone calls, and yes, even our messages here on Matches-R-Us. There is no such thing as a hack-proof system. Remember that, Kassie. No matter what you say, or to who, it can always come back to either bite you in the ass or help you.

I'm sorry you have to deal with assholes. I have to as

well, but not in the same way as you…at least I can shoot them. *grin* Kidding. (Sort of.)

And good job on Googling my MOS. :) Just think, twenty years ago that kind of information at your fingertips was impossible. It certainly makes a criminal or terrorist's job easier sometimes. Speaking of which, if you don't hear from me for periods of time, don't panic. It's just work. Sometimes I can't log in if I'm busy on the job.

With that being said, I like you, Kassie Anderson (and if your name was any more unique, I would scold you for giving me your full name, age, and where you live…but since there are over a hundred and fifty women with the name Kassie Anderson in a hundred-mile radius around Austin, I won't give you too much crap—and yes, I looked you up!). We've been messaging back and forth for a while now and I can say with one hundred percent certainty that I'd like to get to know you better. Would you ever consider meeting in person? We can do it however you like. I can drive down there, it's only about an hour or so, or you can come up here. We'll keep it to a public place so you'll feel safe.

And so you know, I've never done this before. Never wanted to meet anyone I've talked to online. And I'm not blowing smoke up your ass. Think about it.

~Graham

To: Graham
From: Kassie
Subject: I'm sorry

I'm sorry I haven't written in a while. I admit, your last message freaked me out. I mean, it shouldn't have, because I like you too, but I got to thinking about how stupid it was to talk with a man I don't really know online. Then how much stupider I'd be to meet you in person.

But the fact of the matter is that I *want* to. I never thought I'd ever be interested in someone else in the Army after my experience with my ex. Austin isn't really a straight-laced military town, if you know what I mean. But after thinking about it, I decided I don't really have a choice. I'm really drawn to you and would like to give it a shot.

But Graham, please know, when I first messaged you, I didn't think you'd write me back. I thought it was a lark. That I'd shoot you a note or two, and you'd ignore me, and that would be that. But then you *did* reply. I got swept up in how nice you were, and forgot that real life romances don't typically work out for me. There's a reason I'm an introvert.

So whatever happens, it's not you, it's totally me. Okay?

~Kassie

To: Kassie
From: Graham
Subject: Don't apologize

I'm sorry I freaked you out. It wasn't my intention at all.

Real life romances don't work out for you? You *are* who is depicted in your profile picture...right? Because I find that woman fascinating. You look like the girl next door...and I have to tell you, I had a crush on my next-door neighbor all the way through elementary school. She was in middle school, wore glasses, and would sit on her back deck and do homework every night. *grin*

All I'm asking for is a meet. We'll take it from there.

And don't think I didn't catch that there's something else going on with you than what you wrote. I'm pretty observant, and can read between the lines. But we'll keep it low-key. Yeah?

I hope you had a good week at work and didn't have to shoot anyone. :)

~Graham

To: Graham
From: Kassie
Subject: No shooting

You'll be glad to know I didn't have to shoot anyone today...but it was close. *grin* We probably shouldn't be joking about that, you know (but I think it's funny anyway).

Thanks for understanding about the meeting thing. I'll continue to think about it.

Do you happen to watch *Criminal Minds*? It was crazy creepy last night. I have a pretty warped mind, and see bad guys behind every corner, but that was insane! Garcia is my hero though. There's no way in real life information can be gotten as easily as she gets it, but it's still fun to watch (and yes, I remember what you said about everything being able to get hacked and tracked, and it might be sick of me but I think that's pretty cool...especially because if you kill me, all our messages will be around for someone to find and track you down). *grin*

Okay, I'm exhausted. I'm going to keep this short. Hope your week went well.

~Kassie

P.S. Do you have a nickname? I've been thinking about it and in all the movies and shows I've watched, military guys have cool ones. :)

To: Kassie
From: Graham
Subject: Nickname

I do have a nickname. It's Hollywood. You know how these things come about, right? Usually it's something embarrassing a soldier does or says, or how they look, and their buddies christen them with a name and it sticks. So yeah, Hollywood. I was told once that I was so pretty I should be in Hollywood. Of course one of my asshole friends overheard it, and that was that.

I didn't see the episode of *Criminal Minds* the other night, but I'm gonna look it up online now. If you got freaked, I wanna know why...so I can keep the monsters at bay in the future. And you'd be surprised at how much information can be at someone's fingertips...

I need to go to a friend's wedding today, but I wanted to send you a short note and let you know I was thinking about you. Have a good weekend.

~Hollywood

To: Graham
From: Kassie
Subject: I like it

I like your nickname. I examined your profile picture again (okay, I admit it...I've looked at it quite a few times), and even though you're wearing a baseball cap and it's pulled down low over your eyes, you do kinda remind me of Colin Egglesfield. :)

I'm sorry I haven't been around. Work's been crazy.

~Kassie

To: Kassie
From: Graham
Subject: Checking in

I just wanted to check in. I haven't heard from you in a while. Everything okay? I miss our messages.

~Hollywood

To: Graham
From: Kassie
Subject: Just busy

I'm good. Just busy.

That's kinda a lie. I'm a mess. You should delete all contact info for me and forget I exist. Seriously. For your own good.

~Kassie

To: Kassie
From: Graham
Subject: I can't

I can't forget about you. Somehow you've crawled under my skin and I can't stop thinking about you. And now I'm worried. What's wrong? You can talk to me. I'm a good listener.

~Hollywood

To: Kassie
From: Graham
Subject: Army Ball

Hi. I don't have long, so I'll keep this short and sweet. We've been talking long enough now for me to know that I really like you. You're funny, sweet, and I'd love to meet in person. I don't want you to feel threatened though. There's an Army Ball in a few weeks. It's a dress-up thing, and it's being held in Austin. I thought maybe you might want to meet me there? We could see if the chemistry we have online transfers to face to face. If so, great, we can go from there. If not, no harm, no foul. What d'ya say?

~Hollywood

KASSIE ANDERSON LOOKED down at her phone in trepidation as it dinged in her hand. She was hoping to hear from Hollywood again, but was also afraid of what he'd say. She was in over her head, but didn't know how to get out of the situation she'd found herself in.

Seeing the email wasn't from Hollywood, Kassie wanted to shut the phone off and ignore it, but she couldn't. She knew it. She clicked the email open, not surprised by what she read.

Jacks is pleased with your progress. Time to step it up. Report back ASAP.

Kassie wanted to throw up.

Her ex-boyfriend wasn't going to leave her alone. Ever.

She'd thought when he'd gotten arrested for kidnapping and assault, she could finally relax. That she was done with him. But she'd been deluding herself. It didn't matter that he was behind bars. He had enough friends to keep tabs on her. If she didn't do what he wanted, she'd pay.

Her phone made another dinging noise. Another message.

This was the one she'd been expecting from Hollywood.

Kassie read the email twice, her eyes filling with tears. He wanted to meet her. Because he *liked* her. Not only meet, but take her to an Army Ball. She'd read about them online when she'd been obsessively Googling everything she could about the Army. They were a big deal. And he'd invited *her*.

Richard hadn't ever taken her to a formal ball, but he'd made her go to one of his own military get-togethers. He'd told her what went on at the fancy military formal balls, and he'd "recreated" one at his apartment.

The worst part was drinking from the grog bowl. Richard had told her it was tradition, that everyone who attended had to drink...and if you couldn't answer a question, you had to drink...and if you looked at someone the wrong way, another drink.

And it was horrible. Awful. Richard had put in any

kind of alcohol he had on hand, as well as hot sauce, Worcestershire sauce, and anything else that would make it unpalatable. The grog was meant as a punishment, and he'd taken great delight in punishing *her* as often as he could...asking questions he knew she couldn't answer and laughing as his friends held her still while he forced it down her throat.

Kassie shivered and hoped like hell Hollywood wouldn't make her drink from the grog bowl at the ball.

But the bottom line was that Hollywood didn't deserve what she was doing to him. The shit thing was, she honestly liked the man. He didn't seem at all like her ex, or what Richard's friend told her he'd be like. She felt the chemistry between them. And if it was this potent online, what would it be like in person?

What had started out as a revenge thing at the request of her ex had turned into something else entirely. All she was supposed to do was get Hollywood interested in her so Richard's friend could set him up for whatever they had planned, but she'd gone and screwed that up too.

Kassie wanted to tell Hollywood no, that she didn't want to see or talk to him anymore, but that was impossible. Jacks was holding all the cards.

She slowly typed out a response, hating herself with every word.

I'd love to. I can't wait to meet you. ~Kassie

Chapter Two

"**I** LOVE THAT you're finally going out again," Karina said with a huge smile on her face as they thumbed through a rack of dresses.

"It's not that big a deal," Kassie told her little sister for what seemed like the hundredth time.

"It is," she countered. "You haven't been out with anyone since Richard. I was beginning to think you never would."

Kassie tried not to sigh. Her parents and sister knew some of what she'd gone through with her ex, but not all of it. It was embarrassing that she'd stayed with Richard for as long as she had. And she felt dirty and disgusted with herself that she still couldn't seem to move on with her life. Of course, it wasn't by choice.

Karina continued to let Kassie know exactly what she thought about her upcoming date to the military ball. "I mean, Richard was cute and all, but it wasn't fair that he wanted you to sit at home and wait for him while he got to do whatever he wanted. If I ever date a military guy, there's no way I'd stay here in Austin while he goes off and does his thing. I'd insist on him marrying me and I'd move to wherever he was stationed."

Kassie flinched at the dig. She knew her sister didn't mean it in a derogatory way, but that didn't stop the words from hurting. Richard had stated over and over that he wanted to marry her, and when they did she'd move to wherever he was stationed, but that hadn't happened. After he'd been injured, talk of marriage disappeared and he became more possessive of her. Kassie would've married him in a heartbeat...before the accident, but even if it made her a bad person, she was relieved she hadn't because of the man he was now. After the horrible incident with the grog bowl at the fake military get-together he'd had, she'd slowly tried to distance herself from Richard...to no avail.

"I can't believe you actually agreed to go out with another Army guy," Karina went on. "I mean, you've been so adamant that you'd never date anyone in the military ever again."

"I know, but I realized it wasn't exactly the military that I didn't like...it was Richard himself."

"Oh my God!" Karina suddenly exclaimed loudly, scaring the shit out of Kassie and making the three women standing near them whip their heads in their direction. "I found the perfect dress!"

Karina took a dress off the rack and held it up, showing it to her sister.

Kassie was speechless.

She and Karina were close. Even though they were thirteen years apart in age, Kassie made a point to talk to her sister almost every night and go over to their parents' house to see her at least once a week. They had similar tastes, even if the younger girl was much more outgoing and gregarious than her older sister.

The dress her sister was holding up was beautiful. Kassie's hand reached for it before she knew what she was doing. It was a deep purple, almost black. It had short capped sleeves and a vee neckline in the front and back. It looked like it would be snug around her upper body, but then it flared out at her waist with what looked like miles of wispy material. Kassie could almost imagine it swirling around her legs as she walked. It was the most beautiful dress she'd ever seen.

"It looks like it'll be too long," she said softly.

"Try it on," Karina urged. "You can always get it altered."

Kassie nodded then swallowed hard. The whole I'm-going-to-a-military-ball thing hadn't really sunk in until right this moment. Being around military guys was intimidating, especially after meeting Richard's friends. Talking with Hollywood on the computer was one thing, but being face to face with him was another altogether. She liked him, yes, but she was also deceiving him, and that ate at her.

She'd only written to him because she'd been forced to. But the fact that she liked him was almost worse. If he'd been an asshole, it would've made what she was being forced to do easier.

"Come on, silly. Get a move on," Karina urged.

Kassie looked at her sister and nodded. They walked side by side to the dressing room and Kassie didn't even hear her sister's idle chatter as they moved. Karina looked a lot like her, but Kassie knew she'd never been as pretty as her sister. Karina was a cheerleader, had played on the volleyball team, and participated in a couple of plays. She didn't let anyone pigeonhole her into a stereotype and had friends from just about every walk of life at school. She was outgoing, friendly, and didn't have a care in the world.

And Kassie wanted to keep it that way.

The thought of Richard's friend, Dean, getting his hands on her made Kassie want to throw up. When Richard went to federal prison up at Fort Leavenworth, Kansas, Kassie had thought his reign of terror over her was finally finished. But apparently if you were an obsessed asshole, bars and barbed wire couldn't stop you.

He'd gotten his longtime friend to take up where he'd left off. Dean was around six feet tall, muscular, with dark brown hair that he kept long in the back, like an eighties mullet. Most of the time he pulled it back in a ponytail. It hung limp down his back, and more than once Kassie had wanted to take a pair of scissors and chop it off it was so gross.

He had thin lips that he pressed together when he was upset, making it almost look as if he didn't have any in the first place. His nose was long and skinny and if she had to describe his eyes, she would've said they were "beady."

He wasn't attractive, but he was strong. She'd learned that the hard way when he'd held her while Richard made her drink the disgusting grog concoction.

Dean followed her everywhere. Kassie wouldn't be surprised if he was lurking outside in the parking lot of the mall, watching and waiting for her and her sister to emerge. He knew who she spent her time with, and the one time she'd tried to go on a date after Richard went to jail, he'd shown up at the restaurant and had sat at the bar near the table she and her date had been sitting at. He'd taken pictures of her with his cell phone throughout the evening.

The next day, Dean had called and told her that Richard wasn't happy after hearing she'd tried to cheat on him.

Kassie wanted to move away from Austin. Away from Dean. Away from the memories of Richard. And she'd almost been ready to do it when Richard raised the stakes.

He no longer used Dean to threaten *her*; he'd turned his sights to her sister. When Kassie did something Richard didn't like, Dean kept her in line by threatening *Karina*.

She wanted to go to the police, but she was scared to death of what Dean would do. So she kept putting it off, hoping Richard would get too busy with his new life behind bars and he and Dean would forget about her and her family.

When Dean said that Richard wanted her to get close to one of the Army guys who'd "ruined his life" so he could get insider information to figure out how to bring them all down, Kassie had outright refused. She didn't want any part of being a spy, and bringing any more grief to the group of soldiers Richard had already terrorized. The fact that he'd kidnapped a woman and child sickened her.

Yet here she was. Trying on a dress for a military ball. Exactly what she didn't want to happen. But she'd do whatever it took to keep Karina safe. Even face her fears by going to this type of function.

"Come on! Hurry up!" Karina ordered from outside the dressing room. "I want to see!"

Kassie let her jeans fall to the floor and stepped into the dress. She zipped it up and turned to the mirror.

The dress fit perfectly. As if it was made for her. It wasn't too long at all. If she wore a pair of heels it would be the perfect length. The vee in the front came down low enough to be sexy, but not enough to show too much. Kassie had always felt she was too curvy, but this dress accentuated her curves and somehow made them sexy rather than making her feel fat.

She turned and eyed the back of the dress. The material dipped low, exposing her bra strap. She made a mental note to stop by the lingerie section before leaving. A regular bra just wouldn't do with this dress.

Kassie spun, and the material billowed out in a swirl of purple, then settled around her legs once more. Her brown hair did as well, brushing against her breasts as she stopped. She had thick, lush hair. It took forever to dry, but Kassie secretly loved it, considering it one of her best features.

For the first time in a long, *long* time, Kassie felt pretty.

Apparently done waiting, Karina opened the door to the dressing room. "You're too slow, so I—Oh my God. I knew it'd fit!" she said excitedly. "We can put your hair up and you have that necklace that will be perfect for this. You know, the one that has the dangly thing at the end; it'll dip down into your cleavage, bringing attention to your assets."

Kassie rolled her eyes at her sister, but she continued without pause.

"We need to find you a bra that'll push up your

boobs, but you can't see the strap in the back. And stockings. You can't wear a dress like that without them. Thigh highs, definitely. You've got that pair of black heels that'll work with it too. Oh my God, Kass. I love it!"

Kassie grinned. "Me too."

The sisters smiled at each other.

"I can't wait for my dance next month," Karina said. "Has anyone asked you yet?"

Karina shook her head. "No, but it's still early."

"Got your eye on anyone?" Kassie teased.

"There's a new guy in school who is extremely hot."

"Yeah?" Kassie asked absently, her eyes trained on her reflection in the mirror. She could hardly believe how nice the dress looked on her.

"Yeah. He's got sandy-brown hair that falls over his forehead. When he tosses his head to get it out of his eyes, I just wanna swoon. When he looks at you, it's as if you're the most important thing in the world. His blue eyes just bore into you. It's intense and awesome. Oh, and he's tall and muscular, but not all bulgy, which would be gross. He's a senior and looks a lot older than eighteen." She shrugged. "The rumor is that he had to sit out a year or two because of family issues. But he just moved to Austin and wanted to get his actual diploma rather than a GED. Anyway, enough about me. Get that dress off, and let's go see if we can find you some undies!"

Kassie laughed at her sister's unbridled excitement. Shopping wasn't her favorite thing to do, but any day she got to spend time with Karina was a good day in her eyes. She'd do anything for her. Including going on a date with an Army guy she met online, intending to deceive him to give information to her ex-boyfriend's thug of a friend so they could continue to find ways to torment the man.

God, she hated herself for what she was doing.

"I'll wait out there. Hurry up!" Karina ordered, then left the small dressing room.

But to keep her sister safe, Kassie would do whatever she had to. She just needed to meet with Hollywood, see if she could get any information that Dean might consider useful, and she never had to see the hot soldier again.

She looked at her reflection once more before closing her eyes in despair. The shit thing was that she knew this wouldn't be the end of it. The second she gave Dean any information, he and Richard would want more. She was deluding herself if she thought the night of the ball would end Richard's threat to Karina or herself.

Kassie suddenly felt tired. Exhausted. If it was only her, she'd tell Dean to pound sand. She didn't care what he did anymore. He could hit her—wouldn't be the first time—get her fired—again, not the first time Richard or Dean had made her get a new job—but when they involved her family, she wouldn't fight back, and apparently they'd figured that out.

Tears sprang to her eyes as she unzipped the dress and stepped out of it. If only she had someone to have her back she wouldn't feel so alone. But she might as well wish for ten million dollars. It wasn't going to happen. Not with Dean watching her every move and reporting back to Richard.

Taking a deep breath, Kassie hung up the dress and put her clothes back on. Crying about her life wasn't going to change anything. She just had to get through today. Then tomorrow. Then the day after that. One day at a time. It was how she'd gotten through everything she'd been through so far. It's how she'd get through anything life had up its sleeve in the future.

The most important thing in her life was family. She'd be damned if Richard would take that away from her.

Chapter Three

"I 'M DONE," HARLEY announced.

"What?" Rayne asked at the same time Emily said, "Not yet."

"We've been here for two hours. You guys have tried on every dress in the store. You found what you wanted to wear, but there's no way I'm going to do this for another two hours while you try to find the perfect accessories, shoes, underwear, hose, purse, and whatever else you think you need for this stinkin' ball," Harley told them.

She stood with her arms crossed, glaring at the two women.

"Are you sure you don't want to try any other dresses?" Rayne asked. "You picked the first one you tried on."

"I'm more than sure," Harley said. "Seriously. At this point I'm ready to say to hell with it and sit at home in my fat pants and work on my code. I know how important this is to Coach, but I'm done."

Emily gave Harley a one-armed hug. "Okay. No

problem. I can take you home, then come back here and Rayne and I can finish up."

Harley shook her head. "Nope. I've already texted Coach. He's in the middle of something, but he's sending Hollywood. He'll be here as soon as he can."

Rayne narrowed her eyes. "You already made your getaway plan?"

"Absolutely," Harley told her without an ounce of remorse. "I didn't want you to come up with anything that would guilt me into staying."

Rayne and Emily giggled.

"Okay, okay, you've been a good sport," Rayne acquiesced. "Thank you for coming with us. The dress you got is beautiful. Coach will lose his mind when he sees you in it."

"I know," Harley said without conceit.

Her phone toned and she looked down and read the text. "That's Hollywood. He's outside." Harley hugged both Rayne and Emily. "I'll talk to you guys later."

The two other women said their goodbyes and Harley headed outside with her new dress flung over her arm. She immediately spotted Hollywood in Coach's Highlander. He had parked next to the curb and was standing beside the passenger door, arms crossed over his chest, fingers drumming impatiently on his biceps. He was wearing the pixelated Army battle dress uniform he and the other men wore on a daily basis, not anything unusual in this part of Texas.

Like all of the men on the team, Hollywood was good looking, but he had that something extra that made women, no matter their age, sit up and take notice. Harley saw no less than five women do double takes when they saw him standing by the vehicle. She appreciated his looks for what they were, but she only had eyes for Coach.

"Hey, Hollywood. Thank you for rescuing me," Harley told him as she approached.

"No problem," he told her.

Harley knew it probably *was*, but she didn't call him on it. She allowed him to open her door and take her new dress before she got in. She wasn't comfortable with the way all the guys went out of their way to treat her like she was the Queen of England, but she'd learned to accept it.

Hollywood hung her dress on a hook in the backseat and climbed into the driver's side. They were driving down the street to her place when Hollywood's phone beeped. He glanced down at the phone clipped to his belt and then back at the road.

When it made another beep, Harley asked, "You want me to check that for you?"

Hollywood hesitated, but finally grabbed the phone, unlocked it with his thumb, and held it out to her. "Normally I wouldn't care, whoever it is could wait. But we're in the middle of something at work and in case it's Ghost, I need to check it."

"No problem," Harley told him, glancing down at his phone. "It's an email from someone named Kassie." She looked up at Hollywood, surprised to see his impatient, no-nonsense expression morph into one of pleasure. "Want me to read it?"

"Yes, please."

She was even more surprised he was going to let her read his personal email, but thrilled too. She, Rayne, and Emily knew Hollywood had a date for the Army Ball next weekend, but didn't know anything about the woman he'd invited. He'd been closemouthed about how he'd met her, and really everything else, so getting this small glimpse of the mysterious woman was irresistible.

She clicked on the email and read it aloud.

"Since you're an Army guy, you know how to hide a body so no one can find it, right? I'm about done with assholes at work. I just had to deal with a woman who wanted to return a dress. She claimed it didn't fit, but it was obvious she'd worn it to a shindig. It smelled like perfume and even had sweat stains in the pits. When I confronted her and told her we couldn't take back clothing that had been worn, she pitched a fit. Threatened to get me fired, said she'd tell all her friends not to shop here anymore and generally made an ass of herself.

It'd be like me wearing the dress to the ball next week and then taking it back. I'm cheap, but I'm not *that* cheap. Good Lord. Anyway. I hope your day is going better than mine. And to answer your question, no, I'm not staying at the hotel. It's hard for me to justify the expense when I live so close to downtown (told you I'm cheap). Hope you're having a good day. Kassie."

There was silence in the cab after Harley stopped speaking. She looked up at Hollywood and saw the grin that had been on his face before she'd started reading had blossomed into a full-fledged smile.

"You like her," she blurted.

"What?"

"You like her," Harley repeated.

Hollywood shrugged. "Yeah. I wouldn't have asked her to the ball if I didn't."

"How did you meet her?"

"Online."

"Really?"

"Yeah, really." Hollywood looked over at her. "Why?"

It was Harley's turn to shrug. "I don't know. It's just amusing. I mean, you're the hottest guy on the team. For you to meet someone online is just funny. You asked if she was staying at the hotel?"

Luckily Hollywood was used to the way Harley could shift topics in conversation. "Yeah."

"And she lives in Austin?"

"Harley, *yeah*. Why all the questions?" Hollywood griped.

"Because we don't know anything about this woman. If she's gonna become one of us, we want to know about her."

Hollywood's eyes jerked to Harley's, then back to the road. His voice got quiet. "Don't go thinking I'm gonna marry her. It's not like that. I haven't even met her in person. Yeah, I like her, but I don't know her. Not really."

"What *do* you know?" Harley asked, not letting him off the hook.

Hollywood sighed, then said, "She's thirty and has a sister who is a senior in high school. As you gathered, she works in retail, and doesn't particularly like it. I get the feeling she's not that comfortable with the fact I'm in the Army, but she's trying not to let it bother her. But..." His voice trailed off.

"But what?" Harley asked.

"I don't know. She's funny and she makes me laugh. But I can tell she's hiding something."

"Of course she is," Harley told him immediately.

Hollywood chuckled under his breath, but Harley ignored it and continued.

"She met you online. You've never met in person. You're extremely good looking. She's intimidated,

Hollywood. I know how I was with Coach when I first met him. You have to understand, most normal women aren't used to drop-dead gorgeous men having any interest in us. I don't know what she looks like, but I'm guessing she's probably more like me, Rayne, and Emily than a Dallas Cowboy Cheerleader. Of course she's hiding part of herself from you. It's up to you to make her feel comfortable and drop her shields so she can tell you her real thoughts and feelings."

"Asking me to hide a body isn't her real feelings?" Hollywood joked.

"You know what I mean," Harley insisted, her lips not even twitching at his attempt to lighten the mood.

"I do, and I realize that meeting someone online will mean that there are a lot of things left unsaid. But it's more than that. I can't put my finger on it, but it seems like there's more she's hiding than just being uneasy about meeting a guy online," Hollywood explained.

"Be careful," Harley told him. "I've come to like you too much to have you be murdered by a chick you met online."

Harley turned her head and looked out the window. They'd pulled up to her apartment without her even realizing it. She leaned down, grabbed her purse, and went to open her door. Hollywood's hand on her arm stopped her.

"She's not going to murder me, but you're right. I

like her. I'm not an idiot, I know what we have right now is somewhat superficial. We get along great via email, but I'm scared when we meet it won't be the same. And that would suck because I do like her so much. I hate that she gets treated like shit at her job, but I can't do anything about it. The only thing I can do is try to make her smile and continue her jokes. But I can't help but feel that she's hiding way more than merely hating her job. *That's* what I meant. I'm more than a pretty face, even if that's what most people see when they look at me."

Harley looked into Hollywood's intense brown eyes. "I know. Me and the girls'll see what we can find out for you at the ball."

"No, don't," Hollywood returned immediately. "I don't want you to be a spy for me. I'd hate that. I want to learn everything about her myself. It's underhanded and sneaky to sic you guys on her. Promise me you won't pump her for information."

"I promise," Harley told him immediately. "I'd hate to find out anyone did that to me if I was in her shoes."

"Exactly."

"Now, let me go so you can get back to whatever war game you're playing with my man, would ya? I wasted too much time as it was at the mall with Rayne and Emily. I have a million things to do for the new *This is War* game I'm working on. Do you know what time Coach might be home tonight?"

Hollywood shrugged. "Not sure. If things go the way we want them to, probably around six. If not, it might not be until the morning."

Harley paused with one foot outside the SUV and asked, "Are you guys going to have to leave? Will we *get* to go to the ball?"

"We'll be at the ball," Hollywood said firmly. "I'm not going to miss my chance to meet Kassie."

"Good," Harley said with a nod and got the rest of the way out of the SUV. She shut the door and got her dress from the backseat. Hollywood had rolled down the passenger window and she told him, "Kassie. I like her name."

Hollywood smiled. "Me too. See you later."

"See ya. Thanks for rescuing me from the mall."

"Anytime."

Harley watched as he rolled up the window and drove out of the parking lot. Her mind was going in a thousand different directions as she headed up to her apartment. It was obvious Hollywood was more than intrigued with the mysterious Kassie, but now, so was she.

Chapter Four

KASSIE SAT ON the large couch, more nervous than she could remember being in a very long time. It didn't help that there were men in their fancy dress blue uniforms all around. She couldn't help but remember the military party she'd been to with Richard. It had been horrifying, and the last straw in their relationship. She'd hated to throw away two years of dating, but after that, she knew without a doubt she wanted nothing more to do with the man…or his friends.

Wanting to keep her hands busy and not look like she was about to puke waiting on Hollywood to arrive, Kassie resisted the urge to pull out her phone and pretend to be engrossed in it.

Karina had come over to her apartment and helped her get ready for the ball. She'd given her tips on her makeup and they'd taken a million pictures. It was a Saturday, and Karina couldn't stay long because she'd needed to get to the high school. There was a football game and the cheerleaders had to be there early to help loosen up the crowd and welcome the team to the field.

Kassie hated to miss the game, she tried to go to all Karina's events, but her sister didn't hold her skipping this one against her.

They'd giggled and gossiped as they'd gotten Kassie ready for the evening. Karina talked more about the new mysterious guy at school and told Kassie she thought he might be interested in her. Kassie wasn't thrilled with that news, but Karina was almost an adult, so she let it go. It was nice to see her so excited about a boy.

Kassie had tried to hide Richard's crazy from her sister for the longest time, but the last time he'd been around, Karina had witnessed him yelling at her. She'd even tried to intervene, but Richard had just turned his sights on Karina. It hadn't been the best night, and as a result, her little sister had been reluctant to really get involved with anyone...until now.

After Kassie had been dressed, made-up, and lectured about having a good time and "getting some" by her little sister, she'd left to head downtown. It was still fairly early—Kassie was always early wherever she went—and now she was sitting in the lobby of the Four Seasons in downtown Austin, anxiously waiting for Hollywood.

She'd started out calling him Graham, but since he signed all his emails "Hollywood," she'd begun calling him that in her mind.

Kassie tried not to fidget as she took in the people

around her. The women were dressed in amazing floor-length gowns of all colors. Most were dark, black or navy, but there were the occasional orange or yellow dresses as well. Kassie knew she was supposed to be bowled over by all the men in their fancy uniforms, but honestly, they brought back so many bad memories of the "ball" Richard had in his apartment, complete with all his friends wearing their dress uniforms, that it was more comfortable for her to focus on the women than the men.

She had a wristlet in her lap, and she felt her phone vibrate with an incoming text or email. Kassie thought about ignoring it, figuring it was her sister, but then had the thought that maybe it was Hollywood. Maybe he was canceling and she could leave.

Unzipping the small purse, Kassie pulled out her phone and glanced down, expecting to see an encouraging note from her sister or one from Hollywood. That's not what she'd received.

Have fun tonight. Suck his cock, let him stick his dick inside you, it doesn't matter, just get the job done. By the way, Karina looks lovely in her cheerleading out-fit tonight. Later

Kassie drew in a quick breath and clicked the phone so the screen went dark. She robotically put it back in her purse and stared straight ahead. She held back her tears by sheer force of will. Dean had threatened Karina before, of course he had, it was why she was sitting in this hotel lobby in the first place, but nothing like this.

The fact that he was there at the football game, watching her sister, made her want to scream in frustration.

Kassie made the decision right then to warn both her parents and sister. She was done hiding the evil that was Richard and Dean from them. But neither man was stupid. The text from Dean just now didn't sound exactly friendly, but it didn't have anything that could be construed as a blatant threat…even though it was.

Kassie wasn't an idiot either. And keeping the threats to herself any longer was just plain stupid. Hell, it had been to keep them secret for as long as she had, but she'd honestly thought Richard would get tired of her and fade away. Kassie had evidence of the vague threats in the texts and emails from Dean. The rest of the things Richard had done to her were going to be her word against his, but it was something.

She needed to go to the police and get a restraining order, not that it would do much good, but it was better than nothing. She needed to get her life back.

Kassie glanced at her watch. It was about time for Hollywood to arrive. She knew vaguely what he looked like, but not really. The picture on the dating website was okay at best. The hat on his head hid most of his face from the camera. She could tell he was tall and in shape. His arms looked buff as he held up the fish in the picture.

A trio of women entered through the front doors of the hotel and Kassie could only stare at them in awe. They were amazing. If the women she'd seen walking around were pretty, these three gave new meaning to the word.

They were all around the same height, fairly tall, especially with their heels. The tallest woman was wearing a black dress that hugged her slender body. It was the most modest of the three, as it had long sleeves, a high neck, and not an inch of skin below her neck was showing. It was sexy on her, and even though it was form fitting, it wasn't slutty in the least. It was classy, and somehow made her tall height seem even greater.

Another was the complete opposite of her taller friend. She was also wearing a black dress that fell to the floor, as was appropriate for the formal military event, but it was sleeveless with a scoop neck. It had an empire waist and the material had several layers. The dress sparkled with the rhinestones sewn into the bodice. And where the first woman was slender, this one was curvy. The dress hid some of those, but it was obvious the woman was confident in herself and her body. She laughed at something her friend said, throwing her head back in the process, and Kassie noticed that several men turned to stare at her as a result.

The third woman was wearing a light blue gown. It had more of a mermaid skirt, the back dragging slightly on the ground as she moved, the front just high enough for the beautiful blue shoes she was wearing to peek out from the bottom of the material as she walked. She had a white shawl thrown over her shoulders, but Kassie could see the lace covering her from neck to waist underneath.

They looked comfortable with each other and not at all self-conscious about their appearance. They didn't move into the ballroom, but instead stayed near the front doors, obviously waiting for whoever had dropped them off.

Kassie smiled to herself. Even when she'd been with Richard and had thought she'd marry him, he'd never been courteous enough to drop her off at the door of an establishment while he parked the car. The thought had probably never even crossed his mind. Kassie hadn't ever cared before, but seeing the three friends laughing and talking together, and knowing they had men who cared enough to let them out at the front door so they didn't have to walk through a parking lot in their heels and maybe dirty their gowns, was bittersweet.

Kassie's eyes roamed the lobby once more. She and Hollywood had made arrangements to meet there prior to the festivities and he'd even suggested maybe getting a drink in the bar before the ball started. They didn't have a lot of time, but Kassie appreciated the chance to talk to him one-on-one before having to go through the formalities and traditions of the ball. She shuddered thinking about the latter, but took a breath to calm herself.

Kassie hated that she was deceiving Hollywood. She'd heard all about what Richard had done to the woman named Emily and her daughter, Annie, and was appalled that her ex had lost it so badly he'd resorted to almost killing people. But a part of her was selfishly relieved that it wasn't *her* who had been in that position. Richard had hit her a few times, enough to know without a doubt that if he hadn't gone to prison, he probably would've ended up really hurting her...possibly even killing her.

But spying on one of the men who Richard blamed for his being in prison wasn't something she was comfortable doing. Even though it was to keep Karina safe. Something had to change. And she'd start with telling her family about how Richard and Dean had been terrorizing her. Maybe if they knew, then the hold Richard and Dean had over her would lessen. She'd figure out what to do next after that.

The doors of the lobby opening again drew her attention, and Kassie turned her head to watch a group of men enter the hotel. Three went to the women she'd been admiring earlier. It almost felt as if she was watching something she shouldn't, as the men greeted their girlfriends as if they hadn't seen them in a year rather than what was probably only a couple of minutes.

The public displays of affection were appropriate for the occasion, but so intimate they somehow weren't. A caress here, a look of adoration there, and the way they kissed their women…wow. Kassie looked away from the couples, simply for something else to focus on, and her eyes landed on the other men. They were outfitted alike, all in their dress uniforms, but in actuality were very different.

Two men immediately caught her eye. First was the tallest and biggest man of the group. He had to be at least six-seven or so, and had a fierce scowl on his face, made even scarier looking because of the scar running down his cheek. Kassie made a mental note to stay away from him at all costs. The irritated and impatient look on his face reminded her too much of Richard when he was pissed off at something she'd done, or hadn't done.

The other caught her attention simply because he was beautiful. A man shouldn't be allowed to be so good looking. He had dark hair that was a tad bit too long. It curled around his neck and fell onto his forehead and he had to keep pushing it back. He had strong cheekbones, full pink lips, a perfect nose, and Lord, when he smiled, Kassie swore she heard several women standing around gasp.

It was almost scary how attractive the man was. The dress uniform fit him perfectly, the black bow tie, white dress shirt, dark blue jacket and pants...if she didn't know better, she would've thought he was a professional model wearing the uniform for a photo shoot. Kassie could appreciate a handsome man, but this one was beyond handsome.

She forced herself to look away. It didn't look like he was with anyone, but she knew without a doubt he was probably meeting someone there. Men like him never went stag.

She glanced down at her watch again and sighed. She hated when people were late. It was strike one against Hollywood...not that she was counting. The more she thought about what she was doing there and what the night would entail, the more nervous she got. She couldn't wait to get the night over with. If only Hollywood would get there.

"HEY, HOLLYWOOD, WHERE'S your date?" Beatle asked in his distinctive southern drawl. When they were on a mission, the man could lose the accent and sound like just another citizen in whatever country they were in, but when he was home, relaxed and with friends, his natural accent came through thick and easy.

"I'm pretty sure that's her over there on the couch," Hollywood told his friend, gesturing toward a woman sitting by herself in the lobby.

As if it was planned, Truck, Beatle, and Blade all turned their heads in perfect tandem in the direction Hollywood indicated.

"The chick in the purple dress?" Blade asked.

Truck didn't say a word, but his low whistle said it for him.

"Damn, you always get the pretty ones," Beatle whined.

"Stop it, assholes," Hollywood ordered, shoving Blade's shoulder. "Can't you tell she's already nervous? You jackals checkin' her out as if she's a piece of meat isn't going to make her feel any better.

"Is that her?" Harley whispered from next to him.

Hollywood turned and saw Harley grinning from ear to ear.

"Yeah."

"Then go get her!" Harley ordered, shoving his shoulder just like he'd done to his teammate a second ago.

"You guys go on in," Hollywood told the group. "I'll catch up with you before it's time to go through the receiving line. We're gonna go grab a drink in the bar first."

"Smart," Rayne said. "The alcohol should relax her

and you can get to know her a bit before you have to do the formal stuff."

"Exactly. Now go," Hollywood pleaded.

"Afraid she'll see us and wonder why she's stuck with you?" Truck asked, grinning.

"Stuff it," Hollywood retorted, and turned his back on his friends and started toward the woman on the couch.

He heard his friends laughing as he widened the distance between them, but lost interest as he saw the woman's eyes widen comically as he came toward her.

As soon as he got close enough to see her eyes, Hollywood knew it was Kassie. He'd looked at the picture she had on the dating site so often, he'd recognize her pretty hazel eyes anywhere. She stood as he got close, but the wide-eyed look on her face didn't change. It was a mixture of terror, confusion, and desire. He didn't mind the arousal or confusion, but he loathed the fright he saw on her face.

"Hi. Kassie, right?" he said softly, holding out his hand in greeting.

She looked down at it, then back up to his face. For a second, Hollywood thought she wasn't going to shake his hand, but finally she reached out to him.

"Yeah. I'm Kassie. Graham? Hollywood, I mean?"

Her hand was cold, but soft. Hollywood's other hand came up to enclose her delicate fingers in both of his, wanting to reassure and warm her up at the same time. "That's me. It's so good to meet you, Kassie. You look beautiful." And she did.

Hollywood couldn't take his eyes off her. She'd left her hair down, and the brown tips curled around the material at her breasts. He didn't think she knew it, and would most likely be appalled if she did, but it only brought his attention to her chest more, rather than hiding it behind the strands. The deep purple of her dress was beautiful against her skin. He wanted to steal her away, sit in a quiet room and get to know her. The last thing he wanted was to have to deal with the stuffy officers and protocol of the Army Ball.

"Thanks. You look great too."

The words were said politely, but he heard an undercurrent of what he thought was...disappointment? He dropped her hand and took a step back, giving her room. It wasn't often he was immediately attracted to a woman, and it sucked that it seemed as if she didn't feel the same way. He must've read the look of desire in her eyes wrong earlier.

"Look," he began softly, "if you've changed your mind, that's okay. I mean, meeting online is a crap shoot. I'm guessing what you thought I looked like doesn't mesh with the reality. I was already attracted to you based on your photo on the site, but I get that just because I'm attracted to *you*, doesn't mean it's reciprocated. We can call this off right now if you want. No harm, no foul."

She looked stunned for a moment, then looked down at her hands clutching a small purse. She fiddled with it for a moment, then raised her head, met his eyes and blurted, "You're good looking."

"Uh...thanks?" Hollywood said, not understanding her point.

"I didn't expect...your picture wasn't that clear and I..." Her voice trailed off as she tried to gather her thoughts. Then finally she said, "We don't go together."

"Kass, I don't know what point you're trying to make," Hollywood told her.

"I just...I didn't think you'd be as handsome as you are."

"And that's a problem?"

"Well..." She shrugged.

Hollywood ran a hand through his hair, sighed in frustration and said under his breath, "I hate these balls." Then in a more normal voice, he said, "Please. Give me a chance to show you how much I like you." He couldn't tell her he wished he *wasn't* so good looking. It would sound shallow and stupid. But all his life he'd been judged by his outer appearance. He purposely put a crappy picture on the website because he wanted a woman to get to know who he was. Not message him because he was hot.

He watched her swallow hard, then she took a deep breath. "I'm sorry. I'm being so rude. I just didn't expect you to be so good looking. I was expecting someone more like the guy next door."

"You want to date your neighbor?" Hollywood asked with a grin so she'd know he was teasing. He relaxed when she chuckled.

"Figure of speech. If you met my neighbor you'd know how far off that statement is. He's in his twenties and thinks he's God's gift to women." She held out her hand to him again. "Can we start over? Hi. I'm Kassie Anderson. It's nice to meet you."

Taking her cold hand in his once more, he returned, "Graham Caverly. You can call me Hollywood. It's good to meet you, Kassie."

They smiled at each other for a moment before Hollywood asked, still holding on to her hand. "Are you cold? Do you have a wrap?"

"I'm okay," she told him. "My hands always seem to be cold. Poor circulation or something I guess."

"Let me know if you get chilly. Once we get through the receiving line, I can give you my jacket."

She stared up at him as if he'd just told her he'd give her a million dollars. Hating that she was so surprised by his gesture, Hollywood asked, "You want to get a drink before we go in?"

"I'd like that."

Hollywood dropped her hand, feeling silly that he wanted to snatch it up again, and held out his arm, gesturing toward the hotel bar on the other side of the lobby. "Ladies first."

He got to check out her ass as they headed to the bar. He should've felt like a letch, but Kassie Anderson had the kind of ass any red-blooded man would admire. Curvy and full. She was smaller than his six feet, but not too much so. He couldn't see her feet, but assumed she was wearing heels, which would make her about six or so inches shorter than he was. He liked Rayne, Emily, and Harley, but preferred smaller women, and Kassie Anderson fit the bill nicely.

They entered the bar and Hollywood urged her toward a small table off to the side. He pulled out a chair for Kassie then took the seat across from her, which allowed him to see the entrance. As much as he wanted to focus solely on Kassie, the Delta Force soldier was too ingrained in him. He noted the hallway, which led to the kitchen on the left, could be a possible exit point, as well as the emergency exit door on the other side of the bar.

"Hi. Can I get you something to drink?" the waitress asked as she placed two napkins on the circular table in front of them. She smiled at Hollywood, and leaned over a bit, showing off her cleavage.

"I'd like a margarita on the rocks. No salt," Kassie

told her.

"Whatever you have on tap is fine with me," Hollywood said, not looking at the ample female flesh being offered up from the waitress.

The waitress nodded and ran her fingers down Hollywood's arm in a barely there caress before saying, "My name is Becky, if you need anything, just let me know."

Ignoring the blatant flirting of the waitress, Hollywood drank in the sight of the woman in front of him. She bit her lip nervously, but otherwise held his gaze. She had the longest eyelashes of any woman he'd ever seen, and they made her hazel eyes stand out all the more. He could look at her forever, but because it was making her nervous, he said, "Thank you for agreeing to meet me. I feel like I know you really well, but in reality, we're almost complete strangers."

"I wouldn't say *complete* strangers," she teased. "I know you like to fish, are in the Army, and could probably quit tomorrow for a job in the movie industry if you wanted to."

"If I could change my looks, I would," Hollywood said in a low, intense tone. Not giving her a chance to respond, he went on. "All my life, women have seen my looks rather than who I am as a person. I'll admit, in my twenties, I ate that shit up, but now that I'm older, I hate it. Women couldn't care less that I love cats more than dogs, or that the best feeling in the world to me is getting up early and going for a run before the rest of the world wakes up. All they care about is taking a picture of me to post on social media, or seeing if they can get me into their beds. The best thing about meeting you online is that I could get to know you, and you could get to know me, without our outer trappings coming into play."

He hadn't meant to blurt all that out, but he couldn't take it back now.

Kassie was silent for a moment before she said, "I imagine that's what women feel like most of the time. If they're even ten pounds overweight, they're judged because they don't look like the actresses on the big screen or models in ads. And if a woman is fifty pounds, or a hundred pounds heavier than what the fashion industry has deemed 'pretty,' they're made to feel like they're less somehow. I admit, I'm intimidated by your looks, Hollywood. I'm not hideous, but like most women, I also don't feel like I'm all that pretty. So you'll have to cut me some slack as I adjust from you being the guy-next-door redneck who likes to fish, to the most beautiful man I've ever met."

"I can do that," Hollywood told her immediately, loving her candor.

"Although," she said, wrinkling her nose at the same time she grinned to let him know she was teasing, "I'm not sure about the going-for-a-run-in-the-morning thing. I'm neither a workout nor morning person."

Hollywood laughed with her and reached for her hand. He picked it up and leaned over to bring it to his lips. He kissed the back, noting anew how cold her fingers felt against his own, and said softly, "I'll have you know, you are certainly not hideous; you are not only pretty, but breathtaking."

"Wait until you see me in the morning with no makeup, hair all crazy from sleeping on it weird, and in my lounge-around-my-apartment clothes."

Hollywood couldn't imagine anything sexier than what she just described. He'd always preferred the natural look on a woman than the dressy, made-up, and formal look...although on Kassie, the look was amazing.

As if she realized what she'd just said was presumptuous, she stammered, "I mean...that wasn't an invitation, it was just..."

Hollywood chuckled and tried to reassure her. "I know what you meant, Kass. But you should know, a real man loves what his woman looks like no matter what society thinks is pretty. Size twenty-eight, two, or anything in between. As long as the woman loves him, and is a good person, the packaging is just that...packaging."

They smiled at each other for a moment, until their waitress returned, interrupting the intimate moment. "Here we are. A margarita and a Lone Star on tap for the handsome soldier."

Hollywood refused to let go of Kassie's hand, he merely moved their clasped hands to the edge of the table, giving Becky room to put the drinks down.

"Can I get you anything else?" she purred, not taking her eyes off Hollywood.

"We're good. My *boyfriend* and I will let you know if we need anything else," Kassie said in an even tone, a bright, fake smile on her face.

"Of course," Becky said, standing up straight. "Enjoy."

Hollywood picked up his beer with his free hand and held it up. "A toast. To a good night and getting to know each other." He paused a fraction when she picked up her own drink, then added, "And to my date protecting me from overzealous and overstepping-her-boundaries waitresses."

A flush blossomed over her cheeks, but Kassie merely said, "To a good night," and clinked her glass to his.

He smiled broadly at her as he took a sip of his beer. He'd been nervous about meeting Kassie and seeing if the chemistry he felt through their online correspondence would transfer to in person. It did. He couldn't wait for her to meet his friends and continue to learn more about her. The night could only get better from here.

Chapter Five

*T*HE NIGHT CAN *only go downhill from here.*

Kassie wasn't usually a pessimistic person, but as she and Hollywood made their way from the bar toward the ballroom, she couldn't help but get nervous. The military traditions Richard had told her about were bullshit, she'd Googled them after his so-called ball, but even though she knew her ex had lied about what went on at an actual military function, she was suddenly unsure and nervous. But Kassie had said she'd go to this thing with Hollywood, and she couldn't back out now.

She surreptitiously wiped her free hand on the material of her dress and hoped for the best.

"You said you had an ex that was in the Army," Hollywood stated. "Have you been to a ball before?"

Taking a deep breath, Kassie said, "No, not really. He had some friends over and they all dressed up and said they were following proper military protocol, but I looked online after it was over because some of the things that happened didn't seem right." She knew she was talking too much, but couldn't seem to make herself stop. "I mean, most of the things he did were *based* on military traditions as far as I could tell, but he changed them and…anyway…the answer to your question is no."

His lips twitched, but he didn't comment on her babbling. "So you might know basically what to expect. But to recap, there's a cocktail hour first where we all mingle. Then we'll go through the receiving line. I'll introduce you to the adjutant and then we'll go down the line. I'm not sure who's here tonight, but whoever the highest-ranking officers are will be in the line, along with their dates. Then we'll eat dinner, then the traditional speeches will start. After that is dancing. Do you have any questions?"

Kassie shook her head. No. She understood the concept from her online research, but what she'd gone through with Richard and his friends was still pretty fresh in her mind, even though it had happened over a year ago.

"Good. I can't wait to introduce you to my friends."

"Have you known them long?" Kassie asked, trying to get her mind off the ball.

"The guys, yeah. We've worked together for a couple of years. They're like my brothers. Two have steady girlfriends and another is married."

"Hmmm," Kassie intoned, not wanting to seem uninterested, but she was remembering some of the things Richard had made her do and hoping like hell her research was correct. It wasn't as if all these men and women, dressed in their fancy clothes, would do some of the awful things Richard and his friends had...at least she didn't think so.

"Truck got his nickname because he once ate an engine, and Beatle has three secret wives he keeps in the basement at his house."

"Cool," Kassie said, her eyes flicking back and forth as they entered the ballroom. It wasn't dark, thank God, but the lights weren't exactly on full strength either. She looked around, curious as to what a real military ball looked like. Granted, Richard's apartment couldn't compare in the slightest, but she'd wondered if the ballroom would look like a cheesy prom venue, or more distinguished, as she imagined a true ball would be.

When Hollywood lightly took hold of her shoulders and backed her up against a wall, she looked up at him in surprise. "Wha—"

"You're not listening to a word I've been saying, Kass. What's going on?"

"I was," she protested.

"What'd I just say?" he asked gently.

"Um..." Kassie wracked her brain trying to remember, but realized she had no idea what he'd just been talking about.

"Relax," Hollywood ordered. "You're acting like we just walked into a torture chamber. Jeez, I thought *I* hated these things," he said, more to himself than her.

"I'm sorry," Kassie told him, looking him in the eyes this time. "I'm just nervous."

"There's nothing to be nervous about," Hollywood reassured her.

"I don't want to make you look bad," she told him.

"Kass, unless you strip off your dress and dance naked on the tables, you can't make me look bad."

She looked up at him and gave him a small smile. "I'm not planning on doing that…I only strip when I'm at my night job." Kassie tried to control the shaking of her limbs as she joked with Hollywood.

He smirked at her attempt at humor, but didn't comment on it other than to say, "Good." He stared down at her for a moment. "I might be overstepping my boundaries here, but I'd like to give you a hug."

"Really?"

"Really."

Kassie thought about it and decided she could really go for one right about now. "I'd like that."

Without a word, Hollywood stepped into her space and wrapped his hands around her. One landed on her back and the other between her shoulder blades. He gently pulled her into him.

Kassie's eyes closed as she tentatively put her hands at Hollywood's waist. The feel of his strong body holding hers went a long way toward making her relax.

Hollywood wasn't Richard. Not even close. He wasn't trying to cop a feel, he was just hugging her. And it felt awesome.

"Relax, Kass. It's going to be fine," Hollywood whispered. The hand that had been between her shoulder blades went up to her head and encouraged her to lay it on his shoulder.

She put her cheek against the dark blue jacket and moved her arms a bit farther around him so they were resting on his back.

"Breathe," he murmured.

Kassie took a deep breath. Then another. Then one more. Hollywood smelled awesome. She could smell the chemicals used to dry-clean his uniform, but it was the woodsy one that made her tilt her chin up and put her nose against his neck.

Kassie felt Hollywood's hand move from the back of her head to her nape, but she was concentrating too hard on finding the source of the amazing smell coming from him to really register it. She inhaled again. There. It was definitely stronger at his neck.

"Are you smelling me?" Hollywood asked in a quiet voice.

Embarrassed that she'd been caught, Kassie tried to step out of his embrace, but his arms tightened around her, cutting off her escape. Deciding that it was better if she didn't have to look at him, she laid her cheek back down on his chest and said, "Maybe."

She felt his chest move with the huff of air that escaped his mouth. "Can't say a woman has ever smelled me before."

"They don't know what they're missing," Kassie joked.

"You like it?"

She nodded against him. "It's subtle. But it shows that you went through the effort tonight. Maybe you didn't and it's just your soap, but I like it."

"It's probably my aftershave," Hollywood told her.

Kassie couldn't resist. She shifted in his embrace and ran her nose along the underside of his jaw once more, inhaling as she went. "You smell good," she told him unnecessarily.

Hollywood took a small step back and brought a hand to her chin, lifting her head so she had no choice but to look at him. "You're a mass of contradictions, Kassie Anderson. One second you're funny and I'm laughing my ass off, and the next you're acting as if you think the boogey man is going to jump out of a corner. Then you're sniffing me and saying how good you think I smell."

She shrugged a little self-consciously. "I don't mean to be contrary."

"I like it. But if you go around smelling my friends like you just did me, I won't be happy."

She grinned up at him. "I won't. Promise. But you should know…I love the way men smell. At least when they're putting in the effort. Rich…err…my ex never bothered. Said cologne and aftershave were for pussies. I've been known to compliment strangers in an elevator or waiters on how nice they smell."

"Noted. And your ex was wrong. Wanting to smell nice for your date or woman doesn't make a man a pussy. *Not* wanting to do something that pleases her does."

Oh Lord. Hollywood was saying and doing all the right things. The guilt threatened to overcome her again. Kassie hated that she was deceiving him. So far he'd been amazing. Definitely not the asshole Richard or Dean had said he was.

She swallowed hard. Karina. She had to remember her sister. She was doing this for her.

"Shall we go and find your friends?" Kassie asked. The sooner she got this over with the better. She didn't know what kind of information Dean wanted her to get, but maybe someone would say something she could pass on.

"Yeah," Hollywood said absently, his eyes searching hers. For what, she had no idea, but hoped the guilt she felt for lying to him wasn't shining like a beacon on her face.

He dropped his arms and threaded his fingers with

hers, giving her a squeeze before turning to the large room. They wandered through the space, Hollywood nodding at people as he went. Kassie held on to his hand as if it were a lifeline.

After a couple of minutes, he steered them to the same group of men and women Kassie had noticed earlier. If she'd been intimidated before, now she was even more so.

"Hey, Hollywood," one of the men greeted as they came up to the group.

"Hey, Beatle. Everyone, this is Kassie Anderson."

Kassie gave a little wave, feeling awkward and out of place. "Hi."

"Oh my God, I love your dress!" one of the women exclaimed. "That color is so cool. I thought it was black at first, but I can see now it's dark purple."

"Thanks," Kassie said. She gripped Hollywood's hand unconsciously.

"I'm Rayne," the woman who complimented her dress said, holding out her hand in greeting.

Kassie had to drop Hollywood's hand to shake Rayne's, but she felt his hand move to the small of her back as she leaned forward to greet the woman. "It's good to meet you," she told her.

"I'm Emily," one of the other women said in an even tone. "It's so good to meet you."

Kassie shook her hand too.

The last woman also introduced herself. "And I'm Harley. Yes, it's a weird name. My parents were bikers and named their kids after their favorite thing in the world."

"I'm Kassie," Kassie said. "With a K." She shrugged. "My parents thought it'd be cute to be unique with my name, and when my little sister came along, decided to stick with the K theme and named her Karina."

"The guy next to Rayne is Ghost, Emily is married to Fletch, and Harley is with Coach. The others are Beatle, Blade, and Truck." Hollywood finished the introductions.

After she nodded at each of the men, Truck said, "You ladies want some punch? I'm going to get a round."

Kassie looked over to where the large man had indicated and flinched. She'd been looking for the grog bowl, and wasn't sure how she'd missed it. On a long table against the opposite wall were two large punch bowls.

"I don't want any grog," Kassie blurted.

"Pardon?"

"Grog? Did she say grog?"

"What?"

The murmured questions came from Hollywood's friends, but Kassie only had eyes for Hollywood. "I don't know what I did wrong, but please don't make me drink it." She knew she was panicking, but couldn't help it. The grog bowl was one thing she'd researched that was true about Richard's farce of a military function.

"Kass—" Hollywood began, but she cut him off.

"I promise I'll be good. I won't embarrass you. Just don't make me drink it. I'll gag. I know I will. I just—"

"Kassie," Hollywood said sternly, putting his hands on either side of her neck and forcing her to look up at him. "There isn't a grog bowl here. It's punch. Just punch."

Her brows furrowed, Kassie looked up at him in confusion. She gripped his wrists as if her life depended on it. She saw nothing but concerned eyes looking down at her. Didn't hear his friends whispering to each other. "Punch?"

"Yeah, Kass. Plain ol' watered-down Hi-C, most likely. Fruit punch. Not grog."

She swallowed hard. "Are you sure? There's always grog. I Googled it."

Hollywood turned his head, but didn't take his eyes from hers. "Blade. Can you tell Kassie the grog bowl tradition?"

"Sure. They're commonplace at dining-ins. It's a tradition dating back to the Knights of the Round Table. Because of the weight of armor back in the day, it was hard to move and get a drink. So it was used as a punishment for someone who was out of order or unruly. The same thing applies today. There's usually an alcoholic and non-alcoholic version and people who are found to be in violation of any kind of rule have to drink from the grog bowl."

"And what's a dining-in?" Hollywood asked, still holding Kassie's eyes.

"It's a formal military ceremony for members of a unit to foster camaraderie," Blade said immediately.

"And are spouses, girlfriends, or significant others invited?"

"No," Blade said succinctly.

Hollywood's eyes narrowed, and he asked Kassie in a low voice, "When did you partake of a grog bowl, sweetheart?"

"I...uh..." Suddenly Kassie was more than aware of all the men and women around her, staring. She swallowed hard, embarrassed, but the terror hadn't left her.

"Did your ex take you to an event with a grog bowl? You saw people drinking from it?" Hollywood pushed.

"He had an event at his place one night that included it," Kassie told him, then bit her lip. "I told you about that. His friends dressed up in their fancy uniforms and came over. I usually messed up the most and had to drink from it all night. They thought it was funny to make me."

Hollywood's eyes closed momentarily and Kassie

swore she heard one of his friends say "motherfucker" under their breath, but before she could say anything, Hollywood's eyes opened and he said earnestly, "I'm sorry you had to do that, Kassie. As Blade said, the grog bowl is reserved for special soldiers-only functions. I can't deny it's gross, we've all had our share, but it's supposed to be all in good fun. And I swear to you, all that's in the punch bowl tonight is punch. Nothing gross. Okay?"

Kassie nodded. Embarrassed now. She'd made a fool out of herself. She should've known Richard hadn't been following proper military protocol. The grog bowl was a real thing, but only for closed ceremonies…not for friends or family members.

"I don't think I like this ex of yours," Hollywood said, straightening, and reaching down for her hand once more.

"That makes two of us," Kassie said with a nervous chuckle.

"Now that we have that out of the way…anyone want a cup of watered-down, barely drinkable fruit punch?" Truck asked dryly.

"Oh, with that description, how can we say no?" Emily asked with a laugh.

"Four cups, coming right up," Truck said, lifting his chin at Kassie in what she thought was supposed to be a reassuring gesture, but in fact was just confusing.

The large man returned after a couple of minutes and handed out cups to the women.

Kassie looked down at it, still not one hundred percent believing it wasn't a mixture of vinegar, hot sauce, and whatever other gross thing Richard had found to pour into the grog bowl at his parties. She tried to surreptitiously smell the drink before she sipped it, but Hollywood had his eyes on her and caught her at it.

Without a word, he gently took the cup out of her hand and brought it to his own lips, taking a sip, showing her that it was safe to drink. He then handed it back and nodded at her.

Feeling like an idiot, Kassie took a drink of the red liquid. It was exactly as Truck had described, nothing but watered-down punch. Feeling even *more* like an idiot, she let the conversation carry on around her, listening more than participating.

"I can't believe Mary didn't come with us tonight," Rayne pouted. "One of you should've asked her," she said accusingly, glaring at Beatle, Blade and Truck.

"I did," Truck said nonchalantly.

"You did?" Rayne gaped at the large man.

"Yup. She said no." Truck didn't look that upset that he'd been turned down.

"Damn. She doesn't tell me anything anymore," Rayne said sadly.

Ghost put his arm around her shoulders and hugged

her, but didn't say anything.

"Don't take it personally," Truck said. "She'd adjusting to her new job, a new city, and the fact that her best friend is practically married."

"It doesn't matter," Rayne protested. "We've been as close as sisters for as long as I can remember. When she went through chemo, we spent almost every day together. Something's up with her and it's killing me that she's closed me out."

"I don't think you should take it personally," Emily said quietly. "After Annie and I were taken, she was amazing. She cooked for us and babysat Annie several nights when me and Fletch were trying to get our heads wrapped around what happened. Give her some time. Friendships as close as yours don't just dry up. She's just trying to figure out where she fits in your life now that you have Ghost."

Kassie choked on the punch she'd been drinking. She looked at Emily with wide eyes. *This* was Emily? *The* Emily? "Is your name Emily Grant?" she asked.

Everyone's eyes turned to her as Emily responded.

"It was. Now it's Emily Fletcher. I got married a couple weeks ago."

Kassie's mind whirled. She'd known this group of men were the ones Richard hated, but it hadn't really solidified in her mind. She'd pictured them as more redneck, rougher, more assholey. But they'd all been really nice to her so far. She couldn't reconcile Richard and Dean's rants against them with the men standing in front of her now.

"Do you know her?" Fletch asked in confusion.

Kassie quickly shook her head. "No, not really. But I read about you in the paper," she said, trying to come up with a reason that would make sense to these men on how she might know Emily's last name.

"Damn papers," Fletch grumbled.

Emily smiled a bit ruefully. "Yeah, I never thought I'd ever be famous. And certainly not for being kidnapped by a psychotic soldier."

"But, you're okay? You and your daughter?" Kassie asked, needing to know.

Emily nodded. "Yeah, we're both great. Annie thought it was an exciting adventure. I hate that it happened at all, but thank God my daughter is resilient and more adventurous than skittish."

"Good," Kassie said in a heartfelt tone. The more she got to know the men and women around her, the more her anxiety rose. If they knew why she was there, they'd hate her. And that thought was becoming more and more abhorrent.

A chime rang throughout the room and the men all looked toward the door.

"It's time for the receiving line," Blade said.

"Good. It's my favorite part of the evening," Coach

said, putting his arm around Harley.

Kassie stiffened. God. The receiving line. Images of what Richard had made her do swam through her brain. Once again, because of her research, she knew his version was perverted and twisted, but she couldn't help shuttering when she thought about it.

"It's not as bad as you think," Hollywood whispered into her ear as he gently took the now-empty cup from her hand and placed it on a nearby table. "I'll be right next to you the whole time."

Everyone started walking toward the doors and Hollywood pulled Kassie with him. Her mind went back to that night in Richard's apartment.

They exited the room into the lobby, where a line had formed headed into a second, larger ballroom. After going through the receiving line, they'd have dinner…if Kassie could force anything into her stomach. She was nervous and unsure about everything going on around her.

"You're really tense. Are you okay?" Hollywood asked quietly as he leaned down and spoke next to her ear.

Kassie nodded tersely.

"I don't think you are," Hollywood countered, and once again turned her so she was facing him. "What's wrong?"

"Nothing."

"Kassie," he warned.

"I just…I've had a bad experience with a receiving line," she blurted out.

"Christ," Hollywood muttered. "What did that asshole make you do at his so-called fucking ball this time?"

Beatle and Blade were standing on either side of them, and Kassie didn't really want to admit what Richard had made her do. She pressed her lips together nervously then finally said, trying to joke, "What do they say? When you're nervous, try to picture everyone standing in their underwear?"

Hollywood sighed, as if he realized she wasn't going to tell him what had happened with her ex. "That's when you're about to give a speech, Kass. The receiving line is another tradition that goes back a long way. It's annoying and somewhat archaic, but it's nothing to be afraid of. We'll tell the attendant our names, and he'll announce us. Then we'll walk down the line of the highest-ranking officers and non-commissioned officers who are attending tonight. You'll shake their hands, say hello, and move on. That's it. That's all that's going to happen."

"I know." She did. But it didn't stop the memories from flicking through her brain.

"What did he make you do?"

She licked her lips nervously, but didn't answer. If

she'd thought she was embarrassed back then, it was nothing compared to the thought of admitting to Hollywood what Richard had made her do.

"Tell me so I can reassure you, and you can get that wide-eyed look of consternation off your face. I hate it, sweetheart. I hate that this is freaking you out. Do you want to leave? We can totally go. In fact, I think we will. Beatle, tell Ghost that—"

"He made me kiss all his friends as I went down the line." Kassie blurted out.

Hollywood looked her with such an expression of horror on his face that she hurried to joke, "I know that's not what's going to happen tonight. I mean, can you imagine what the men would look like with all that lipstick on their faces by the time it was over?"

"When you say kiss, what do you mean?" Hollywood asked in a lethal tone. "Like on the cheek?"

Kassie shook her head.

"A peck on the lips?"

She shook her head again and bit her lip. He was really pissed. She should've kept her mouth shut.

"Let me get this straight. He made you go through a line of his friends and make out with them? When he was standing right there? What the fuck is wrong with him?"

Hollywood's voice had risen enough so Blade and Beatle easily heard him. Kassie glanced at their faces and winced. They looked equally horrified.

He turned to Blade and said tersely, "We'll be back." Then he grabbed hold of Kassie's hand and towed her toward the front of the line.

Panicked, Kassie tugged on her hand, but he wasn't letting go. "Hollywood, please, I know it's not true, he's an asshole and..." Her voice trailed off when he pushed past the people waiting at the doorway to the ballroom and pulled her to the side against the wall. He leaned against it and pulled her so that her back was to his front. He put both arms around her belly, and held her tightly against him.

Then he leaned over until his chin rested on her shoulder and he said in her ear. "Watch, Kass. This is what the receiving line at an Army Ball is like. What a *real* one is like, not what your ex made you do."

Without a word, eyes huge, Kassie watched. Couples and single soldiers alike would introduce themselves to the attendant at the front of the line, and he would in turn say their name when they greeted the first person in the line. Then they walked down it, shaking hands with each person. No one lingered. No one kissed anyone else. Everyone was smiling and polite. It was exactly like what she'd seen online.

Feeling humiliated once more at what she'd admitted to Hollywood and what Richard had made her do, Kassie's entire body shook. Hollywood tightened his arms around her, keeping her from breaking into a million mortified pieces at his feet.

Putting his lips at her ear once again, Hollywood said softly, his warm breath sending shivers through her body as it wafted against her sensitive ear, "It's obvious everything that asshole of an ex told you and made you go through was complete bullshit. He used and abused you—and that is not acceptable. No way in hell. I'm so sorry that happened to you. I'm glad you were smart enough to go online and find out what a real ball is about, but I'm still sorry you had to go through what you did in the first place. The Army is about respect, sweetheart. Yeah, we can be outspoken assholes, but traditions are meant to honor those who came before us. Not to demean and insult."

He took a breath and ran his nose gently up the side of her neck, just as she'd done to him earlier. Kassie heard him inhale deeply before he continued. "There's no way in hell I'd let anyone treat you with disrespect. When you're with me, no one will touch you. No one will kiss you. And I certainly wouldn't stand next to you and let it happen in the first place. I'm kinda possessive when it comes to my girlfriends. I don't share. I'd *never* share you." He pulled back and turned her in his arms.

Kassie felt her heart beating way too fast, but she liked being in Hollywood's arms. Instead of feeling trapped, as she had in Richard's, she felt protected and safe.

He leaned down and kissed her forehead gently before asking, "You okay?"

"I'm sorry. I don't mean to keep freaking out on you."

"I don't blame you. If I'd been through what you obviously have, I'd be freaking too. But trust me when I say that nothing that happens tonight is going to embarrass or humiliate you. We're going to eat, then there will be speeches that will probably bore you to tears. There will be toasts to the Army, Fort Hood, and our units. Then there will be dancing. Nice, respectable dancing. No one will have to take their clothes off. Okay?"

Kassie knew he was trying to make a joke, and she appreciated it. "Darn, and I wore my pasties and everything."

He grinned and shook his head in amusement. He ran his index finger down her nose and said simply, "If you're concerned about anything, just ask me about it. I won't laugh."

"I will. Although you do know that if something is on the Internet, it has to be true. I can't wait for the parade of lions, tigers, and bears that are supposed to come at the end of every Army Ball."

The look on Hollywood's face was priceless, as if he hoped she was kidding, but wasn't one hundred percent sure. Kassie tried to keep a straight face, but couldn't. Her lips twitched and she bit her lip to keep her smile from escaping.

"Jeez," Hollywood breathed. "I thought you were serious for a second. I can see I'm gonna have to stay on my toes around you."

"I have a tendency to joke when I'm nervous," Kassie told him. "I'll try to curb it."

"Don't. I like it," he told her, leaning down and kissing her once more on the forehead. He took her hand in his own again and headed back through the doors to their spot in line.

"All okay?" Truck asked when they returned.

"Yup," Hollywood said.

"Do I want to know what her asshole ex did with the receiving line?"

"Nope," Hollywood answered succinctly.

"I'll tell you later," Blade told Truck, sounding pissed.

Kassie blushed and bit her lip nervously. Man, these guys had to think she was a complete idiot. She refrained from making a bad joke...barely.

They shuffled along in the line until it was their turn. Kassie watched carefully as Harley, Rayne, Emily, and their men went through the line. Then it was Blade, Truck, and Beatle's turn.

"Just keep breathing, sweetheart," Hollywood murmured before he gave the attendant their names.

Before she knew it, they were through the line and it was done. Hollywood kept his hand on the small of her back the entire time, giving her the support she didn't know she needed to keep her memories at bay.

"Where do you want to sit?" Rayne asked no one in particular. Ghost led their group to a table at the outer edge of the room.

Following everyone's lead, Kassie stayed standing next to her seat. As the ballroom filled up and it got noisier, she leaned into Hollywood and asked, "Why are we all still standing?"

Without telling her she was stupid for asking, or belittling her, Hollywood simply answered her question. "We're following the lead of the ladies at the head table. It's considered rude to sit before them."

"Oh," Kassie said. At Richard's gathering, she'd had to serve the men, and because that hadn't seemed weird to her—he always made her serve him and he ate first— she hadn't researched it.

Finally, the women at the head of the room sat, and the men at their table held out the chairs for them. Kassie smiled up at Hollywood and carefully sat. He immediately pulled out his own chair and settled himself next to her.

Kassie picked up the program on the table and followed along as the night commenced. First they all stood as the colors were presented. They stayed standing for the invocation and as several toasts were made.

Then a spotlight came on over a table near the front of the room. It had a white tablecloth and there was a single red rose in a vase with a yellow ribbon tied around the top. A place setting with an upside down glass, a single candle, and an empty chair completed the setup.

The lights dimmed and a man at the front of the room began to speak.

"The cloth is white—symbolizing the purity of their motives when answering the call to serve.

The single red rose reminds us of the lives of these Americans...and their loved ones and friends who keep the faith, while seeking answers.

The yellow ribbon symbolizes our continued uncertainty, hope for their return and determination to account for them.

A slice of lemon reminds us of their bitter fate, captured and missing in a foreign land.

A pinch of salt symbolizes the tears of our missing and their families—who long for answers after decades of uncertainty.

The lighted candle reflects our hope for their return—alive or dead.

The glass is inverted—to symbolize their inability to share a toast.

The chair is empty—they are missing. A moment of silence for the lost heroes."

No one moved in the large ballroom. No one coughed, nor said a word. After a few moments, the man at the podium spoke once more.

"Let us now raise our water glasses in a toast to honor America's POW/MIAs, to the success of our efforts to account for them, and to the safety of all now serving our nation."

Everyone in the room raised a glass and toasted to the missing men and women—and Kassie closed her eyes to hold back the emotion she was feeling.

She felt a hand on her thigh and turned to face Hollywood.

He didn't say anything, but stared at her as if he could read her mind. As if he knew the awful thing Richard had done. And as if compelled to tell him, Kassie said, "Before we ate at my ex's get-together, he called it the 'traitor table.' He said the white tablecloth is there because it more easily shows the blood that fell because of his actions, the empty plate is because he doesn't deserve to eat, the rose represents the tears of the women and children who weep for their loved one, the yellow ribbon is for revenge, and the empty chair is because he doesn't deserve to sit at the table with civilized society."

The anger in Hollywood's eyes was piercing in its

intensity, but Kassie knew it wasn't directed at her.

"By this point in his stupid event, I knew he was whacked. Everyone knows what a yellow ribbon symbolizes. They'd have to be an idiot not to. When I was researching formal Army events the next day, I found a picture of the exact table he called the traitor table, and read the words the man here just said."

She paused and looked back up at the front, toward the heartbreaking symbolism of the empty table. "It was much more beautiful read aloud tonight," she whispered.

The speeches continued, but Kassie couldn't pay attention. She felt Hollywood lean into her and once again his lips were at her ear as he spoke.

"I wish I could have one minute alone with your ex. Kassie, he deliberately bastardized the most honored traditions of the Army."

"I'm embarrassed I stayed with him as long as I did."

"You have nothing to be embarrassed about. *He's* the one who should be about what he did. Embarrassed and ashamed."

"I'm sorry about the traitor thing," she mumbled. "Even though I knew it couldn't be true, he made it sound so believable."

Hollywood brought a finger up to her chin and turned her until she was facing him. "There's nothing to be sorry about. He might've made it sound believable, but you were smart enough to still know something was wrong and research it yourself."

Without another word, Hollywood's mouth came down on hers, and he gave her the sweetest kiss she'd ever had. It was just a brief touch of his lips to hers, but it was the most intimate kiss she'd ever received.

Kassie stared up at him with wide eyes, her breaths coming fast and hard.

"Now you know."

She nodded and licked her lips. Kassie swore she could taste Hollywood on them, but that was stupid, he hadn't even really kissed her.

His eyes went to her lips and she saw his pupils dilate.

Good. Lord. She, Kassie Anderson, was turning this man on. This beautiful man who could have any woman in the room. She had no idea what to do with that.

Everyone around them repeated a toast, shaking them both out of the moment. Kassie turned and raised her water glass, having no idea what or who they were toasting now, but going with it nonetheless.

How this night was both the worst and best one of her life was something Kassie would never understand, but it was. It seemed as if Hollywood liked her, really liked her, and she cared about him right back. He was understanding, sweet, funny, gentlemanly, hot, and he'd kissed her. But she was only there because Richard wanted information about the men and women sitting at the table that he could use against them. She didn't know what he wanted to do to them, but if kidnapping a woman and child wasn't enough, she didn't *want* to know what he had planned.

Making the decision right then as the servers began to bring out plates of food, Kassie knew she had to come clean to Hollywood before the end of the night. She couldn't in good conscience continue any relationship they might have with this big secret between them.

He wouldn't be happy, she knew that. But hopefully after he heard why she'd done it, he'd understand.

She smiled over at him, somehow thankful that her ex-boyfriend had blackmailed her into messaging the soldier sitting next to her.

Chapter Six

HOLLYWOOD SMILED DOWN at the woman in his arms. Somehow, after the misunderstanding at the beginning of the night, things had calmed down once the meal started. He couldn't believe she'd agreed to come to the ball with him after her experience with her ex. What a douchenugget.

Kassie had relaxed enough to talk openly with the other women. She'd laughed and joked with his teammates too. All in all, this had to be the best date he'd ever been on. He'd actually enjoyed one of the formal Army balls for once, which was a huge deal for him.

The only weirdness in the night, other than Kassie thinking she'd be forced to drink grog, came about halfway through dinner. Truck's phone had rung and he'd gotten up and left the table as soon as he heard who was on the other end of the line. Excusing himself, Hollywood had followed him, wanting to make sure everything was all right.

Truck had shared more with him about his situation with Mary than with any of their teammates. She'd started chemo again, but hadn't told Rayne. Both men hated keeping the secret from their teammate's woman, but Mary had begged Truck not to say anything.

Hollywood didn't agree with Mary's thought process, that she'd taken up so much of Rayne's time her first bout with cancer, she didn't want to do it again, but it wasn't his decision to make.

He caught up with Truck in the lobby and heard his end of the conversation.

"...me an hour to get back there. Will you be all right until then? And Annie's asleep? Good. No, you did the right thing, and no, you're not interrupting anything. The ball is boring anyway." Truck chuckled, but Hollywood could tell there was no humor in it. "Mary, I already told you it was fine. You absolutely did the right thing. I'll be there in an hour. No, I won't tell them why I'm coming back to help babysit Annie. You're just going to have to trust me, aren't you?"

His voice dropped. "Don't cry, Mare. I know you hate this. But we'll get you through it just like last time. I don't care what the statistics say, you *will* beat this a second time. Yeah, all right. Go lay down. Relax. I'll be there as soon as I can. Bye."

As soon as he hung up, Hollywood asked, "Mary and Annie okay?"

"Yeah. Annie's asleep. Mary had chemo yesterday and can't stop throwing up. She's worried that she can't look after Annie properly. If something happens, she said she'd be useless to do anything. So I'm gonna head back and take care of them both until Fletch and Emily get home tomorrow."

Knowing there was a lot more going on between Truck and Rayne's best friend, Hollywood asked, "You want me to let Em know?"

"Would you?"

"Of course."

"Don't tell them about the chemo," Truck warned.

"Of course not," Hollywood said, not offended.

"Thanks. I appreciate it."

"You know what you're doing?" He had to ask.

Truck nodded firmly. "Yeah, I know *exactly* what I'm doing."

"Mary hasn't been very nice to you in the past." Hollywood told Truck something he undoubtedly knew.

"Look, I know you guys worry about me, but don't. Mary was protecting Rayne. She was pissed at Ghost and taking it out on me. Any snark she's thrown since then hasn't been because she *doesn't* like me."

Hollywood eyed his friend, then nodded. "She gonna be all right?"

"Fuck yes, if I have anything to say about it," Truck said emphatically.

"Good. Drive safe. I'll see you later."

Hollywood had gone back into the ballroom and told the group Truck went home to give Mary a hand with little Annie. He'd had to reassure Emily and Fletch, and Rayne, a hundred times that it was nothing and that Mary and Truck could take care of Annie until they returned home the next day.

Now Hollywood was on the dance floor with Kassie. She fit perfectly in his arms, and even though they weren't really dancing, more like swaying back and forth, Hollywood didn't care because he could hold her.

"Can we talk?" Kassie asked after they'd been dancing for several songs.

"Sure, sweetheart."

"Not here. Is there someplace we can take a walk or something?"

Hollywood looked down in concern at Kassie. It was never good when a woman said she wanted to talk, but he really didn't like that he couldn't read what was going through Kassie's head at the moment. He'd thought her revelations about what had happened to her at the hands of her ex were over. He wondered what else the man had done disguised as an Army tradition. He didn't like the man. Really didn't. Kassie had already run a gamut of emotions, and he was liking the relaxed and easygoing woman currently by his side, and didn't want anything else to upset her tonight.

"I think there's a small garden off the lobby. We

could go there."

"Great."

Hollywood pulled away and led her out of the ballroom, lifting his chin at Coach as he passed his teammate, letting him know he was leaving for the moment. They might be in the States, at a formal function, but no one on the team ever lost their attentiveness and support of each other. It had saved their lives many times.

Hollywood and Kassie wandered out of the lobby into the small walkway area behind the hotel. There were lights strung up in the trees, giving the entire area a romantic but safe feel. Benches lined the walkway and Kassie walked straight to one and sat.

Hollywood followed, suddenly more nervous than he'd been all night. He'd wanted to ask Kassie out again at the end of the evening. He not only wanted to see her again, he *needed* to. They'd clicked on a basic level, and he'd been overjoyed to find out that the funny woman on the other end of the emails and messages was exactly the same in person.

"What's up?" he asked, taking one of her perpetually cold hands in his own. It seemed natural already, to take hold of her fingers and hold them against his leg as they sat next to each other. He couldn't keep his hands off her.

"I've had a really good time tonight," Kassie started.

"And before I say anything else, I want you to know that I'd like to see you again."

"Good," Hollywood said in satisfaction. "I want to see you again too."

She smiled shyly at him. "I wasn't sure what to expect tonight, and you know about my experience with my ex's military shindig. Even though I'd researched what to expect, I still wasn't quite sure about it all."

"I'm surprised you agreed to come. Especially if you thought you'd have to drink out of the grog bowl," Hollywood said honestly.

"About that," Kassie said with a bit of reluctance. "I…"

"What? You can tell me anything, Kass."

"Okay, well, you know I have an asshole of an ex. He's not in the picture anymore, but he has this friend who has been following me around and making my life miserable. I've tried to ignore him, but that hasn't worked."

Hollywood stiffened next to her. "He's stalking you?"

Kassie shook her head. "Not really. But—"

"If he's following you around and you don't want him to, he's stalking you," Hollywood told her sternly. "Have you gone to the cops?"

"No. But I'm going to next week." She held up her free hand and smiled at him as he continued to glare.

"Swear. I can't do this on my own anymore. I realize that now. But I need to talk to my family first."

"You want me to come with you to the police station?" Hollywood asked, not sure why the question popped out, only knowing that he hated the thought of anyone harassing the woman sitting next to him. They weren't exactly dating, but they were something. And he cared about her.

"Maybe. But Hollywood, there's more."

"More?"

"Yeah," Kassie said. "Anyway, so my ex's friend has been annoying me for a year or so. He and my ex were thick as thieves growing up. But you have to know when I first started dating Richard, he was sweet and kind. It wasn't until he went overseas that he changed. He said an explosive went off too close to him or something. He was okay, but it rattled his brain. The doctors said he was fine, but I don't think he was. It changed him. He'd asked me to marry him, but when he came home he was mean. He wasn't the same man I'd been dating. I tried to be sympathetic, the last thing I wanted to do was break up with him after he was injured while deployed, but after the thing at his house, I had to.

"His childhood friend tried to join the Army with him, but didn't make it through basic. The two of them would train on a course my ex made himself. Day and night, they'd run through it. Richard taught his friend everything he learned. When Richard got back from overseas, he somehow got his friend to buy into everything he was saying and doing. It was like they were a cult or something. They scared me. Both of them. I tried to break up with Richard, but he wouldn't let me."

Hollywood didn't like the sound of the story he was hearing, but he stayed quiet and let Kassie continue.

"I'm ashamed to admit I let our relationship go on too long, partly because I was hoping Richard would go back to being the man I fell in love with, and because I think I was scared what he'd do if I involved the police, but the bottom line is that I didn't know how to extricate myself. The times when my ex was at Fort Hood were bliss for me because I didn't have to worry about him. But he always had his friend, Dean, keep an eye on me. It got really bad in the last few months. My ex was crazy, talking about all sorts of insane things about revenge and stuff."

All of a sudden, Hollywood got a bad feeling. The hair on the back of his neck stood up and he stiffened.

"I tried so many times to tell him that he was imagining things and needed to go to the doctor, but he didn't listen. I couldn't do anything right, and he was always so angry. I was scared of him. I'm *still* scared of him. When Richard went to prison last year, I thought I was free. I thought I could finally get on with my life."

She'd said it a couple of times, but it finally clicked

in Hollywood's head. He hoped like hell it was a coincidence, but he had a bad feeling it wasn't. He loosened his hold on Kassie's hand, feeling the loss acutely but ignoring it, and asked, "What was your boyfriend's name?"

"You have to understand how scared I was of him," Kassie said urgently, wiping her hands on the skirt of her dress. "Dean was still following me around and giving me messages from my ex."

"What's your ex's last name, Kassie?" Hollywood asked again.

"Jacks. His name is Richard Jacks," she whispered.

"Jesus fucking Christ," Hollywood swore.

"I know," Kassie said quickly, her words running together now. "When he said I needed to find you on the dating website I didn't want to, but I wasn't given a choice. And I didn't think I'd like you so much."

"So you're spying on me," Hollywood said in a flat voice, all the good feelings about the woman sitting next to him now gone.

She frantically shook her head. "No, it's not like that at all. I—"

"You messaged me because Jacks told you to. Then you befriended me and got me to ask you here tonight so you could report back to him."

"Sort of, but—"

Hollywood wouldn't let her finish. "What a joke,"

he spat. "Here I was thinking I'd finally met someone who liked me for me instead of my looks, but instead I find out it's worse than that. You're no better than the barrack bunnies who just want to fuck for a night."

"Hollywood, no, I—"

"So what are you going to report back, Kassie? You going to tell your boyfriend that Coach is now dating someone so he can go after her too? Maybe you'll tell him to go after Mary, that she's Rayne's best friend and vulnerable."

"No, listen. I would never—"

"Spare me," Hollywood bit out and stood up, glaring down at her. "I don't want to hear it. I honestly thought you were different. I was so pissed when I found out about the grog bowl and receiving line thing. But it was most likely all an act, wasn't it? A story you two concocted to make me feel sorry for you. You've probably fucked all his friends, haven't you? Did you guys all laugh about how scared little Annie was when she was drugged and ripped out of her wrecked car? Maybe you thought it was funny how Emily was blackmailed all those months and got sick because she didn't have enough money to eat because she was giving it to Jacks?"

"No! Dammit, Hollywood, stop interrupting and listen to me, I didn't—"

"Why should I listen to you?" Hollywood was on a

roll. He saw her through a haze of red that had filled his vision. He couldn't remember ever being so angry. Part of it was that he'd liked Kassie so much and the other was because Jacks wasn't done fucking with him and his team. "You're with Jacks. He's in prison and still trying to make our lives miserable. Pass a message on to him for me and my friends, would you? Tell him to bring it. It doesn't matter what he does, we'll still kick his ass. Jacks is a miserable little coward and he'll always be a loser."

Hollywood continued to glare at Kassie. She'd stood up as well and was facing him with her arms crossed over her chest. She looked beaten down and scared. He hated that, but her betrayal was eating away at his soul.

"I know he's a loser," Kassie said quietly. "That's what I'm trying to tell you. If you'd let me finish a sentence, you'd—"

Simply listening to her speak hurt his heart. He couldn't let her talk. If he did, she might say something that would make him feel sorry for her and he'd cave. His friends were more important than her. "Why would I let someone who deceived me, and my friends, tell me more lies? You go on home and tell Jacks whatever the fuck you want. But Kassie—if that's even your name—if one hair on any of my friends' heads gets hurt, I'll make *you* pay."

She didn't try to say anything else, simply stared up

at him as he glared down at her.

"Nothing to say now?" he taunted.

"You won't listen to anything I do say, so why should I bother?" she asked flatly.

"Tonight's been a complete waste," Hollywood said bitterly. "*You're* a waste." He turned from her then, trying to block out the look of hurt on her face as his last jab hit its mark. He stalked back into the lobby of the hotel and went straight to the bank of elevators. He punched the button and seethed inside as he waited for the lift.

He needed to let his teammates know that Jacks was still out to get them and had no problem involving others from inside his jail cell. He entered the elevator when it arrived and pressed the button for his floor.

The last glimpse he had of Kassie Anderson was of her back as she walked out the front doors of the hotel. Her head was bowed and shoulders slumped. She certainly didn't look like a woman who was proud of what she'd done...but that didn't change the fact she'd done it.

Hollywood loosened the bowtie around his neck and sighed, suddenly tired. The adrenaline was being reabsorbed into his body, leaving him exhausted and heartsick. Thirty minutes ago he was on top of the world, and now he felt as though he'd been tortured for days by the Taliban.

As he exited the elevator and walked down the hall toward his room, he planned what tomorrow would bring. He'd give his friends their night off, then they'd need to figure out what the hell they were going to do.

Jacks was back, and he would use anyone and everyone to get what he wanted. Revenge.

Chapter Seven

"LET ME GET this straight," Ghost said in a pissed-off tone. "Kassie's ex is Jacks, and she targeted you on the online dating site so she could learn more about us to pass on to that motherfucker?"

"Yes," Hollywood bit out.

"Are you sure?" Coach asked. "I honestly didn't get the sense from her she was that kind of person."

"I'm sure. She told me herself," Hollywood told his friend. "I didn't want to believe it either."

The six men were in Hollywood's room, discussing the information he'd found out the night before about Kassie and their old enemy, Jacks.

Rayne, Emily, and Harley were still sleeping when Hollywood had texted his teammates for a meeting. Truck was back in Temple, but they'd fill him in on what was happening when they got home.

"I don't get it," Beatle interjected. "What did he really hope to learn from her? It's not like you go around talking about our missions and shit. So what…she was supposed to report back what you ate for dinner and how you kiss?"

Hollywood ran his hand through his hair and shrugged. He wished that he'd had the foresight to kiss her, *really* kiss her, instead of just a peck on the lips, before she'd dropped her bomb on him. "I have no fucking idea. Who the hell knows with Jacks. But it pisses me off she was using me."

"It didn't look like she was," Fletch said easily. "In fact, from the way you were holding her hand, I thought you two were definitely hitting it off."

"Why aren't you pissed?" Hollywood ground out. "It was *your* wife and kid who were kidnapped by that asshole. You should be spitting nails that Kassie tried to do this shit."

Fletch sat forward and pinned Hollywood with a look he couldn't interpret. "I know that it was my wife who had a gun pointed at her head by Jacks. I'm *fully* aware of it, and I've wished a hundred times that Rock had put a bullet in that asshole's brain. But, Hollywood, it was *Jacks* who held that gun. Not Kassie. I don't think the woman I met last night could hurt a fly. Emily told me when they went to the restroom, she giggled and laughed with them as if she didn't have a care in the world. My wife liked her, and I trust Em's judgement one hundred percent."

Hollywood shook his head, not convinced. "She lied, man. The only reason she messaged me was because she was trying to get information."

"Maybe in the first place. But why did she *keep* messaging? She could've told Jacks that you didn't take the bait. Or you didn't seem interested in her. But apparently she didn't. She kept emailing you," Fletch pushed.

"Because she needed information!" Hollywood yelled.

Fletch leaned back in his chair and shook his head. "I don't think so."

"Fuck, I don't believe this," Hollywood grumbled.

"Why did she tell you about Jacks?" Ghost asked, his anger from earlier banked.

"Who the fuck knows," Hollywood clipped.

"No, seriously," Ghost insisted. "You were getting close. You'd been holding hands all night. She had you where she wanted you. Can you honestly say you wouldn't have taken her up to your room if she gave the slightest clue she wanted that?" he asked. "Why would she tell you about Jacks if things were going so well?"

The room was silent for a moment before Hollywood ventured, "Because she felt guilty."

"Yeah," Ghost agreed. "I'm sure she did. But she *still* didn't have to tell you shit. She could've ended the night, gone home, then made up some excuse not to see you again if she really felt bad about what she'd done. But instead she owned up to what she did. And while we're on the topic...why *did* she go along with what

Jacks told her to do?"

Hollywood stared at his friend. The question seemed to echo in his brain. *Why?* He brought his fingers up to his forehead and tried to massage out the headache that had been there since he'd found out what Kassie had done the evening before.

"Did she tell you why?" Beatle pushed.

Hollywood tried to think back to the night before. "She said Jacks had a buddy—Dean, I think Kassie said his name was—who didn't make it through basic, but had learned military shit from Jacks and was following her around. After I figured out that Jacks was her ex and she admitted what she did, I didn't exactly give her a chance to explain."

"He's threatening her," Fletch said without a trace of doubt in his voice.

"He's behind bars," Hollywood reminded his friend.

"But his friend isn't," Ghost added.

"Dammit," Hollywood swore. And suddenly *he* felt bad. He was the one who had been wronged in this situation, but somehow he still felt guilty about not listening to Kassie's explanation.

"Keep your friends close, and your enemies closer," Blade said dryly.

"What?" Hollywood asked.

"Keep your friends—"

"I heard you, asshole," Hollywood interrupted.

"What the fuck are you talking about?"

"If Jacks is still out there planning on doing whatever he's hoping to do to us...wouldn't we want someone who has an inside track to him on our side, giving us intel? Wouldn't we want Kassie to help us figure out what he has up his sleeve and who he has helping him? Otherwise we're going in blind, which is asking for a FUBAR situation."

"This situation is already fucked up beyond all repair," Hollywood said dryly. "But you have a point."

"You should email her," Ghost suggested. "Say you're sorry. Tell her you want to talk."

"So I should lie to her just like she did to me?" Hollywood asked his friend.

"*Would* you be?" Ghost responded immediately, with uncanny insight.

Fuck. He loved his friends and the fact that sometimes it seemed like they could read each other's minds, but at the moment it was highly annoying. He wanted to hold on to his irritation. Wanted them to rant and rail about how horrible Kassie was and how what she'd done was unforgivable. But instead they used logic and made him really think about what she might be going through.

Before he could respond to Ghost, Hollywood's phone chimed, indicating he had a new email. Glancing at the device, Hollywood blinked. Then looked again.

"Fuck me," he said under his breath.

"What?" Blade asked urgently. "Is it Truck? One of the women? Annie?"

"No. It's Kassie. She sent me an email," Hollywood told his friends.

When he didn't move, but continued to stare down at his screen, Ghost ordered impatiently, "Go on. Read it."

Hollywood nodded and clicked on the email. The men in the room were quiet as he silently read the words Kassie had sent.

When he stopped and closed his eyes, Ghost said. "Care to share? If it's about Jacks, it involves us all."

"I know," Hollywood said, running his hand through his short hair. He'd gone from being angry when he'd first started talking about the situation with his friends to frustrated and confused in a heartbeat. "She's upset. And has a right to be. I was an ass."

"I don't think—" Coach began, but Hollywood interrupted him.

"No, I was. I appreciate the support, but I didn't let her talk. I kept interrupting her, all pissed off for myself because I liked her and was humiliated that she seemed to only be with me because of Jacks."

"What'd she say?" Ghost asked.

Hollywood cleared his throat, and read Kassie's email to his friends.

To: Hollywood
From: Kassie
Subject: I'm sorry

I'm sorry. I'll say it as many times as I have to until you hear me. I'm sorry. So sorry.

I'm sorry, but I'm also kinda pissed. At you.

I didn't have to tell you about Richard. I didn't have to admit why I'd messaged you that first time, but I did. And you wouldn't even listen to me when I tried to tell you why.

Richard hit me. It hurt. So much that I'd do anything to keep it from happening again.

He made me kiss his disgusting friends.

He made me drink that shit he called grog.

He made up Army traditions like the fucking "traitor table" and wanted me to blindly believe him.

I never felt safe with him after he got hurt. Not once.

But I felt safe with you. Even after only knowing you for a couple of hours, I knew you'd never hurt me. But then you did. You didn't use your fists, but you still hurt me.

You want to know why I messaged you?

Because Richard's friend, Dean, is threatening my little sister. I wouldn't care if he threatened me; that's nothing new. He does it all the time. But he's following Karina. He said if I didn't message you and try to get information from you (what information? That you look hot in your uniform? Those idiots wouldn't know a good plan if it bit them in the ass.) that he was going to make Karina disappear and I'd never see her again.

THAT was something I couldn't ignore. If I got hurt because of my actions, that's one thing, but if Dean hurt Karina, I couldn't live with myself.

That's why I did it.

Even though I was reluctant to do anything Richard and Dean told me to, I did. But you made me trust you. You made me think that I had someone on my side for once. I knew you would be upset, and I didn't blame you, but if you'd at least listened to me and *then* decided that you wanted nothing to do with me, that would've been one thing. But you didn't even give me a chance.

For what it's worth, I'm sorry I first messaged you for the wrong reasons, but once you wrote back, I talked with you because I liked you. You.

I hope you and your friends stay safe. Richard is (obviously) still pissed at all of you. I don't know what he's planning, but I'm pretty sure it involves you all dead and in the ground. Even though I'm upset, sad, and angry at you, I'd hate to see you dead. So be careful.

Good luck.

~Kassie

Call him crazy, but Hollywood couldn't help but feel proud of Kassie. When he didn't give her a chance to apologize she could've slunk back to her home and never talked to him again. But she'd reached out, not knowing if he'd reject her email as badly as he had her in person the night before. Even after she'd been abused by Jacks and his friend, she wasn't afraid to stand up to him. He'd been an asshole, even if he was justified in his reaction to her news, but he should've at least listened to her. He liked her stubbornness and that she refused to let it go.

What he *didn't* like was that Jacks was using his friend to blackmail someone else. It was bad enough he'd done it to Emily. They had to shut this shit down. Yesterday. He stood up.

"You going to her place?" Ghost asked.

"I want to, yes. But I need to figure out where that is first."

Ghost grinned at him. "You gonna ask Beth?"

"Yup," Hollywood said with no remorse. Finding an address should be child's play to the hacker they'd gotten to know over the last couple months.

"Need a wingman?" Blade asked. "She tore you a new asshole. I'm even a little scared of her."

Hollywood glared at his friend, who was grinning from ear to ear. "No."

"You want me to get with Tex or Beth to get info on this Dean guy?" Coach asked.

"Abso-fucking-lutely," Hollywood told him. "We also need to know how he's communicating with Jacks. His letters are supposed to be monitored, as well as phone calls. Anyone know someone at Leavenworth?"

Everyone shook their heads and Ghost said, "I'll

check with Truck. He seems to have connections everywhere."

"Appreciate it. Now if you don't mind, I have a woman to grovel to."

His friends grinned at him.

"Seriously, Hollywood," Fletch said. "You need anything, let me know. Em wants to go down to Sixth Street, so I'll be here for a few hours."

"I will. Now I just need to figure out how in the hell I'm going to keep Kassie safe when she lives an hour from me. And her sister. And get Dean out of the picture. And make Jacks understand that he's never to even *think* about his ex-girlfriend again," Hollywood muttered.

"Hey…is Kassie the reason you asked me about my apartment being available for rent?" Fletch asked suddenly.

Hollywood shrugged, a little embarrassed. "She mentioned in passing once that she was looking to get out of Austin."

Fletch got up, walked over to Hollywood and put his hand on his shoulder. "If she needs or wants it, it's hers. For as long as she needs."

"Even though Jacks is her ex?" Hollywood asked. It was kind of a dick thing to say, but he had to know if Fletch would hold it against her in some way.

"*Especially* because Jacks is her ex. I'm more than

aware of how that buttmuncher can ruin people's lives. After what happened to Em, and then those assholes robbing our wedding reception, my place is as safe as Fort Knox. No one farts on my property without me knowing and being notified by my phone app."

Hollywood chuckled. "Thanks, man, I appreciate it. Don't know if she'll need, or even want it, but it's nice to know the option is there."

"Anything for you. We might not be blood, but we sure as hell are brothers."

Hooahs echoed around the room, and Hollywood smiled to himself, thinking about what Kassie had said about the word.

"Now," he said, holding his hotel door open, "everyone get out so I can go and apologize to Kassie."

After everyone left, and Hollywood had received a text from Beth with Kassie's address, he tried to think about what he would say to her…and failed. She'd apologized to him, but in actuality he should be the one saying sorry to *her*. He was allowed to be upset, but it wasn't cool that he didn't let her explain. And to know that she'd done what she did because her sister was being threatened only made him feel worse.

If someone had threatened his sister, Jade, he'd do whatever it took to keep her safe. Hollywood knew he needed to start out by begging Kassie's forgiveness for not listening to her last night, then work his way up to helping her figure out how to use Jacks's desire for revenge against him. If the man didn't know that Kassie had told him everything, they could use that to figure out what he had planned and take him, and his asshole friend, down.

Chapter Eight

K ASSIE WAS EXHAUSTED. It was late Sunday afternoon and she hadn't slept much last night after getting home from the ball. Too many thoughts had been going through her head. She'd alternated between being sad and heartbroken, then thoroughly pissed off. Hollywood hadn't even given her a chance to speak. To tell him why she'd gone along with Richard and Dean's stupid plan.

He still would've been pissed, and might've stormed off, but at least he'd have all the facts. She knew part of her upset was because she'd liked the man so much and he'd let her down badly. Just once she wanted a champion in her life. Someone who would stand by her, hold her hand, and generally tell her things would be all right. She'd never had that. She thought she had with Richard, but then the stupid explosion while he was overseas had screwed that up.

By the time she'd crawled out of bed, she'd been not only sad about what had slipped through her fingers, namely the first man she'd genuinely liked since Richard, but also a little disappointed. So she'd sent Hollywood an email. Apologized, again, and explained what he wouldn't let her the night before.

Then she'd put on her big-girl panties and headed out to do what she should've done way before now.

Her first stop had been her parents' house. Jim and Donna Anderson needed to know exactly what was going on in their oldest daughter's life. What had been going on for the last couple years or so. They needed to know the kind of man Richard Jacks was.

They'd been understandably shocked at first. Her dad had liked Richard when he'd first met him. He hadn't been around him much after he'd been hurt, and hadn't wanted to believe what the newspapers said he'd done to Emily and her daughter. But listening to Kassie tell him how miserable she'd been toward the end of their relationship, and how he'd verbally and physically abused her, had hit her dad hard.

She was his firstborn. Daddy's little girl. And showing him the emails and texts from Dean, which supposedly came from Richard, had also been hard. Really hard.

Then she'd unfortunately had to tell them that the threat wasn't over. She explained how Dean was now threatening Karina. Her dad had gone a little crazy then. Stomping around the room, ranting about how there was no way Dean was going to get his hands on either of his baby girls. It made Kassie feel good that her parents were taking the threat seriously. She knew she'd been an idiot for not sharing with them earlier.

Then she had to tell her sister that someone was watching her. The terror on Karina's face about broke her. This was why she hadn't said anything before now. She hated that her little sister had to go through this. It was her senior year. She had her Homecoming Dance in a couple weeks. She shouldn't be concerned about anything but which university she wanted to attend next year, cheerleading routines, and grades.

Kassie had left after Karina promised to be careful, and assured her they'd talk more about the entire situation later.

Then she'd gone to the police station to report the harassment by Dean. She had no proof that Richard was involved since he was behind bars, but at least they listened to her. They copied all the evidence, texts and emails that Kassie had brought in. They'd told her to be extra vigilant, to let them know if she got anything more, and advised her to get a restraining order against Dean.

She promised to look into it, but was satisfied for the moment that if anything happened to either her or her sister, God forbid, the police would have something to go off of.

Kassie hadn't eaten anything that morning because

she'd been too anxious. Now she was starving, but she only wanted to get home after dealing with the detective. Karina had been texting her all day, worried about the situation, and all Kassie wanted to do was crawl into bed and pull the covers up and over her head.

She pulled into a parking space in the lot of her apartment complex and looked around. She didn't see anything that looked out of place, but then again, Dean could be inside any one of the cars and she'd never know.

Hating that she was so paranoid, Kassie shivered but took a deep breath and opened the door. Even if she wasn't feeling brave, she could fake it. She grabbed her purse and messenger bag, which held all the evidence she'd been carting around all day, and climbed out. Using her hip to shut the door, she clicked the lock on her key fob and walked quickly toward the front of her apartment building.

She took the stairs, as usual, to the second floor—and stopped dead when she opened the door to her hallway.

Leaning against the wall next to her apartment door was Hollywood. He had his feet crossed at the ankles, his arms over his chest, and his chin down as if he was sleeping.

For just a second, Kassie thought about turning around and making a run for it. He hadn't seen her yet.

But then she took a deep breath. No. She hadn't done anything wrong, and she was sick of being scared all the time. She didn't think she had the strength at the moment to be yelled at, but whatever. This was her life; she'd brought this on herself, so she had to deal with the consequences of her actions.

She walked down the hallway with her head held high. She hadn't taken more than five steps in his direction when Hollywood's head came up, and he pinned her with his gaze as she came toward him.

Kassie couldn't read the emotion behind his eyes. She was exhausted, and the thought of dealing with another harangue from Hollywood made her want to cry. For all her pep talk of being strong, she really wasn't at the moment. She looked down at her keys and fumbled with them until she had her apartment key at the ready.

She passed Hollywood, not saying a word, and stuck the key in the lock.

"How'd you find out where I live?" she asked, deciding to go on the offensive.

"A friend of mine is a hacker," he said calmly, as if he hadn't just admitted to having someone break the law to find her address. "Can we talk?" Hollywood continued in a low voice.

"I think you said everything you needed to last night," Kassie told him, proud of the way her voice didn't quaver.

"I was a dick," he said baldly. "I should've listened to you. I'm glad you emailed."

"Yay. Go me," Kassie mumbled, as she turned the key in the deadbolt and pushed the door open. She turned to Hollywood and looked up at him, standing next to her door, hoping her nonverbal language was loud and clear. "You're forgiven. Now go away."

She would've been good if he hadn't touched her. She could've shut the door in his face and gone on with her evening.

But before she could escape inside, he put his hand on her arm and said softly, "Please. Let me come in so we can talk. I've been waiting for you since before lunch."

She looked up at him in shock, trying to ignore the warmth of his fingers on her arm. "You've been here all day?"

"Yup. Six hours."

Sighing hugely and closing her eyes, Kassie tried to bring back her anger from that morning when she'd emailed him. But she simply didn't have the energy. "Fine. But I'm really tired, so it'll have to be quick."

He nodded, but didn't say anything.

Kassie moved her arm so his hand fell away and entered her apartment. He followed behind and she could feel his eyes on her as she threw her keys into a bowl on a table right inside the door. "Please lock it behind you," she told him, still not looking at him, and wandered farther into her space.

It wasn't much, but it was affordable. A small but functional kitchen, sofa, coffee table, decent-sized television, and a bookcase full of books. When her life went to shit, she'd always been able to fall back on books to get her through. Pictures of her family were everywhere, as was evidence that a less-than-neat woman lived there.

Junk mail on the coffee table, dirty dishes in the sink, a blanket scrunched up at the end of the couch, two pairs of shoes lying haphazardly on the floor near the couch, and half-burnt candles here and there. Kassie mentally shrugged. Whatever. It wasn't like she'd invited him over.

She put the bag with the evidence she'd showed the detective and her parents on the floor by the couch. Her purse landed next to it. Then she sat, feeling as if the weight of the world was on her. It wasn't exactly the strong, take-no-shit attitude she should be showing Hollywood, but she just didn't have it in her at the moment.

The gray suede cushions enveloped her and she sighed in relief. The sofa had been one of the first things she'd bought when she moved in, and she hadn't regretted the purchase for one second. It had been expensive, but it was extremely comfortable and exactly what she needed at that moment.

Closing her eyes, Kassie pretended she was alone. Pretended that her life wasn't in the toilet. That her little sister hadn't cried her eyes out after finding out a creepy, slimy asshole was spying on her and wanted to do her harm.

"Can I get you something to drink?"

Hollywood's voice burst the little solitude bubble she was pretending she was in. Opening her eyes, she turned her head and saw him standing next to the arm of the couch looking down at her with concern.

"No. Can we get this over with?"

Hollywood walked around the low coffee table in front of the couch and sat next to her. He turned toward her, hitching one leg up, his knee touching her thigh. He reached out and grabbed her hand, intertwining his fingers with hers as he'd done the night before. Except now, instead of feeling safe, Kassie felt trapped.

She tugged at her hand, but he tightened his grip. "Relax, Kassie."

"Relax? No way." She tugged again, frustrated that he wouldn't let go. "I don't know what you want me to say. Let go of me, Hollywood."

"No. And you don't have to say anything. *I* do. I was an ass last night. In my defense, you surprised me, but that's not an excuse. You have to understand that I view Jacks just like I see any terrorist. ISIS, Taliban, extremist…you name it. Seriously, that's how I see him. And there I was, enjoying the shit out of our first date, wondering how in the world I'd managed to find you, loving how perfect you seemed to be for me, when you dropped your little bombshell."

Kassie whimpered and pulled harder, and Hollywood merely tightened his hold on her. She didn't want to hear this. She really didn't. She reached over with her free hand to try to pry his fingers away. But he merely put his other hand on top of both of hers, easily stopping her. He spoke faster, as if he sensed she was on the verge of losing it.

"I can't deny I was pissed, but I was upset because of the connection I'd felt between us. Then I woke up this morning feeling as if I'd lost something precious. That I'd made a big mistake. I spoke with my friends and they helped me figure out what I already knew. Kassie…" He paused and looked into her eyes. "I know you didn't have to tell me why you messaged the first time. The fact that you did shows me how much integrity you have. If I gave you a chance to explain last night, I know I would've settled my shit and realized how brave you actually are."

Kassie closed her eyes, scared to give in. She was hanging on by a thread. The entire day had been too much. She felt his fingers tuck a piece of hair behind her ear as he spoke.

"I'm sorry you've been living with Jacks hanging over your head. I'm sorry he put his hands on you. And I'm really sorry you're dealing with his friend. Let me help you, Kassie."

"Why?" she whispered.

"Why do I want to help you?" Hollywood clarified.

Kassie nodded and opened her eyes. She had to see his face when he answered. Surely she'd be able to tell if he was genuine or blowing smoke up her ass.

He didn't shy away from looking her straight in the eyes as he spoke. "Because I've never felt a connection with another woman the way I do with you. A year ago I might not've realized what we had. But since I've seen my friends experience true love, I'm not willing to give up what I feel in my heart is the same thing. In the past, if someone had told me they'd done what you did, I would've blown them off and not thought about them again. But I literally can't do that with you. You've somehow crawled inside me and taken root."

Ignoring the "true love" statement—no way was she touching that one—her lips quirked involuntarily. "So I'm a virus? That's what you're saying?"

He smiled back. "No, sweetheart. I'm just saying that as hard as I tried to write you off last night, I couldn't. We got to know each other pretty well with only emails back and forth. Meeting you last night solidified the fact that there's something special between us. I'm thinking you feel it just as strongly as I do, otherwise you wouldn't have risked telling me about Jacks. You get me and I you. I don't want to throw that away. So you messaged me because Jacks told you to. Whatever. If I didn't hate that motherfucker so much, I'd thank him."

Kassie looked up at the man next to her with big eyes. She couldn't believe he'd gone from completely pissed off and never wanting to see her again last night to saying that he thought they clicked. "I'm perfectly willing to work with you and your friends to tell you what I know about Richard and what he's planning, even though I have no idea *what* he's planning. But I'll be the go-between and give you any information you want. I'll feed false info to him and I'll even be bait if that's what it takes. I'll do all of that without being your friend, Hollywood. I hate what he did to Emily and her daughter. You don't have to give me pretty words and pretend to like me just to get to Richard."

Now he looked pissed. Kassie should've been scared of him, but she knew he wouldn't touch her in anger. Last night had proved that. He'd been furious, but hadn't hit, grabbed, shoved, or otherwise done anything physical to hurt her.

"I'm not telling you how much I like you to get you to be bait. Jesus, Kassie, I can be an ass, but I'm not *that* much of one. I'm not here because I want you as a go-between either. Me and my friends can take care of that asshole without your involvement. I want to get to know *you* better. Take you out to dinner. Watch movies with you. Get to know Karina. Watch her cheer in games. The bottom line is that I want Kassie Anderson. No hidden agenda, sweetheart. Just two people dating and hopefully getting closer."

"Oh." It was a lame response, but it was all she could come up with.

"Is that an 'oh, yes,' or an 'oh, no?'" Hollywood asked.

"I guess...yes."

"Even though it's not a hundred percent yes, I'll take it," Hollywood told her. "Now, are you hungry? I'm starving. I didn't want to take the chance you'd show up if I left to grab lunch."

"Didn't my neighbors say anything? I can't imagine they'd like you lurking in the hallway all day," Kassie asked, trying really hard not to feel bad that he'd been there so long.

"A couple of people asked who I was and what I was doing there." Hollywood shrugged. "I told them I was your boyfriend and we'd had a disagreement. I was here to grovel for your forgiveness. They seemed to be okay with that response, a few even giving me tips on how best to get back in your good graces."

"I don't even want to know," Kassie mumbled.

"Roses, make dinner for you, foot massage, and letting you tie me to the bed so you can have your wicked way with me," Hollywood informed her with a straight face.

Kassie's chin dropped. "Seriously?"

"Seriously. I don't have any flowers with me, and I don't think we're quite ready for bedroom gymnastics, although I have to say, the thought of being at your mercy isn't a turn off, just so you know, as long as turnabout is on the table where that's concerned. But I can make something for dinner if you don't mind. And I've never done it, but I could probably manage a halfway decent foot massage as well."

Kassie was shaking her head before he'd finished. She refused to think about this gorgeous man in her bed. It wasn't going to happen. He'd get to know her, find out she was too boring for his tastes, and back off. "I'm tired, Hollywood. As soon as you go, I'm crashing."

"You need to eat," he said with concern.

"No, I don't. It's not like I'm wasting away. I'll live if I skip a meal." She gestured to herself with her chin.

Hollywood frowned for a moment, then strangely asked, "Where were you today?"

"Uh…" Kassie couldn't think of a response fast enough.

"I waited for you all afternoon. You didn't have any shopping bags with you when you got here, so you weren't at the grocery store or mall. Were you with your family?"

He was astute, she'd have to remember that if he stuck around. She nodded. "Yeah, I try to go over there most weekends."

Hollywood put his hand on the side of her neck, his thumb gently stroking the underside of her jaw, his fingers warm against the sensitive skin behind her ear. "You tell them about Dean and Jacks?"

Kassie nodded. "They weren't happy."

"I can imagine. And Karina? She knows to be careful?"

Kassie nodded again, and pressed her lips together to try to stem the tears lurking behind her eyes. The last thing she needed was sympathy. She'd been like that her entire life. Stoic and strong…unless someone showed her compassion. Then she'd lose it.

"Oh, sweetheart. I'm sorry."

She squeezed her eyes shut, trying to hold back her tears. She waited a beat, then croaked, "It's fine. I should've told them a long time ago."

"You've had a hard day," Hollywood murmured, pulling her to him.

That was it. She couldn't hold back the tears if someone offered her a million dollars. Hollywood's sympathy and the fact he was there in the first place did her in. Her arms were tucked in front of her and she gripped the front of his T-shirt as she cried.

Kassie didn't really know why she was crying. Stress, not sleeping the night before, the ups and downs of dealing with Hollywood, knowing her sister was freaked…it was all of it.

Hollywood didn't say a word, just held her to him with one hand on her back and the other brushing her hair soothingly. Over and over. From the top of her head to the middle of her back, then back to the top.

When she thought she'd finally gotten control of herself, and feeling embarrassed, Kassie pulled back. She used her fingers to wipe away the tears from under her eyes and looked anywhere but at him.

"Feel better?"

She shook her head. "Not really. Now I've got a head full of snot and still have no idea what to do about Dean." She couldn't lie to him at the moment, not with the day she'd had and him showing her sympathy.

He chuckled and shifted to the edge of the couch. "Fair enough. Why don't you lie down? Rest your eyeballs while I make us something to eat."

Kassie looked up at Hollywood then. He didn't look disgusted by her tears or what had to be her incredibly puffy face. He didn't care that she was still sniffing as if she had allergies from hell. "What are you doing?" she whispered, completely confused.

He leaned down, kissed her forehead, then said, "About to make dinner."

Kassie shook her head. "No, I mean, here. With me."

"As I said, making dinner. Lie down, Kassie. Relax."

"I can't," she mumbled, but brought her feet up to the cushions and curled them under her.

"Then don't. Just lie here and think about all the awesomeness I'm going to make you to eat."

She smiled at that. "Can you cook?"

"Guess you'll just have to wait and see, won't you?" he returned, his face mirroring her smile.

"It's a long drive back home for you." Kassie told him something he undoubtedly already knew.

Hollywood merely shrugged. "Not really, just an hour."

"That's a long drive."

He leaned over her, bracing his hands on the cushion on either side of her shoulders and said softly, "Driving to El Paso is a long drive. An hour up the road is nothing. And so you know, you living down here and me up by Fort Hood isn't going to keep me from making the effort to see you. If that means I get here at six-thirty at night and leave at ten because I have to get up at oh-four-hundred for PT, then that's what I'm going to do. I'm perfectly willing to make the two-hour

SUSAN STOKER

round-trip drive if it means I get to spend even thirty minutes getting to know you."

"That's insane," she told Hollywood.

"Nope. It's determination," he retorted, kissed her on the forehead once more, then straightened. "Close your eyes, Kass. I've got food to make."

With nothing else to do, Kassie did as Hollywood demanded.

Chapter Nine

"**H**EY, HOLLYWOOD," KASS said in his ear.

It had been two weeks since the Army Ball.

He'd stayed that first night at her apartment and made an easy dinner of spaghetti and homemade garlic bread. They'd exchanged small talk as they'd eaten. She told him she'd been to the police station, and updated him on everything Dean had said and done since Jacks had been arrested. Hollywood once again had felt guilty he hadn't let her talk the night before, but firmly put it aside. He was there now. He'd do everything he could to keep her safe.

And he had. He'd asked Beth, the same woman who had gotten Kassie's address for him and now worked for his friend, Tex, to find out what she could about Dean. He'd talked to his commanding officer about the situation with Jacks communicating with Dean and threatening Kassie from behind bars, to see if there was anything he could do about it, and Hollywood made a point to try to make sure Kassie never felt as if she was fighting this by herself. He hated that she'd felt alone with no options.

He'd also talked to Emily about Kassie, and she didn't hold any hard feelings about the other woman. She'd explained how she'd felt when Jacks had been blackmailing her...how she didn't think she'd had any options other than to pay him the money he'd demanded. Jacks might be an asshole, but he wasn't stupid. He knew by threatening the most vulnerable person in Emily's life, and now Kassie's, that they would do what he wanted.

Hollywood had seen or talked to Kassie every day since he'd made her dinner two weeks ago. Some days he'd done just what he told her he would, driven up after work to visit with her for a few hours before heading back home. Other days, if he or Kassie worked late, he settled for talking to her on the phone. And he'd emailed and texted her every day, several times in fact. Just saying hi, telling her about his day, and generally touching base.

The tenuous bond they'd formed had grown. Kassie was the first person he wanted to talk to when he got up and the last before he went to sleep. Hollywood hated that she lived down in Austin, but he hoped once he helped get Jacks and Dean off her back, he might be able to convince her to move up to Temple. It was a long shot, but he'd never felt as protective, concerned, or as excited about a woman before. Kassie was quickly becoming the most important person in his life. It was crazy, but his soul seemed to settle when he was with her.

She was it for him. He knew it down to the marrow of his bones. He wanted to ask her to move in with *him*, but just because he knew she was the woman meant for him, didn't mean she felt the same way. It was more than obvious she'd take some convincing, but Hollywood was up to the challenge. He'd court her every day for years if the end result was her wearing his ring on her finger.

This weekend Kassie was coming up for the first time. She'd been complaining about how stressed she was. So Hollywood had arranged with Fletch for her to stay in the apartment over his garage. She had the weekend off from work and he wanted her to be able to really relax and not worry for at least two days.

He wanted her to stay at his place, but even though they were growing closer, he didn't want to pressure her into doing anything she wasn't ready for. Hollywood knew she was fast becoming vital to his well-being, but she probably wasn't there yet. Especially not after everything with her ex. It was a testament to how stressed Kassie was that she'd agreed to the trip without too much cajoling.

Hollywood didn't have a lot planned for them to do over the weekend, it was enough that he'd get to spend more than a few hours with her at a time, but one thing they *did* need to do was meet with the other guys and discuss the Jacks situation. Dean had been out of town, but when he got back, Hollywood had a feeling things would escalate quickly...especially once Dean found out how close he and Kassie had gotten while he'd been gone. The plan for her to spy on him and the rest of his team hadn't exactly gone as Dean and Jacks had planned.

"Hey, Kass," he responded, holding the phone to his ear with his shoulder. "Where are you?"

"I just left. I should be there in an hour or so. Is that okay?"

"Of course," Hollywood reassured her. "You're coming straight to my place, right?"

"Yeah. I've got your address programmed into the GPS and it looks straightforward enough."

"How's your sister?"

"She's okay. Neither of us have seen Dean, but I'm sure he's still around somewhere. The longer he waits to contact me, the more nervous I get. But if I'm honest, I'm not sure Karina is really watching for him. She's kinda got her head in the sand about the entire situation. She was freaked out when I first told her, but since then I think she's just trying to forget about Dean in order to cope with the fact he's been watching her."

"She needs to be careful," Hollywood warned.

Kassie sighed. "I know, and I think she does too, but I can't be with her twenty-four seven. She has school and I have to work. I'll talk to her again. I'm doing my best, Hollywood."

"I know you are, sweetheart. I didn't mean to imply otherwise," he soothed, hearing the defeat in her tone. Hopefully after the weekend, he and his team would have a plan to deal with both Dean and Jacks that would make her feel better. Hollywood caught Truck's eye and gave him a chin lift and head jerk, letting him know he was leaving. "Have you talked to the detective you showed the texts and emails to lately?"

"Yeah. He said they were looking for Dean, but hadn't been able to find him yet. It's so weird that someone can hide like that. Heck, every time I turned around he was there. I can't believe they can't find him."

"It's fairly easy to stay out of sight if you don't want to be found," he told her. Then asked, "Did you get a restraining order yet?"

She paused, and Hollywood knew what she was going to say before she said it.

"No, but I meant to."

"We'll talk about it this weekend. You can't keep putting it off," Hollywood told her sternly. Before she could argue with him—he knew what her objections were to getting it filed, and he would nip those in the bud—he said quickly, "I'm going to let you go so you can concentrate. Drive safe. Let me know when you get close. I'll be waiting for you."

"Okay. See you soon."

"Bye."

"Bye."

Hollywood hung up and climbed into his car. He'd seen Kassie three days ago when he'd driven down there after work on Tuesday, but he was ridiculously excited to see her again. On *his* turf this time. Dating had never felt like this before. He'd been happy to spend time with a woman, but hadn't ever felt this anticipation, this eagerness to be with another person as he did with Kassie.

He felt more himself with her than with anyone, outside of his family and teammates. She liked how he looked, but he knew she wasn't with him *because* of it. Until he'd met her, he hadn't realized just how much that mattered to him.

Hollywood glanced at his watch and nodded to himself. He had plenty of time to shower and change before Kassie arrived. He hadn't forgotten how she'd run her nose along his neck, inhaling his scent. If she liked his aftershave, he'd go out of his way to make sure he always smelled like that for her.

An hour later, Hollywood waited outside his apartment complex for Kassie to arrive. She'd called five minutes ago saying she was getting off the interstate and should be there soon. He watched as her four-door Honda Accord pulled into the lot. By the time she parked, he was at her door, holding it open when she climbed out.

Without thought, Hollywood caught her around the waist and pulled her into him. He dropped his head and caught her lips with his own. They'd kissed before, but not like this. Hard, long, and passionately. Hollywood could smell the scent of shampoo mixed with her essence as he devoured her mouth. He hadn't even looked at what she was wearing; his only thought was that he needed to kiss her.

He felt her hands gripping the sides of his T-shirt and shifted her in his grasp until he could feel every curve. Pulling back long enough to mumble, "Hey, sweetheart," he put his hand on her back, pressing her harder against him. He didn't give her a chance to respond. Taking her mouth again, Hollywood swore he heard birds singing and bells ringing. It was ridiculous, but nothing in his entire life felt as good as Kassie's lips and tongue moving under his own.

After several more blissful moments, he finally pulled back. He kept her lower body flush to his and asked, "You okay?"

"Yeah," she breathed. "Better now that I'm here."

"Good."

They smiled at each other for a beat.

"You need anything before we go up?" Hollywood asked, strangely reluctant to move even an inch.

Kassie shook her head. "Since I'm staying at Fletch's place tonight, I'll keep my bag in the car."

Turning them, Hollywood put his arm around her waist and shut her car door. He led them up the stairs to his apartment, for some reason anxious to get her into his space. He wasn't able to keep her safe day to day, so now that she was here, he wanted to lock her away from the world. The only place he knew for certain Jacks or Dean couldn't get to her was behind his door. So that's where he wanted her.

Sighing in relief when the door clicked behind him, and trying not to think about the fact that she'd be leaving later to go to the apartment over Fletch's garage, Hollywood smiled at Kassie.

"The drive was okay?"

"Yeah. Surprisingly, the traffic actually wasn't too bad. I thought getting out of Austin would suck. I guess everyone saw me coming and got out of the way," she teased.

"As they should. Want the grand tour?"

"Sure."

Hollywood showed Kassie around his apartment. It wasn't much to write home about. The door opened into the main living area. The space was an open concept, so the kitchen was visible from the doorway. It had stainless steel appliances and granite countertops. Hollywood didn't have a kitchen table, but there were stools pushed in under a bar.

"As you can see, this is the kitchen and living area," he said unnecessarily.

He tried to look at his place from her perspective. He had a few pictures of his family on the bookshelf against the wall, including his sister and her family. There was also a framed shot of him and all his friends taken at Emily and Fletch's wedding. Emily had insisted on taking it before the shit had hit the fan that night, and then had gotten it framed and gifted a copy to each of the men. Ghost, Fletch, Coach, himself, Beatle, Blade, Truck, and Fish were wearing their dress blue uniforms, standing next to each other, grinning like fools.

Kassie went straight to it, smiling. She picked up the heavy frame and examined the eight-by-ten print. "I recognize everyone but this guy," she said, turning the photo to him and pointed to Fish.

Hollywood smiled and said, "That's Fish."

"Fish?"

"Yup. He can swim like one."

"Hmmm, I didn't see him at the ball," Kassie commented.

"That's because he wasn't there. He doesn't do so

well with crowds. The short story is that he was in a situation in the Middle East and all the guys in his platoon were killed. Truck saved his life, and we hauled his carcass to safety. So now he's one of us."

Kassie wrinkled her brow. "But he's okay?"

Hollywood shrugged. "He will be. He lost part of his arm, and will be medically retired from the Army, but he's almost done with therapy. He's come a hell of a long way and we're happy to call him brother."

"I love that for him," Kassie said softly. "I wish every wounded soldier had the kind of friends to come home to that he did."

"Me too," Hollywood agreed, wondering anew how in the world he thought Kassie would ever deliberately and maliciously use him to feed information to Jacks. She was considerate and kind to just about everyone she met, even Fish, who she'd *never* met.

"You wanna see the rest of the place?" he asked quietly.

Kassie nodded, but her eyes didn't leave the photo for a long moment. Finally, she placed the frame back on the shelf and turned to smile at him. "You're hot in your uniform, but I think I like you better like this,"— she gestured to him—"jeans, old T-shirt and ratty sneakers. It's more...you."

God. She killed him. Not able to say the words that would do justice to the way she made him feel, Hollywood took her hand, kissed the back and led her through his living room. He steered her around the black leather couch, coffee table, and recliner. He went down the hallway, gesturing to a closet, a utilitarian bathroom, a bedroom that he used as a workout room, a linen closet, and finally to the master bedroom. Swallowing hard, feeling as if he was opening the door to a whole new life, he turned the knob.

Kassie took a step inside, then snorted under her breath.

Hollywood smiled. "What?"

"You don't have a bed," she told him, as if he didn't know.

"I've got a bed," he countered, looking at the mattress sitting on the floor. It wasn't the most put-together master bedroom he'd ever seen, but he had a place to sleep, a dresser to keep his clothes in with a TV sitting on top of it, and a small bedside table where a digital clock sat and his pistol resided when he was sleeping. It worked for him.

"No, you have a mattress," she corrected.

Hollywood smiled, loving how relaxed and happy Kassie looked. "Right. Then I have the most important part of a bed. I'll have you know that mattress is as comfortable as anything I've ever slept on, and I've never seen the need to go to the trouble of buying a contraption to put it on." He didn't tell her that when he was on a mission, he usually slept in the dirt, mud, and sand. *This* was actually luxurious by comparison.

Kassie shook her head at him. "You have to have a bed, Hollywood."

"Why?"

Instead of answering, she asked, "Do you really bring women to your place to seduce them, then back here to your room, only to have them see this?"

Hollywood knew she was joking with him, but it was important for her to know how things were. "I've never had a woman here, Kassie."

The smile faded from her face as she searched his eyes. But she didn't say anything.

"I don't pick women up anymore, sweetheart. I'm thirty-two, way beyond the bar-hopping stage. I've only been with two women in the last four years. Partly because I've been busy, but I've also gotten sick of them wanting to be with me simply because of my looks. That sounds conceited, I know, but it's been what I've experienced. And neither of those two stepped foot in my space. Not in my kitchen. Not in my living room. And definitely not in my bedroom. This mattress has known the weight of my body and mine only."

Hollywood wasn't sure what Kassie's response would be to his impassioned statement. Maybe delight that he didn't sleep around. Maybe surprise that he had the balls to bring it up. But what he *didn't* expect her to do was smile broadly, then take three steps toward his mattress and throw herself down on it.

She giggled as she lay back and wiggled her butt back and forth. Her arms moved up and down and her legs in and out, as if she were making a snow angel on his sheets.

"What are you doing?" he asked, bemused.

"Now you can't say that you've been the only person on this mattress," she got out between giggles. "Now it's been contaminated by girl cooties."

Hollywood knew he'd only known Kassie for a couple of weeks, but it was right at that moment, watching her giggle and writhe on his mattress, teasing him, that he fell irrevocably in love. No shit, not fucking around, madly in love. He knew some people wouldn't believe him, would tell him there was no way he could be in love with a woman after meeting her online and only seeing her in person a handful of times. But they'd be wrong.

He absolutely loved Kassie Anderson and she'd be his, no matter what.

Not giving her any warning, Hollywood pounced.

He crouched over her, pinning her body under his. She was still giggling, but pushed at his chest, trying to move him. "Oh no, Hollywood, it's too late. It's already contaminated. There's nothing you can do now."

It wasn't until he dropped down fully on top of her

that Kassie stopped giggling, even though the smile stayed on her face. Aligning his crotch to hers, knowing she'd be able to feel his erection, Hollywood grabbed her hands, pinning them over her head and holding them there with one of his. His chest rubbed against her now stiff nipples as he came down on an elbow over her.

She inhaled deeply once and wiggled under him before stilling.

He smiled as she closed her eyes and arched her back, pressing herself harder against him. "I don't mind your girl cooties," Hollywood told her. "In fact, I'm hoping you'll someday infect the shit out of this mattress with your...cooties."

The smile on his face grew when she blushed. But she gamely opened her eyes and looked up at him. "I'll infect yours if you infect mine."

Hollywood was speechless for a moment, then he dropped his head and nuzzled her neck. She tilted her head to give him more room and he felt her inch her legs apart and shift until her knees were bent and pressing against his thighs. "Damn, woman."

She laughed at him and Hollywood pulled back. "How did I get lucky enough to have you here in my bed?" he mused more to himself than her. But, of course, she answered him anyway.

Kassie shrugged. "I think you're delusional because *I'm* the lucky one. But whatever."

"You are absolutely one hundred percent wrong," Hollywood told her softly. "I know a good thing when I see it. If Jacks and all the other men you've run into during your life didn't see it, it's their loss. But now you're mine. They had their chance. I'll spend every day making sure you know how precious you are. I hate that he made you feel as if you weren't an amazing, wonderful woman. But if you want to continue to believe as if *you're* the lucky one, have at it."

"You're crazy, Hollywood."

Without smiling, he returned, "No, sweetheart. You just haven't been treated as you should be. But that shit's over. I'm going to make it my mission in life to show you what you've been missing. To show you how a woman who is the most important thing in a man's life is treated."

Her brows furrowed in confusion, but she obviously chose to move the conversation on. She lifted her head and ran her nose down his jawline, inhaling as she went. "You always smell so good. I love it."

"Thank you."

"You're welcome."

"But I should warn you, Kassie. I don't always." He smiled down at her and touched his index finger to her nose in a gentle caress. "Forty-five minutes ago, if you sniffed me you would've shrunk back in horror and refused to even be in the same apartment with me, nevertheless the same bed."

She giggled. "Well, I appreciate the effort."

Hollywood asked, "You get a chance to grab something to eat on your way?"

She shook her head. "No. I was too excited to get up here."

He liked that answer. She hadn't said she was too excited to see *him*, but it was implied. He'd take it. "You hungry?"

Kassie nodded. "I could eat."

Knowing he needed to move, or he might not let her leave at all, Hollywood pushed himself up, getting to his hands and knees over her. "I'm making steaks, green beans, and salad. That okay?"

"Perfect."

He stepped off the mattress and held out his hands. "Come on, I'll help you."

"For some reason, I feel like I'm sitting on the floor," she quipped.

"That's because you almost are."

She put her hands in his and he grimaced at the coldness of her fingers. Once she was standing, he sandwiched her hands between his own and briskly rubbed them. "I can't get over how cold your hands always are."

She shrugged. "It doesn't bother me."

"Well, it bothers me," he told her honestly.

After he'd rubbed them for a while, he grasped one, intertwined his fingers with hers and led her out of his bedroom. He got her situated at the bar in the kitchen and poured her a glass of red wine. He took out the steaks he'd been marinating and got to work.

Forty-five minutes later, stuffed from dinner, they were both sitting on his leather couch. The television was off and they were talking.

"I love that you're so easy to talk to," Hollywood told her. "From the first message we exchanged, I noticed it. You had no problem talking about whatever popped into your mind."

"Don't remind me," Kassie moaned. "I can't believe I babbled on about dick pics."

Hollywood chuckled. "I'm still holding out for a boob pic from you."

"You're just gonna have to keep holding out, buster," she scolded. "There's no way I'm sending naked pictures to anyone. With my luck, Richard would figure out how to hack my phone or computer and they'd end up on Porn Hub or something."

He laughed and pulled her closer to him. "I don't need pictures, Kass. I'm holding out for the real thing."

Kassie bit her lip and said hesitantly, "I'm not exactly porn star material, Hollywood."

"And?"

"And I just thought I'd warn you before we get to

the point where we exchange cooties," she tried to joke.

"I don't want perfection, sweetheart," Hollywood reassured her. "I want a woman who is passionate. Who wants me as much as I want her. I want someone I can laugh with. Who doesn't care about looks as much as she does about what's inside a person. And I know for a fact from that kiss earlier that the only thing I'm going to care about when we do get naked together is how you like to be touched, where, and how quickly it'll take you to come for me."

She shivered and murmured without looking at him, "I don't think it'll take long."

Hollywood tipped her chin up with his finger. "I like what I see when I look at you, Kass. You have nothing to worry about."

"I'll remind you of that if you're disappointed when we get naked."

Loving that she'd said *when*, and not *if*, Hollywood merely grinned and tugged her closer to him.

As she did most nights when he'd visited, she snuggled into his side at his urging. They were quiet for a moment before he changed the subject. As much as he wanted her naked in his bed, tonight didn't seem to be the right time. If he was honest with himself, he wanted the threat of Jacks and Dean eliminated before he took her to bed. He wanted to slay all her dragons for her. "Why haven't you gotten a protective order, Kass? It seems to me that would be the next step."

She sighed and buried her head deeper into his chest. She was sitting next to him, her knees drawn up with both arms around him. "Two reasons," she said, not even trying to put him off. "One, I'm afraid it'll piss either Dean or Richard off enough that they'll decide to stop fucking around and do something drastic. And two, because it costs a lot of money to hire a lawyer. I've got some saved, but I have no idea what those two assholes have planned. If they do something to get me kicked out of my apartment, or hurt me, or God forbid my family, I want to have the money to be able to do something about it."

Hollywood turned and kissed the top of Kassie's head before running his hand reassuringly up and down her arm resting on his belly. "I'm not going to sit here and tell you that the protective order will keep you safe. I think we both know that isn't the case, but I honestly don't think either Jacks or Dean will care if you file it or not. They're both arrogant enough to dismiss it as unimportant."

"Then why should I do it?" Kassie asked reasonably.

"Because it's just one more nail in their coffins if they do decide to do something stupid. The cops will know there's a history between you and if something happens, they'll be more apt to mark it down to something Dean did than blow it off."

Kassie huffed out a breath. "Yeah, you're right."

"And to address the second point—"

"I'm not letting you pay for it," Kassie said, interrupting him.

"I wasn't going to offer. Although if I thought for a second you'd take me up on it, I'd hire a lawyer for you tonight and gladly hand over my credit card. What I was *going* to say was, first, I haven't ever had to file one, but I don't think simply doing it is all that expensive, and two, Harley's sister is a lawyer. A damn good one. I know she'd help you."

Kassie sat up at that and looked at him.

Hollywood traced a finger over her furrowed brow. "What you are thinking about so hard, Kass?"

"I don't understand what we're doing."

"What do you mean?"

"This." She gestured between them. "You and me. I mean, how we met is so fucked up it isn't funny. But you forgave me and I you for being a jerk. But now we're...I guess dating...but we haven't really even talked about Richard, what he did, and wants. You drive an hour to see me several times a week, we've only kissed once, I mean *really* kissed, and it's just...I don't know what we're doing," she finished in frustration.

"Do you like me?" Hollywood asked.

"Well...yeah. I wouldn't be here if I didn't," Kassie told him without hesitation.

"And I like you. I was a jerk *because* I liked you so much. And that's what's most important between us. I haven't forgotten about Jacks. Not for one second. But he isn't going anywhere right now so Dean is the bigger threat to you and your family at the moment. I've wanted to get to know you without those assholes hovering over us, even if they were the reason we met. I haven't minded going down to Austin to see you. I've actually enjoyed the time to myself to decompress during the drive. I know where I'd like our relationship to go, and that includes me not having to drive to Austin three or four times a week because you'd be living here in Temple where I could see you every day."

"I could make the drive up here," Kassie said tentatively, ignoring his last sentence.

"Absolutely not," Hollywood told her immediately. "I don't want you on the roads that late at night. It's not safe."

"How is it for you, but not me?" she argued reasonably.

"Honestly? It's not. But I'd much rather I got hurt if something happened, than you."

"That makes no sense whatsoever," she shot back. "You know that, right?"

Hollywood shrugged. "You heard me say that I liked you, yeah?"

"I'm not deaf."

He ignored her snark and continued, "And because I like you, I will *never* put you in a position where you could get hurt. That means you not driving late at night. Not calling you when I know you'll be in your car on the way home from work. Helping you get a lawyer to file that protective order against Dean. Not letting you make yourself bait for that asshole and figuring out how to keep Karina safe while at the same time shutting Jacks down for good. Got me?"

Kassie stared at him for a moment before saying softly, "We've only known each other for two weeks."

"No," Hollywood countered. "We've known each other for a lot longer than that."

"You know what I mean," Kassie protested. "You shouldn't feel responsible for me like you obviously do. I'm a grown woman, responsible for my own actions."

"You can't tell my heart what to feel," he told her honestly. "There's something about you that's irresistible, Kass. I can actually understand why Jacks is as obsessed with you as he obviously is. Of course, he's obsessed in a sick way, and I am in a perfectly normal, I-want-to-get-to-know-you-better, protect you, feed you, and make-love-to-you-until-you-can't-move way."

Kassie shook her head in exasperation, but grinned. "Oh and that's so much different, huh?"

Hollywood loved her sense of humor, but he got serious. "It's night-and-day different, sweetheart. I respect you. I want you to do what you love for the rest of your life. If that's work as a manager at your store, so be it. If it's quitting your job and roller skating around the globe, great. But whatever it is, I want to be by your side cheering you on and supporting you. But I can't do that if your ex is stressing you out, Dean is stalking you, and you're worried about your little sister. But what I *can* do is help you figure that shit out, so you can get on with your life. Hopefully with me."

She stared at him for a beat, then crumpled back into his arms as if she were a ragdoll. "I'd like that."

"You'll let me help?" he pushed.

"Yes."

"In any way I can?"

Kassie half sat up and eyed him. "Why does that sound like trouble?"

"Answer the question, Kass. You'll let me help you get out from under your ex's thumb, and get rid of Dean once and for all so you can start to live your life…hopefully with me?"

"I've dreamed about moving away from Austin," she said weirdly, not answering his question.

"Kass…" Hollywood warned.

She ignored him and said, "But I never had any real idea of where I wanted to go. I thought about Florida, but know it's really humid there and my hair would be a frizzy mess all the time. I love the mountains, so I even thought about moving to Colorado, but I'd probably freeze. Snow *looks* pretty, but since I've lived in Texas my entire life, I'd be a Popsicle the first time it got below twenty. If I thought my hands were cold now, they'd probably fall off if I lived somewhere it got below freezing on a regular basis."

She raised her eyes then, and Hollywood felt as if she could see into his soul. "But maybe I'll start out with baby steps and move to a small Texas town. After all, if my boyfriend is in the Army, he'll probably have to move and maybe he'll get stationed somewhere exotic."

"Fuck me," Hollywood breathed. "You want to travel, Kass?"

"I think so. But not all the time. I'd like to have a home to come back to. Somewhere familiar where I have friends I can talk to about what I saw and did while I was gone."

"I want to give you that." He paused, then asked one more time, "You'll let me help you…my way?" He knew he was pushing, but he needed her to say it.

She caved and gave him what he needed. "Yes, Hollywood. Please help me. I've felt alone for so long. I'm not very good at asking for help, but anything you can do to get Richard and Dean away from me and my family would be very appreciated. I'm ready to move on with my life. To stop looking over my shoulder all the time."

It wasn't the time to tell her that he already had Beth electronically monitoring Dean's email and phone, and that she'd been able to essentially infect his phone with a secret app that allowed her to track his every move. One of the reasons Hollywood had been comfortable not moving her or her sister somewhere safe was because Dean had been in Kansas for the last week and a half. Visiting Jacks and probably plotting against his team, Kassie, and Karina. Assholes.

But he'd learned yesterday from Beth that Dean was headed back to Texas. Hence Kassie spending the weekend in Temple with him. They needed to get a plan in place. Because without a doubt, Dean and Jacks had one, and it probably involved Kassie.

"Tomorrow we're going to meet with my friends and commanding officer at the post. He knows all about Jacks because of what he did before. We need to shut him down, then get Dean to back off. You're not going to have to look over your shoulder forever. I'm going to make sure of it."

"You already set up the meeting?" Kassie asked, sounding surprised.

"Yes."

"You were that sure that I'd agree to your help?"

"Kassie," Hollywood said seriously, "you were going to get this help whether you agreed or not."

"Why?" It came out more a breath of air than an

actual word.

He palmed the side of her face, then leaned in and brushed his lips against hers. "Because from the first second I saw you on that couch in the lobby waiting for me, I knew."

"Knew what?"

"That you were mine. You weren't fiddling with your cell phone. You were trying too hard to look at ease, when I could tell from where I stood you were anything but."

"That doesn't make sense," she protested. "You decided I was yours because I looked nervous?"

Hollywood's lips quirked upward. "Yup."

She looked him in the eye for a long moment, and Hollywood loved the fact she didn't run screaming from the room at his candid words. "Can I ask a question?" she asked.

"Of course. You can always ask me anything. You should know, though, I might not always be able to answer. I won't lie to you, but if I say there is something I can't talk about, then I can't. I'm not being secretive or an asshole. I literally can't."

"That OPSEC thing, huh?" Kassie asked with a smile, obviously remembering one of their first email conversations.

"Exactly."

"Okay. I can respect that. But my question is why?

Why does Richard hate you and your friends so much?"

Hollywood sighed. Then he twisted his body until he was lying down. He pulled Kassie with him until she was tucked between his body and the back of the couch.

"We beat him in a training exercise," Hollywood told her succinctly.

"And?" she questioned, obviously confused.

"And nothing. That's it. There was a completely official, sanctioned training exercise on post. Me and my friends were the 'bad guys' and Jacks and his unit were the 'good ones.' His platoon was supposed to infiltrate our section of the city made out of shipping containers. We killed them—not *killed*, but shot them with the lasers we were using—within moments of them stepping foot into the perimeter of the target area." Hollywood shrugged. "Jacks didn't take it well."

"Are you kidding me?" Kassie asked in a weird voice.

"No."

"You're kidding." It was a statement this time. Kassie pushed up and tried to crawl over Hollywood's prone body.

He grabbed her hips, holding her still. "What's wrong?"

"What's wrong?" she asked, struggling against his hold. "What's wrong is that my ex is insane! I mean, I already knew he was crazy, but that's *really* crazy. Seriously. You were just doing your job! That's no reason to go ape-shit crazy and blackmail a woman and then kidnap her and her kid! He held a *gun* to her *head*, Hollywood. That's not cool! And all because he was throwing a temper tantrum because he lost a *game?*"

"Kassie, seriously, it's—"

"No! Hollywood, it's insane! And he's still not over it! Being shot in the head and thrown in jail wasn't enough for him to come to his senses. He's still trying to win!" She shook her head. "I swear to God he wasn't like this when we first started dating. He was normal. I wouldn't be with someone who likes to drug and threaten to kill other people."

"I know you wouldn't. Come here," Hollywood ordered, pulling her back next to him. She lay down, but was stiff and obviously still upset.

"Tell me you're kidding," Kassie said softly. "Tell me that it's more than that."

"Sorry, sweetheart. I can't."

"I'm not condoning anything he's done," Kassie whispered. "But I wish the Army would've helped him after he got hurt. Maybe if they saw that he wasn't the same person as before the explosion, I wouldn't be in this situation right now."

"The Army's not perfect," Hollywood told her. "They aren't mind readers. I wish I could tell you that they take care of all soldiers who are hurt with the care and concern they deserve, but we both know that'd be a lie. It's a government institution. I think there are a lot of people who work for the VA who care, but they're overwhelmed. But I'll tell you something…" He paused, wanting to make sure Kassie heard and understood what he was about to say.

"What?" she whispered.

"I hate what he's done. I hate what he's doing to you. But if none of this had happened, if Jacks didn't have a brain injury, didn't lose that training exercise, didn't kidnap Emily and Annie…we wouldn't be where we are right now."

Her head came up and she propped her chin on her hand, which was lying flat on his chest. She studied his eyes for a long moment before she said quietly, "You really believe that."

"It's a fact. So yeah, I believe it."

"I probably would've married him," she said.

"And you'd have thirteen kids by now," Hollywood teased.

"And I'd weigh eight hundred pounds."

"And you'd be on a reality show, trying to lose the weight so you could have more babies."

Obviously getting into the game, Kassie said, "I'd be stationed in some far-off place, like Alaska."

They were both quiet for a moment before Kassie commented, "For the last year or so, I've asked, 'why me?' I've had pity parties and been depressed about all I was going through. I didn't understand what I'd done that was so bad I had to suffer at his hands. I was miserable, scared, and confused. But, right now, at this moment, I honestly feel as if it was worth it."

Hollywood's eyes dilated and he felt his heart rate pick up at her words. But she wasn't done.

"I don't know where we're going, if whatever it is we have between us will fizzle out and we'll look back with fond memories of the fling we had with the person we met online that one time. But I swear, Hollywood, this doesn't feel like that. I've never felt this intensely about anyone in my entire life before. So even though I feel like a bitch for thinking it, much less saying it, I'm thankful for what he did…because it led me to you."

Hollywood's hand moved without his brain telling it to. He clasped Kassie behind the neck and pulled her down to him. His lips hit hers, hard. Their teeth knocked together, but it didn't slow either of them down. Hollywood shifted his hand up so it was tangled in her hair and he tugged, moving her so she was at a better angle, so he could get farther inside her mouth.

They made out on his couch as if it was the last time they'd be together. When Hollywood separated his legs and shifted Kassie until she was lying over him, his cock found right where it most wanted to be, lengthening and pressing against her crotch. He swore he could feel the heat from her core burning through both their jeans, branding him.

Her hands snaked up his chest, rubbing and caressing him even as they continued to kiss. Hollywood put all the love he knew he couldn't express verbally into his. Showing her without words how much she meant to him and how he'd keep her safe no matter what.

After several moments, Kassie pulled back a fraction of an inch and whispered, "So I guess you don't think I'm a bitch for thinking that."

"No, I don't think you're a bitch. If you're a bitch, then I'm a dick, because I said it first," Hollywood said, not taking his eyes from her flushed face and swollen lips, which glistened with his saliva. It was sexy as fuck and he wanted nothing more than to bury his cock so far inside her, she wouldn't know where she ended and he began. He struggled to contain his out-of-control lust when she wiggled against him.

"What about this couch?" she asked.

"What *about* this couch?" Hollywood echoed.

"Does it have girl cooties on it? Or can we infect it too?"

The glint in her eyes as she said it, and the way she bit her lip as she smiled down at him, made him throw back his head and laugh. He'd never had this kind of relationship. Where he could be in the throes of sexual lust one second and laughing the next.

"You can infect anything in my life you want,

sweetheart. Kassie cooties are always welcome."

They smiled at each other. Hollywood was still hard, and wanted to be inside the woman lying on top of him, but the need had settled to an ache, one he could deal with. He knew the buildup and anticipation of being with her would make their coming together all the more exciting and explosive. "You wanna watch a movie?"

Obviously feeling the same mellowness he was, Kassie lay her head down on his shoulder, nuzzling the underside of his jaw with her nose. She wiggled until she found what was obviously a comfortable position, one arm folded up under her, the other resting on his chest, her hand tucked behind his neck.

Having her like this, snuggled into him, completely relaxed, just became Hollywood's new goal in life. Giving Kassie this every night. He'd go through whatever he had to as a Delta Force soldier if he could come home each evening and give her this.

"Depends on the movie," Kassie finally said.

They'd been through this in an online chat before, and Hollywood knew exactly what Kassie's tastes were in flicks. "*Full Metal Jacket*?"

He felt rather than saw her nose wrinkle. "No," she emphatically stated. "What else you got?"

Hollywood named a few more films he knew she would reject, laughing inside when she categorically denied each one. He grabbed the remote and turned on the television, bringing up his Netflix account. "Stop me when something looks interesting," he told Kassie.

Before too long, she said, "That one."

"*Sahara?*"

"Yeah. It's got everything. Adventure, humor, action...I like it."

"You sure it's not because it has Matthew McConaughey in it?" Hollywood teased, having no problem watching the movie. He'd seen it as well and enjoyed it.

"Pbfft," she scoffed. "He's fine, but I love Steve Zahn in this one. He's hilarious. He might be the sidekick, but he carries this movie. Every time I see it, I wanna mail him a hat since he keeps losing his."

"He is good," Hollywood agreed, setting the remote on the coffee table and settling back into the couch with Kassie in his arms. He couldn't remember a better evening.

Chapter Ten

KASSIE ROLLED OVER on the surprisingly comfortable bed and frowned, wondering what had woken her up. She was tired, but in a good way. She and Hollywood had watched *Sahara*—well, *she* had. Hollywood had fallen asleep under her within the first thirty minutes of the movie. She figured he'd probably had a tough week, because she didn't think falling asleep like that was his usual MO. She'd spent the next hour and a half or so memorizing the feel of his hard body under her and alternating between watching the movie and him sleep.

She still didn't really understand how he'd somehow decided that *she* was the woman he wanted to be with, but she'd had enough shit in her life that she wasn't about to talk him out of liking her. He'd said that he was the lucky one, but she knew without a doubt that wasn't true. Not by a long shot.

He'd been disgruntled when she'd woken him up after the movie ended, apologizing for zonking out on her. Then he'd refused to let her drive over to Fletch's, insisting on taking her himself.

Kassie had given in, because it felt good to be looked after. He'd kissed her silly when they'd arrived at the small apartment, but had left her alone after making sure everything was all right. He'd reassured her that she was as safe as she could be and told her that he'd be back by mid-morning.

Glancing at the clock on the little table next to the queen-size bed, Kassie saw that it was only a quarter past seven. Not exactly mid-morning.

Then she heard a sound. Tapping at the front door. It had to have been what had woken her up. Kassie had no idea who could be here so early, but whoever it was couldn't be bringing good news. Nothing good happened this early on a Saturday morning.

Suddenly wide awake, Kassie threw back the covers and rushed for the front door. Thoughts of Hollywood arriving to tell her something had happened to her sister ran through her head. The apartment wasn't big. There was just one bedroom, one bathroom, and a small kitchen attached to an even smaller living area, so she got to the front door within seconds and looked out the peephole—then blinked. What in the world?

Kassie opened the deadbolt and undid the chain at eye level as well as the one at hip height. She cracked the door open and stared at the little girl standing there.

"Hi! I'm Annie! You're Kassie with a K, right?

That's so cool. I couldn't wait to meet you! Daddy Fletch and Mommy talked about you all night. They said you were dating Hollywood and staying here for the weekend. They laughed, I'm not sure why, but they thought it was really funny. But if you're Hollywood's girlfriend, then you're *my* friend too. Daddy doesn't let anyone stay here unless he likes them. And trusts them. Anyway, I used to live here before Mommy and Daddy got together. Are you sleeping in my room? Of course you are, it's the only one. Isn't this place great? Can I come in? *Teenage Mutant Ninja Turtles* is on. Wanna watch it with me?"

Looking past Annie, Kassie didn't see any adults with her. "Are you here by yourself?"

"Uh huh, but it's okay. Daddy has cameras everywhere and I can't get stolened again. So…wanna watch with me?"

"Uh…sure," Kassie said, backing up to let the little girl inside. Hollywood had told her about the cameras and security on the property, but she still wasn't sure it was a good idea for Annie to be wandering around by herself.

As soon as the thought went through her brain, she stiffened. This was Annie? The little girl Richard drugged, kidnapped, and threatened to hurt if Emily didn't do what he wanted? Dear Lord. As she closed the door, Kassie felt her hands shaking. She didn't know if she could face Annie knowing what her ex had done. She felt dirty just being in her presence.

Having no idea of the turmoil going through Kassie's head, Annie reached out, grabbed one of her hands and started to pull her toward the couch. "Come on, it's gonna start soon. Wow, your hands are cold. There should be blankets in the closet. Here, you sit. I'll go get one for you."

Annie pushed at Kassie until she sat, then quickly headed toward the bedroom. She ran back into the small living area seconds later lugging a large comforter. It was dragging on the ground behind her, but Annie didn't even seem to notice. She plopped it on Kassie and made a big production out of spreading it out over her lap, then got down on her knees to tuck it in around her legs.

"There. Now you're snug as a bug in a rug. My mommy says that all the time." Then, without waiting for a comment, Annie skipped over to the television and turned it on. She grabbed the remote, climbed up on the sofa next to Kassie, and snuggled in next to her as if she'd known the woman her entire life. She pulled part of the comforter over her own legs and began to change the channels, looking for the cartoon she wanted to watch.

Kassie sat frozen. Paralyzed by thoughts of unworthiness. How in the world this child had such a sunny and positive outlook on life was beyond her. She'd been through hell, but here she sat, making friends with someone because she knew her parents trusted her. Kassie wasn't sure she deserved that trust, but she'd rather cut off her own arm than do anything to hurt the adorable little girl next to her.

Tentatively, Kassie put her arm around Annie's shoulders, and sighed in relief when she merely settled farther into her side. They sat that way for the next forty minutes. Annie keeping up a running commentary about her favorite turtle and how she was going to learn how to fight like they did, and someday she'd be a soldier and 'kick bad guys' butts just like Daddy Fletch did.'

When the knock on the door came, Kassie wasn't surprised. She'd been expecting it long before now, if she was honest with herself. She patted Annie on the head as she got up. "I'll get it."

"Make sure you peep through the hole before you open the door," Annie lectured, not taking her eyes from the screen.

"I will," Kassie reassured her. She looked down at herself and grimaced. She wasn't exactly dressed for company, but it couldn't be helped. At least she had on sleep shorts and not just the oversized T-shirt she usually wore.

Looking through the peephole, Kassie saw Emily

standing on the other side of the door. Relieved she didn't have to face Fletch—Hollywood might be the best-looking man she'd ever seen, but his friends weren't too shabby either; having Fletch see her in her pajamas would be pushing her comfort level at the moment—Kassie opened the door.

"Hi, Kassie. I'm sorry to bother you. I've come to collect Annie. I hope she wasn't a pest," Emily said easily, a wide, apologetic smile on her face.

It wasn't lost on Kassie that Emily hadn't asked if her daughter was there, she'd merely apologized for her *being* there. Hollywood and Annie had obviously been correct about the cameras.

"It's okay. We were just watching TV."

Emily leaned forward and said in a soft voice that her daughter wouldn't hear. "I was going to be here thirty minutes ago, but Fletch decided since we had the house to ourselves that he'd take advantage of it." She blushed, but continued on, "He's also decided that Annie needs a baby brother or sister and takes every chance he has to try to make that happen."

Kassie smiled at the other woman. It should've felt weird that she was basically telling her she and her husband had been going at it, but somehow it didn't. It made Kassie feel like she was an honest-to-God friend rather than some random chick who was staying the night at the guest house on their property.

"As I said, it's fine. I'm glad I could...err...provide a distraction for your daughter." They smiled at each other for a beat, before Kassie added, "Oh, come in. I'm sorry, I should've said that from the start."

Emily waved away her concern. "No worries." She went straight to Annie, who was now lying on the couch under the blanket she'd retrieved, eyes still glued to the antics of the turtles on the screen. Emily leaned down and kissed her forehead. Then said, "Hey, Annie."

"Hi, Mommy."

"Didn't we tell you that it wasn't polite to bother our guest so early in the morning?"

"Yeah, but Daddy said that Hollywood would come over and steal her away as soon as he could, and I wanted to meet her so I had to beat him here."

Emily shook her head in exasperation then straightened. "You want something to eat, baby?"

"Yeah."

"What?"

"Surprise me," was Annie's response.

Kassie just gaped. Good Lord, the little girl sounded like she was in her teens rather than only...she didn't know how old she was, but couldn't be more than eight.

Emily caught her look and chuckled as she went into the kitchen. "I know, I know. She spends a lot of time with Fletch and his friends, and tends to pick up some of the things they say." Emily shrugged. "Unless it's something awful, I don't bother correcting her."

Feeling as if she had to say something—Emily was being really nice to her and Kassie wasn't sure she deserved it—she blurted, "I didn't know what Richard was going to do."

Emily had opened the fridge, and she turned to Kassie in surprise. "Of course you didn't."

"I mean, I was dating him, though honestly I hadn't *really* been for the last several months, but he didn't really want to let me go. If I had known what he was doing to you, or what he had planned to do to you and Annie, I would've gone to the police. I swear I would've."

Emily closed the refrigerator door and walked over to where Kassie was standing. She put her hands on her shoulders and said quietly, "Kassie, I know. Nothing he did was your fault. I know, more than anyone else, how threatening he can be. So relax, okay? Neither me nor Fletch think badly of you for anything."

"If Annie was my daughter, I don't think I'd be as forgiving as you," Kassie said honestly.

Emily chuckled and gestured to Annie on the couch. "You think she'd let you be anything *but* forgiving?"

Kassie's lips quirked. "Probably not."

"Exactly. She wanted to come over and meet you, so she did. Sometimes we worry about how outgoing and fearless she is, but she's smart about it. Fletch and I talked about you in front of her on purpose. We wanted her to know that you were a friend and it was safe for you to be here on our property. Yes, she's tough, but she's also only seven."

"Thank you for trusting me," Kassie said in a low tone.

"You're welcome. Now, if I were you, I'd get showered and changed. I have a feeling Hollywood is going to be here sooner rather than later. We're having a barbeque this evening and everyone is invited."

"Everyone?" Kassie asked.

"Yup. You already met the girls, but Mary will hopefully be here so you can meet her too. You'll meet Fish today though, at the meeting."

"Meeting?" Kassie didn't like echoing the other woman, but she was telling her things she had no idea about.

"Oh man. Hollywood didn't tell you?"

"Oh, yeah, I guess he did. I must've forgot, or blocked it out or something."

Emily chuckled. "I doubt it'll be as bad as what you're probably thinking. From what I gather, Hollywood called a meeting with his commander and the team. Fish is going to be there too, and you. They want to talk about Jacks and what the next step should be to deal with him."

Kassie tried not to panic, but she really didn't want

to think about sitting in a meeting with all of Holly-wood's friends, probably in uniform. Especially not his commanding officer. It all sounded ominous, and brought too many memories of having to sit around with Richard and his friends as they talked. They liked to wear their uniforms and order her around as they had their meetings.

As if she could read her mind, Emily quickly said, "Don't worry. Most of the higher-ranking guys at the post look scary, but they're not. They just want to figure this out and make you and your sister safe as quickly as possible."

Okay. Obviously Emily knew most of what was going on. "And you think Hollywood is going to be here soon?"

"Welllll, Fletch was talking to him when I left the house, telling him that Annie had most likely woken you up at the crack of dawn. And if Hollywood is anything like my husband, which I know he is, if he knows you're up and awake, he's going to want to be here, up and awake with you."

Kassie glanced at her watch and saw that Emily had been there for about ten minutes. "How long did you know Fletch before he decided you were it for him?"

"After he figured out that we'd had a massive com-munication breakdown and he realized Jacks wasn't my boyfriend, but had been blackmailing me?"

"Uh…yeah?"

"About three point two minutes, I think." Emily beamed. "I take it Hollywood hasn't hesitated to let you know that your life has changed now that he's in it."

"Something like that," Kassie murmured. A part of her wanted to be upset or freaked, but the feelings of satisfaction and contentment won out.

"Welcome to the family," Emily told her, completely serious. She pulled Kassie into a brief hug, then said nonchalantly, "It doesn't take too long to get here from Hollywood's place. This time of morning, fifteen to twenty minutes maybe."

"That sounds about right," Kassie told her.

"Right. So you better get that shower then, huh?" Emily said dryly.

"Thank you," Kassie told Emily, hoping she'd understand what she was thanking her for.

"You're welcome. Now go. Tick-tock."

Kassie made a quick detour to say bye to Annie and let her know she'd see her later before rushing into her room to gather what she needed to get ready. Even knowing she'd have to talk about Richard and Dean with all his friends, Kassie couldn't wait to see Hollywood.

Chapter Eleven

"**A**RE YOU SURE you're okay about Annie coming over this morning?" Hollywood asked Kassie as they headed for the post.

"I'm fine, seriously."

"You didn't have any bad moments?" he insisted.

Kassie turned her head to look at Hollywood as he drove. She shouldn't be surprised he was so in tune with her, but she was.

"Maybe one or two, but it's fine."

"Tell me?" he asked.

It wasn't quite a demand, and Kassie appreciated it. She knew he was worried about how she was going to react to the meeting they were going to with all his friends and commanding officer. If she was honest with herself, she *was* worried how it would go down. But in the short time she'd known Hollywood, she knew he wouldn't put her in a position where she'd be attacked.

"Annie shocked me. I'd met Emily at the ball, but seeing how amazing, funny, and cute Annie is with my own eyes made it hit home all the more. I felt guilty that

I even *know* Richard."

Hollywood reached over and grabbed her hand, once more interlacing their fingers. The familiarity was reassuring to Kassie. "No one blames you for what happened. Least of all Annie or Emily."

"Intellectually I know that, but emotionally I'm still wrapping my head around it."

"As long as you don't let it get between us, you can keep doing that," he told her with a serious look on his face. "But I hope after today, you'll get even closer to believing it. You've told me some of what that asshat did to you, and I hate that he touched you at all. But even without knowing all of it, I'm astute enough to know you've been through, and are going through, hell with him. Your hell and their hell might be different, but it's still hell."

Kassie thought about his words for a long moment. He was right. She had to stop thinking about the way Richard used to be before his injury. That man was long gone. She knew without a doubt that Hollywood and his friends would help her get out from under her ex's thumb once and for all. And hopefully take Dean down at the same time. "You're right."

Hollywood chuckled. "You certainly thought about something for a long time before coming to that conclusion."

"Well, you know," she said, not smiling, "First, I

thought about all the good looking men in uniform I'll be seeing once we get to Fort Hood. Then I had to decide if I could get away with taking pictures without them knowing so I could share with Karina when I get home. Then that made me think about you in your uniform at the ball and how I didn't get to properly appreciate it. And *that* made me think about what you might've been wearing under your dress blues…so yeah, sorry, I got distracted."

At the shocked look on his face, Kassie couldn't hold back her grin any longer. She giggled like she hadn't a care in the world. "You should see your face," she got out between giggles. "Priceless!"

"Interestingly enough, I've thought about what you might've been wearing under your gown several times," he retorted.

Without missing a beat, Kassie said, "Nothing."

"What?"

"Nothing. I didn't want any panty lines, and even though I bought a bra to go under the dress, it was uncomfortable. So Karina convinced me to go bare-ass naked under it. I think she was hoping I'd get lucky though, so she might've had an ulterior motive."

Hollywood choked and Kassie pounded him on the back as best she could in the small space of the car. "Are you all right?" she asked, concerned as his face turned red and he continued to cough.

When he had himself under control, he shook his head ruefully. "I need to stop trying to one-up you. You blow me away every time."

"What'd I say?" Kassie asked innocently.

"You know exactly what you said," Hollywood told her, reaching for her hand again.

Gladly grabbing hold of him, Kassie leaned back, resting her head against the seat behind her. "Who's going to be here today?" she asked, getting serious.

Hollywood squeezed her hand. "First, stop worrying. Nothing is going to happen that should stress you out. Everyone already knows your situation; we just need to get a handle on it and shut Jacks and Dean down once and for all. So all the guys will be there...Ghost, Fletch, Coach, Beatle, Blade, and Truck. Fish will too, he volunteered to come up and be involved. My commanding officer will also be there."

"I have absolutely no clue what I should tell Dean to communicate to Richard to make all this stop for you guys," Kassie told him honestly.

"That's why we're meeting as a group. It's how we work best...as a team. We'll throw ideas off each other and by the time we're done, we'll have a plan. You aren't alone anymore, Kassie. You've got me and all my friends on your side. I'm going to do everything in my power to make sure you and your sister are safe."

"What about you?"

"What *about* me?"

"What are you going to do about keeping yourself safe?" she asked. "Richard doesn't really care about me. I've come to the conclusion that I'm like a favorite toy of his. He doesn't want to play with me anymore, but also doesn't want anyone else to either." She grimaced. "That wasn't the best analogy, but you know what I mean."

"I do."

"Anyway, so the only reason I'm here is because he hates you and your friends. We might figure out a way for me to get out from under his thumb, but what about you guys? I was serious when I told you in that email I sent right after the ball that he wants to see you all dead. I would be less than pleased if the guy I've come to care about very much ended up dead. Wouldn't look good on my track record for any future prospective boyfriends."

"First of all, there aren't going to *be* any future ones because I'm not going anywhere," Hollywood told her in what sounded like a huff to Kassie. She would've smiled, but he continued, "Second, I can guarantee that we aren't going to get dead."

"You can't guarantee that," Kassie insisted.

Hollywood took a deep breath, then let it out slowly before saying, "I'm about to tell you something that is top secret. It could get me in big trouble with my commanding officer and the Army. But I'm telling you because as my woman, you need to know. It's not something I'm comfortable keeping from you."

"Oh my God," Kassie breathed, trying to disengage her hand from his. "You're married, aren't you?"

"No," he told her with no ire in his tone. "Settle and listen to me."

Kassie tried to read him, but couldn't. She had absolutely no idea what was so secret that he could get in trouble if he told her. She thought she knew a lot about the Army, but as evidenced at the ball, what she'd learned from Richard probably wasn't accurate anyway.

"I'm Delta Force."

The three words were flat and to the point. And Kassie had no idea what they meant.

"Okay. And?" she asked.

Hollywood's lips twitched, but he merely said, "And what?"

"Is that the big secret?"

"Yeah, Kass. That's it."

She wracked her brain for a moment and came up blank. Finally, she told him, "As evidenced by your demeanor, that's supposed to mean something to me. But I'm really, really sorry, I have no idea what that means. I could Google it, but I figure it'll be quicker if you just told me what you wanted me to know. Is it bad?"

"You seriously have no idea what Delta Force is?" Hollywood asked, his eyebrows raised in surprise.

He didn't sound upset, but Kassie couldn't read his tone. She decided being succinct was the way to go. "No."

"You've heard of Navy SEALs though, right?"

"Duh. Everyone's heard of the SEALs. They're the guys who are all badass and go on super-secret missions overseas. Weren't they the guys who finally took down Osama Bin Laden? I think I saw that somewhere but..." Her voice trailed off as a thought hit her. "Oh."

Now Hollywood was smiling. "Yeah. Oh."

"So you're a SEAL, but for the Army?"

"Man, you're tough on the ego, sweetheart. No, Deltas aren't SEALs; we're more badass than them."

Kassie narrowed her eyes at him as she tried to picture it. Nope, she simply couldn't do it. She kept seeing him in his white tuxedo shirt, bow tie, and pretty blue uniform with all the medals on it. "So you're Delta Force. And your friends are too?"

"Yeah. Unlike the SEALs, our missions are done with a complete media blackout. We don't talk about them, and what we do isn't ever televised or reported on. We'll never get invited to the White House to be commended by the President. We do our thing, come home and live under the radar most of the time. We focus primarily on counterterrorism missions."

"What does that mean?" Kassie asked quietly, worried now.

"We're usually sent into situations to kill or capture high-value targets, or to dismantle terrorist cells. We're flexible, and can operate with just the seven of us or within bigger units. We've worked with the CIA, as well as protected the President when he's made visits in war-torn countries."

"So it's dangerous," Kassie concluded.

Hollywood looked over at her as if she was insane. "Yeah, Kass, sneaking around Iraq without their government knowing we're there to try to kill people tends to be a bit dangerous at times."

She glared at him. "Don't make fun of me."

"I am absolutely not making fun of you," Hollywood told her. "What I *am* trying to do is reassure you that there is no fucking way Jacks and his asshole sidekick will kill me or any of my friends. We're trained in this shit. How do you think we smeared their asses in that training exercise so fast? Hell, when we rescued Emily and Annie, it took us less than twenty minutes. I'm not worried about me or my friends, I'm worried about *you*. And Karina. And anyone else he decides to fuck with in the futile hope he can catch any of us off guard. It's not going to happen. Period."

"Alrighty then," Kassie quipped, not sure if she was relieved or not. "You're a super-badass, top-secret soldier who eats Navy SEALs for breakfast and spits out stupid ex-boyfriend soldiers who think they're God's gift to the military. Does that about sum it up?"

"That's about it."

Kassie breathed a sigh of relief when he grinned at her. They were approaching the front gate of the post and Kassie tried not to be nervous. She'd been here a couple of times with Richard, but it felt different now.

Hollywood held out his hand. "He needs to see your ID, Kass."

"Of course," she said, fumbling for her purse at her feet. She got out her driver's license and gave it to Hollywood, who handed it to the soldier at the window. He scrutinized both then handed them back.

"Have a good day, Sergeant Caverly. Ms. Anderson." He nodded at them and Hollywood nodded back. Kassie just smiled at the young man. Then they were driving through.

"Whew!" she exclaimed, slouching back in her seat. "I'm glad I didn't have to have a strip search that time."

"Did that asshole do that to you too?" Hollywood growled.

Kassie started in surprise. "No, no, no. I'm sorry. I was trying to make a joke. Obviously *that* was a big fail."

"You once told me that you joked when you're nervous, and I hate that you're nervous about being on post, being around men in their uniforms. You've been okay with me, but I can tell that actually being here is difficult for you," Hollywood told her as he drove toward his office. "I know it's a result of that douche-canoe, but it still frustrates me." He glanced over at Kassie. She was gripping her hands together so tightly her knuckles were white with the effort.

"I'm not—"

"You are," he insisted. "And Jacks made you that way. I haven't forgotten all those fucked-up things he tried to teach you about military balls and our traditions. I told you once, and I'll tell you again, if you ever have a question about something, or you feel uneasy, promise me you'll ask about it. Don't be embarrassed. How can you learn if you don't ask?"

"Okay."

"And just so you know, everyone today will be in uniform, except for probably Fish. He's medically retiring and not required to show up in uniform. But you're safe here, Kassie. I don't know what other asinine things that asshole had you do while he and his buddies played dress up and tried to be all macho badass soldiers, but that won't happen here. What *will* happen is that we'll greet each other in a friendly way. We'll grab some coffee, sit around a big-ass table, and talk. We might swear. Okay, that's a lie, we *will* swear. We might get pissed off and upset, but not at you. But you are in absolutely no danger from me or my friends. Got it?"

"Thanks, Hollywood."

"Don't thank me," he told her immediately. "You should never have to thank your man for keeping you safe. It's my privilege, honor, and duty to do so." Hollywood looked over at Kassie and was surprised to see her smiling. "What? I wasn't kidding."

Her smile faded. "I know you weren't. I just...that sounded like something someone would say in a movie."

Hollywood pulled into his parking space and shut the engine off. He turned to Kassie and took her hands in his, chafing them gently to try to warm her chilly fingers. "Your days of trying to do everything yourself are over, Kass. Not only do you have me looking out for you, but you've got seven other men who are waiting upstairs who will do everything in their power to make sure you're safe, happy, and healthy."

"It sounds kinda like a cult," Kassie told him.

"No cult, sweetheart," Hollywood returned immediately. "Friends. The best ones a man could ever have. The kind of men who would give their lives for mine without thought. And I'd do the same for them."

"I'm nervous," Kassie blurted.

"I know you are. If you think I've missed that, you're insane. But that's okay. Because I'm going to do everything in my power to make this easier for you. All you have to do is hold on to me. In a couple hours we'll leave here, go back to my place so I can change, and I'll take you back to Fletch's. We'll hang out with the men you'll get to know here today and their women, and relax. After this meeting, your life will change…for the better. You just have to stick by my side and trust me. Can you do that?"

He saw the emotions swirling in her eyes. He'd never seen any as expressive as Kassie's. He read her acceptance before the words left her lips.

"Yeah. I can do that."

"Good. Now come on. Let's get upstairs. I'll get you a cup of horrible coffee. I wouldn't suggest drinking it, but you can hold it in your hands to try to keep your fingers from falling off. Okay?"

She smiled at him then. "Sounds good."

Hollywood leaned over, kissed her forehead, leaving his lips on her skin for a long moment as he murmured, "There's no way on God's green earth I'm going to let you slip through my fingers now that I've found you. Jacks is not going to win this war."

He pulled back and climbed out without waiting for her to answer.

He was making no mistake. This *was* war. Jacks had started it with Emily, and it would end here and now.

Chapter Twelve

"CAN'T WE JUST beat the shit out of Dean?"

"What if we get someone to whack Jacks while he's locked up? Who knows someone?"

"I think we should feed him a false time and place that we'll be having another training exercise and we can nail Dean's ass when he tries to interfere."

"What about the sister? Do you think Dean will try something with her like he did with Emily?"

"Can we do anything legally?"

Kassie's head hurt. They'd been sitting around the large table for at least an hour and nothing had been decided yet. All the men had been doing was asking questions...not actually deciding anything. She appreciated the fact they were here on a weekend and helping her and her sister, but she hadn't ever been in a meeting like this one. In her line of work, when there was an issue, a manager made a decision and that was that. But now she had more questions than answers, and she was quickly reaching her breaking point.

Hollywood had taken hold of her hand under the

table and hadn't let go since the meeting started. But she was done.

Letting go of him, she pushed back her chair and got up. She began to pace back and forth in the small space behind the chairs pushed into the conference table. She massaged her forehead with one hand and put the other on her hip as she stalked the room.

"Talk to us," Ghost ordered Kassie as everyone fell silent and watched as she paced.

Kassie didn't even turn her head. She'd been nervous when she'd first entered the room, but at the moment was more tired and frustrated than anything else. She wanted to help them, but every time they'd brought up what Richard had done to Emily, or to her, it only made her feel worse about the entire situation.

She ticked off her thoughts on her fingers as she paced. "One, Richard is behind bars, communicating his crazy to Dean who's carrying out his orders. Two, Dean is stupid. He couldn't graduate from basic and barely got through high school. Three, just because Dean is stupid doesn't mean he's not a threat. He's big. And strong. And can easily overpower me and Karina. Four, he's creepy and has been watching Karina. Five, they want me to give information about you guys to them so they can do something. But what? Six, what if I don't give it to them? What do they have planned for Karina? If they do something to her, what will that gain them? Seven, if I do pass information on to them, will they stop threatening me or Karina? Or will they just continue because I did what they said?"

She stopped pacing and turned to the men at the table and said resolutely, "I can't ignore Dean. I can't and won't put Karina in danger. I need to tell him something. But what? That's the question. What can I tell Dean to tell Richard that will end this?"

"As much as I hate to say it," Fletch said, "I don't think anything you tell him will end his threats. He gets off on it."

Kassie huffed out an exasperated breath and held her arms out, palms up. "Then what? I let him continue to threaten me forever? My sister?"

"Of course not," Fletch said easily, not seeming to be irritated at all by her show of frustration. "You'll feed Dean information, that he'll give to Jacks, who will decide what will happen, then we'll end this farce once and for all."

The room was silent for a moment before Fish spoke. "Karina won't be an issue. I'm already down in Austin. I'm officially getting discharged on Monday and free to keep an eye on her."

Kassie gaped at him but before she could say anything, Truck said, "You're done on Monday? Fucking awesome, man. Pleased for you."

Fish gave the other man a chin lift, but kept his eyes

on Kassie. "When Hollywood isn't around, I promise to keep my eye on you and your sister. I'll do everything in my power to make sure Dean isn't a threat to you anymore. Not only that, but I guarantee you, Kassie, you will not have to worry about Richard Jacks after this is over." There was a note of steel in his tone that made her absolutely believe him.

"Fish, don't do anything stupid," the commander stated quietly. "I know you're not under my command, and technically you aren't even employed by the United States of America anymore, so I can't push anything you might do under the rug. The last thing you want is to end up in Leavenworth yourself."

Fish turned then and looked at the older man. "I don't know what you mean, sir. All I'm saying is that I'm sure my friends, and you, will figure out a way to stop Jacks from threatening Ms. Anderson in the future. Am I right?"

No one said a word for the longest time, before the commander cleared his throat and agreed. "You're right."

"All right then," Fish said reasonably. "So what information are we gonna have Kassie give Dean to pass to Jacks?"

Kassie looked from the former badass secret soldier to the rest of the badass secret soldiers sitting around the table. If Hollywood hadn't told her that he and his friends were Delta Force, she never would've guessed, but...she would've known to the marrow of her bones that they were different. More lethal. More dangerous than the average soldier.

Even though she wasn't used to how they made decisions, there was just something about their mannerisms, and the way they spoke and planned, that screamed...competence.

"What did Dean say you were supposed to do the night of the ball?" Beatle asked.

Kassie took a deep breath and wandered back to her chair. Hollywood swiveled it for her and when she sat, turned it back and claimed her hand again.

"He said that I'd done well in getting Hollywood to ask me out. Wanted to know if I'd sent him naked pictures or something."

"Fucker," Hollywood said under his breath. "Asshole wouldn't know a quality woman if she hit him in the ass. He probably can only get pussy if he pays for it."

Kassie couldn't keep her grin from escaping. Looking around the table, she noticed that neither did most of the other men. They were all smiling straight out. So she ignored Hollywood's outburst, merely squeezed his fingers in thanks for standing up for her, and continued, "Anyway, he told me that I was to see if I could get any information from Hollywood, or any of the other guys, about if you'd be going out of town anytime soon, any details about your girlfriends, or anything else I thought might be useful."

"Useful for what?" Blade asked quickly before anyone could get riled up about Jacks wanting to know about Rayne, Emily, or Harley.

"I don't know," Kassie said. "If I did, I'd have told him something by now. After meeting all you guys, I didn't want to say *anything* that might get you hurt."

"Has he contacted you since the ball?" Truck asked.

Kassie nodded. "He's texted a few times. I told him I was still seeing Hollywood and that I was trying to find out something he could use."

"How did he take the delay?" It was the commander who asked that time.

"He called me and said I was a cunt, and that I better tell him something useful soon or Karina would find herself sold to a sex trafficker and flat on her back in Mexico." Kassie shuddered at the thought. That hadn't been a good day, and Hollywood had talked her down from kidnapping her own sister and moving to Timbuktu.

"Shit," Beatle swore.

Kassie heard the others mumbling under their breaths, but didn't catch anything as Hollywood turned her to face him with a hand at her cheek. "You're doing great, sweetheart. Hang in there."

"Thanks," she whispered, not feeling like she was

doing well at all.

"The last thing we want is him turning his attention to one of your women again," the commander noted quietly after the mumbles from the Deltas quieted down. "The trouble is that it's going to be hard to prove *Jacks* is behind any of this. We want Kassie to feed Dean information to give Jacks, but I'm not sure how to prove he's orchestrating this entire fucking thing from behind bars."

"But if we take out Dean, that's who's currently the most threatening to Kassie and her sister," Hollywood mused, "Jacks might recruit someone else to help him, but by then we'll have hopefully figured out another way to take him down...and again, Kassie will be safe."

"Good point," the commander agreed.

"What about another training exercise?" Truck asked.

"Yeah," Blade said, picking up on where Truck was going. "If we have Kassie tell Dean that Hollywood told her he'd be going out of town and he'd be unable to talk or see her for a few days, we could then lie in wait for whoever showed up to try to interfere."

"And if we made it somewhere away from this area, they'd have to travel to get there, which would mean Karina and Kassie would be out of their range while it happened," Hollywood added.

"Galveston," Ghost decided. "It's far enough away,

but we can say it's a maneuver related to ISIS and them trying to smuggle shit into the country via ships."

"That's pretty specific for a generic Army exercise," Fletch noted. "And Galveston isn't exactly remote."

Kassie's head whipped back and forth as the men narrowed down and refined their thoughts. She was kind of in awe at how well they bounced ideas off of each other.

"Not Galveston," the commander said excitedly. "The Brazoria National Wildlife Refuge. It's down there nearby, but mostly all grassland, and of course it's unpopulated. We can set up a fake command center near Christmas Bay. We can use another team of Del— err...men under my command here."

"What're the chances Jacks will decide that all of us being gone is the perfect opportunity to snatch our women?" Coach asked. "There's no way I'm going to leave Harley and the others as sitting ducks while we're down there with our thumbs up our asses, waiting for an ambush that might never happen."

"That's always a possibility," Ghost said. "He's already proved that he'll use our women to get to us. But I'm hoping his arrogance and the opportunity to take us all out with one fell swoop will be too much for him to resist. Why go after them if he can kill us all at the same training exercise?"

"I already said that I'd watch Karina and Kassie,"

Fish stated into the silence that followed Blade's statement. "If Rock isn't working, I know he'd come up and keep an eye on the girls."

"I bet I could get Rayne to have one of her girls' nights in when we're gone so they're all in the same place," Ghost mused.

"They could come here on post," the commander volunteered. "We've got a guest house they could commandeer. They wouldn't be safer anywhere else."

"Don't underestimate this asshole," Hollywood grit out between clenched teeth.

"Annie loves coming on post," Fletch said. "There's that new platoon of female Army Rangers, right?"

The commander and Fletch shared a look before the commander said, "Yeah. What are you thinking?"

"We say that Annie and the women are invited to the post to watch the women go through the obstacle course. Annie loves that shit. Then they're treated to a special dinner where they get to mingle with the women and learn more about what it means to be a woman in a male-dominated organization like the Rangers. Afterwards, they can all spend the night here on post. I'm not saying the Rangers need to be briefed on everything that's going down, but they can be made aware there's a threat against Rayne, Emily, Harley, Mary, and Annie." Fletch had obviously thought it through.

Kassie blinked in surprise. She'd heard of the Army

Rangers, but had no idea women were allowed to join. Richard would *hate* that. He'd tried out for the elite group, but had washed out pretty early in the selection process. Any woman who could make it through would be badass for sure.

"That could work," the commander mused. "They'd be protected in case Jacks doesn't take the bait. Let me see what I can do."

"When?" Kassie blurted. When everyone turned to look at her, she said quickly, "Karina's dance is in two weeks. I don't know what 'watching over us' means, but there's no way she'll want to miss it. She's been looking forward to it for weeks. She's even buying her dress this weekend. She's got a new boyfriend and hasn't been as excited for a dance like she is this one."

"Actually, I think that works out well," the commander said. "If she's at the dance, in public, especially with a new boyfriend who hopefully won't let her out of his sight, I think she'll be safer."

Kassie wasn't sure about that, but didn't say anything.

"While you guys are down at the refuge, I'll be watching Kassie," Fish stated.

"No. Permission to skip the ambush and stay in Austin to protect Kassie," Hollywood stated firmly, staring at his commander. "Fish can stick with Karina. He can't be in two places at once."

"Don't you think you should be at the fake training exercise to lend authenticity to it? If Kassie tells Jacks about it, he'd expect you to be there."

"If everyone is dressed in fatigues and has face paint on, it'll be almost impossible to tell who is who. Especially for whatever ragtag army he's collected. They won't know if I'm there or not. Get someone from the other team of...the other team to stand in as me."

"You don't have to stay with me," Kassie protested. "I'll be fine. It's you guys Richard wants."

"Permission granted," the commander stated, not giving Hollywood a chance to reply.

"Thank you, sir," he told him, then turned to Fish. "I'd appreciate your backup though. Pleased as shit you're done with rehab. Sucks the Army is losing as good a soldier as you though."

"You got it," Fish stated, then smiled. "But don't get used to it. I'm still moving to Idaho as soon as the sale of the house I bought goes through."

"You bought a house?" Truck asked. "Thought you were just looking."

"I was. Found one I liked." He shrugged. "Still have to fill out all the paperwork and give the lending company a kidney or two, but it's in the works. House inspection is next week."

"Couldn't be happier for you," Truck said, slapping Fish on the back. "I can't wait to see it. Hope you don't think you leaving means you'll get away from us."

"Wouldn't dream of it. I'll have a housewarming barbeque when I get there and settled in."

"Sounds like a plan," Truck told him.

"So we're good?" the commander asked.

Everyone agreed, but Kassie looked around in confusion. "Uh...I have no idea what was decided," she said honestly.

Hollywood picked up her hand and kissed the palm before wrapping his fingers around it. "You'll tell Dean that you overheard me talking about a top-secret training exercise down in the Brazoria National Wildlife Refuge near Galveston. You heard me saying that it was going to be a small platoon-on-platoon thing. That should pique his interest because he'll have a better chance of taking us out. The girls will all go to a demonstration by the Army's newest super soldiers...who just happen to be women. Your sister will be safe at her dance. I'll hang with you at your place, Fish'll be on standby, and when Dean and his flunkies show up, we'll kick their asses and get them arrested for interfering in a government training exercise."

"What about Richard?" she asked.

"I'll take care of him," Fish said before the commander could.

"Now, look here, Munroe. You said that before, you can't—"

"I can. And I will. All due respect, sir. You know as well as every man in this room that in order to kill the snake, we have to cut off its head."

Kassie swore she'd be able to hear a pin drop in the room; it was that quiet.

Finally, the commander stated softly, "When are you moving, Munroe? Because the sooner you're out of my hair, the better."

Strangely, his words seemed to make everyone relax.

"As soon as my VA loan goes through and I sign the papers for the house, I'm out of here."

"Anything I can do to hurry that along, just ask," the commander stated as he pushed his chair back and stood. "The rest of you, I'll talk with the general and get this shit sanctioned. But the same rules will apply this time as the last. This is a nonlethal op. The US Army can't go around killing people because of threats against girlfriends."

"This is not about a threat against my girlfriend," Hollywood growled. Kassie hadn't ever heard him sound so angry. She tried to release his hand to give him space, but he wouldn't let go as he continued.

"This is a threat against national security. Jacks is doing all this from behind bars. How's he doing that, hmmm? He has to have help. Traitors working up at Leavenworth aren't an issue anyone can take lightly. Think about the kind of prisoners who are incarcerated there. They're not exactly upstanding citizens, and Jacks is child's play compared to some of the men who are behind bars up there. You want violent criminals or gang members getting information to their followers? Rapists? Murderers? Traitors who made connections with the Taliban or ISIS? No fucking way. I don't put my life on the line with every mission to have some asshole prison guard who makes ten twenty-five an hour turning his head when a prisoner makes a phone call to his contact in fucking Afghanistan, or when he passes information to his cronies when they visit."

"Hollywood—" the commander warned, but Hollywood ignored him.

"Jacks is an amateur asshole. None of us is concerned about him or his flunkies, but we *are* concerned about how easy it is for Dean to drive up to Kansas and meet with him. We're disturbed about how easy it is for Jacks to blackmail his ex-girlfriend when he's supposed to be locked away for the safety of society. If *he* can do it, what else is going on up there? What other information is getting shared and what other collaborations are being made?"

"You've got a point," the older man said in a low tone, "but your disrespect isn't necessary."

Hollywood took a deep breath. "Noted," he bit out.

Mollified, the commander nodded then looked at Kassie. "Talk to Dean. We need to get this shit done.

Reach out to him if necessary, but get it done."

"Yes, sir," Kassie said meekly, relieved when the commander merely nodded at her, then left the room.

She sagged back into her chair after he'd left and said softly, "Good Lord. I thought *you* were bossy, Hollywood."

There were a few chuckles around the room, but Fish wasn't smiling when he asked, "Are you okay with me looking after you and your sister when Hollywood can't be in Austin?"

"Uh, yeah?" Kassie responded, confused. "Why?"

"Because of this," he said, gesturing toward his prosthetic. The hook on the end of his arm opened and closed where it rested on the table, as if making Fish's point for him.

Kassie looked over at Hollywood, who was scowling at Fish. She turned back to the other man. "I'm sorry...I still don't understand."

"I've only got one hand, Kassie. Aren't you worried that I won't be able to protect you as well as one of the other guys who have both?"

Kassie stared at the man for a brief moment, then burst out laughing. It was more a release of tension than anything else, but she couldn't control it. Eventually, she wound down to giggles instead of full-out laughter and took a deep breath, trying to control herself.

"You about done?" Fish ground out.

Kassie sobered at the hurt tone of his voice. Shit, she hadn't meant to insult him. She looked over at the former soldier. He had a beard, which was cut close to his cheeks, but he'd let it grow a bit longer at his chin. The facial hair combined with the sharp, lethal hook on the end of his arm made him look *more* badass than the other men sitting around him. Not less.

"I'm sorry, Fish, but seriously, that was funny. Do I think you can't protect me? Even with missing part of your arm, you look more dangerous and ferocious than anyone I might meet on the streets of Austin. I have no doubt whatsoever that if for some reason Dean shows up at my apartment with an ax, you could singlehandedly take him out and make him wish he'd never even heard my name. So yeah, I'm perfectly okay with you having my back when Hollywood isn't there."

Her words rang out in the austere conference room.

Finally, Truck broke the silence by saying, "Told you, Fish. Maybe now you'll shut up about how crippled you are."

Everyone chuckled and Fish shook his head at his friend. "Fuck off, Truck." But his words held no malice.

Hollywood stood, and held Kassie's chair still as she did too. "We'll see you all later at Fletch's, right?"

Choruses of "right" and "of course" rang out from amongst the group of friends.

"Ready to go, Kass?" Hollywood asked.

She nodded, figuring since he was already leading her to the door of the room with his hand on her back that was the expected answer.

Chapter Thirteen

AFTER THE MEETING, Hollywood whisked her straight out of the building and to his car without more than a chin lift to the few people he passed. He got her settled into his car then quickly got in and headed off post.

"You hungry?"

"Aren't we going to a barbeque later?" she asked.

"Yeah, but that's not for at least another three hours. Then we'll shoot the shit with everyone and hang out while the brats and burgers are cooking. So it'll be four to five hours before we eat. Figured you'd want something to tide you over. The bagel you had for breakfast—he glanced at his watch then continued— "four and a half hours ago, has probably worn off by now. Besides, *I* could eat."

"Right. When you put it that way. Yes, I'm hungry."

He smirked. Hollywood could tell she was uneasy with everything that had just happened, but he much preferred seeing this snarky side of her than the unsure and scared one. "Good. What do you want?"

"Whataburger."

"Pardon?"

"Whataburger," she repeated.

"Really, don't vacillate. Tell me exactly what you're hungry for," Hollywood teased.

She turned in her seat and crossed her arms. "You asked," she accused.

Hollywood smiled huge. "I did."

"So I told you. Would you rather I have said, 'Oh, Hollywood, I don't know. Wherever *you* want to eat is perfectly fine with me. I don't have any opinions about anything, so just say the word and that's where we'll go.'"

He burst out laughing, shaking his head at the same time. "No. Absolutely not. I'm just not used to it. Hell, even when I'm with the guys, it takes a massive fucking discussion to decide on a place to eat. I'm thrilled you can make a decision."

She smiled back at him, not at all put off by his laughter. "Good. Because I have to tell you, I have extreme opinions on fast food restaurants. Some I love, others I hate, a few I'm ambivalent about. But when I'm hungry, I'm hungry, and I want what I like. You *do* like Whataburger, don't you?" she asked suspiciously, raising one eyebrow at him as she asked.

"Of course. What Texan doesn't?"

"Exactly." She nodded happily. "Wait, I don't even know where you're from. Did you grow up here?"

"Nope," he told her easily, as he headed toward the nearest Whataburger. "Fayetteville, North Carolina."

"Fort Bragg is there," Kassie informed him of something he knew. "Is that why you joined the Army?"

Hollywood shrugged. "Maybe. Of course we saw soldiers in their uniforms all the time. But I think it was more because my dad is a history buff. I grew up watching every military movie you can imagine. Being proud of my country was ingrained in me from a young age. When I graduated from high school I knew there wasn't anything I wanted to do other than join up."

"How'd you choose the Army over any of the other branches?"

Hollywood smirked. "They offered me the best deal," he told her honestly.

"Oh my God, seriously?" she asked, eyes wide.

"Yup. I might have been patriotic, but I was also eighteen. I was shallow, what can I say?"

"Do you regret it?" Kassie asked with a tilt of her head.

"Not for one second," he said with feeling.

"Are your parents still there?"

"Yeah. They love it. I think I told you, but my sister, Jade, is married and lives in Chapel Hill. She went to school at UNC and loved it so much, she stayed."

"Does she have kids?"

Hollywood couldn't read Kassie's tone. "Yeah, two. A boy and a girl."

"Uncle Graham," she said teasingly. "Do you get to see them often?"

"Not as much as I should, but we Skype all the time. I love those little rugrats."

"That's great."

Hollywood pulled into the fast food restaurant's parking lot. "Want to eat here, or get it to go?" He didn't like the sad tone that had crept into her voice and wanted to do what he could to make her smile again.

"Depends on where you're taking me after we eat."

"If we eat here, you're coming back to my place until it's time to go back to Fletch's. If you want to get it to go, we're still going back to my place."

"To go then."

Hollywood steered until he was in line at the drive-in and gave her a stern look. "Want to tell me what your weird tone was about when I told you about my niece and nephew?"

Kassie shrugged. "It's just...we don't really know that much about each other."

"We know each other," Hollywood said.

"Hollywood, I didn't even know where you grew up, or that your sister had kids," Kassie protested.

"We might not know the superficial things, but we

know the important ones."

"We do?"

"Yeah, Kassie. We do. For instance, I know that you love it just as much when I kiss you hard as you do when I brush my lips across your forehead. I know you've got a protective streak a mile long, and you've got the kind of strength that knocks me on my ass when I think about it. I know that you're honest, giving, and have a wicked sense of humor. I know that you're unsure about your attractiveness, which is utter bullshit and I can't believe no guy has ever made you feel beautiful just as you are. I know that you have a temper, but it's quick to burn out. I know just from what Emily told me about your interactions with Annie this morning that you'd make a wonderful mother. I know that you have so much passion built up within you waiting to get out that when I take you to bed, I'm going to want to stay there a week until I take the edge off. And finally, I know that I'm a lucky son of a bitch and if you let me, I'll spend the rest of my life making sure you know that you made the right decision trusting me and letting me into your world."

A horn honking behind him made Hollywood jerk his eyes from Kassie's wide ones to the drive-through lane. He inched forward, stopping behind the car in front of him once again, and looked back to Kassie.

"Do you have any other arguments about how we

don't know each other?"

"If I do, will you say some of that stuff again?" Kassie asked. She was blushing, but she met his eyes and didn't look away.

"I'll tell you every day for the rest of our lives if you need to hear it, Kass."

At that, she did finally close her eyes. "That was the nicest thing anyone has ever said to me. Okay, maybe not that I have a bad temper. I know I do, but you didn't have to point it out."

"I said you have a quick temper, sweetheart, but that it burns out fast. Which means you don't hold a grudge and that bodes well for when I piss you off in the future."

Her eyes popped open. "You planning on doing that a lot?"

"No. But with as much passion as you have in you, I can't see any way around it."

"Hollywood," Kassie complained.

"Kassie," he mimicked. But he did it smiling. "It's almost our turn. You know what you want?"

"Veggie burger with everything and the Whataburger Hulk."

Hollywood looked over the menu and examined it for a long moment before turning back to Kassie. "Hon, those aren't on the menu."

Kassie looked at him with her mouth open. Then

finally said, "If I didn't know you weren't a true Texan before now, I would've by those six words." She shook her head in mock disappointment. "You getting a burger?"

Hollywood merely shook his head. "Yeah."

She unclicked her seat belt and pointed forward. "Our turn."

"What are you doing? Put your belt back on, sweetheart." He slowly pulled forward to the speaker to order.

Kassie shocked the shit out of him by kneeling up on her seat and leaning over him. She rested her hands on his left thigh and turned to him and whispered, "I'm ordering for both of us. You'll screw up a perfectly good Whataburger experience."

He couldn't keep his hands to himself if his life depended on it. Having Kassie kneeling over him made him imagine what she'd look like straddling his waist as she rode his cock. Hollywood felt his dick stiffen but didn't give a shit.

"Welcome to Whataburger. What can I get for you today?" a tinny voice said from the speaker.

"Hi," Kassie said brightly. "We'd like a veggie burger with everything and—"

"We no longer have the potato patties, ma'am," the underpaid employee said with regret. "But we do have hash brown sticks that we can use to make your burger."

"That sounds perfect," Kassie told whoever was behind the speaker. "My hungry friend would like a double-double, but *with* the sauce, please."

"Of course. Would you like fries with that?"

"Yes, please. A large order."

"Anything to drink?"

Kassie turned her head and whispered, "Do you trust me?"

"With my life," Hollywood told her without hesitation. And he did. The woman who was kneeling over him, smiling because she was ordering off some secret menu, and enjoying the hell out of doing so, was the woman he'd lay down his life for. He hoped in time, she'd come to feel the same about him.

She beamed and turned back to the speaker. "Two Whataburger Hulks to drink, please."

"That'll be seventeen forty-three at the first window," the boy on the other end of the speaker told them without missing a beat.

Hollywood took his foot off the brake and moved forward just enough to let the car behind him pull up to the speaker, but he wrapped his arm under Kassie's waist, preventing her from sitting back in her seat.

"Hollywood, let me go. You have to pay," she giggled.

He tightened his hold, bringing his other hand to her cheek and turning her face toward him. Without asking, he kissed her. A full-on, tongue-memorizing-her-mouth, I-want-you-in-my-bed French kiss. And she responded in kind.

Hollywood pulled back way before he was ready and licked his lips, tasting a hint of the lip gloss she'd put on earlier that day and her own essence. "Do I want to know what's in a Hulk drink?" he asked with a smile.

She grinned back and licked her own lips. "I'm not telling until you taste it and tell me if you like it."

Moving his hand around her so it rested on the back of one of her thighs, Hollywood squeezed, loving how Kassie squirmed at the feel of his hand on her. "Sit back, sweetheart. I need to go pay," he ordered.

He kept his hand on her, guiding until she once again had her ass on the seat next to him. Then before she could fasten her seat belt, he leaned over and palmed the back of her head. "Thank you."

"For what?" she asked, tilting her head.

"For being you. For making me laugh when all I've wanted to do today is find Dean and beat the shit out of him. For making ordering fast food an event to be remembered rather than a boring, everyday task."

"Oh. Then you're welcome."

"Put on your seat belt," he ordered as he pulled forward to the first window.

"I was," she singsonged. "And not because you ordered me to either."

Hollywood knew the boy at the window probably

wondered what the hell he was grinning at so sappily, but he didn't care. He loved Kassie's sass and, if he was honest, purposely tried to bring it forth. He tried not to think about his hard-as-nails cock as he took the change from the boy and pulled forward to the next window.

He didn't even care that he was going to have blue balls until he finally made Kassie his. Every second he had to wait to have her in his bed would make it that much better when he was finally balls deep inside her. Taking her would change his life. He couldn't wait.

An hour later, Kassie smiled at Hollywood. She was sitting next to him at the bar in his kitchen. They'd finished eating about fifteen minutes ago and were polishing off their drinks while they chatted.

"So? Did you like it?" Kassie asked, motioning toward his now empty cup.

"Surprisingly, yes. Even though it looked like an alien was murdered in my cup…not that I know what aliens look like, but the bright green color just matches what I think the little green men might if they were melted down…yes. Now will you tell me what was in it?"

Instead of answering, Kassie stuck her tongue out at him, laughing anew at the look of horror on his face.

"Your tongue is green, Kass."

"I know. So is yours," she told him smugly. "The Hulk is a fourth Powerade and the rest Vault soda. Isn't it awesome?"

"Is that why my heart is racing so much?" Hollywood asked. "Because you've pumped me full of energy drink and caffeine?"

She giggled. "Yup."

"Didn't Coca-Cola discontinue Vault a while ago because it had an insane amount of caffeine in it?" Hollywood asked.

Kassie looked around as if someone might overhear her before saying in a whisper, "I heard that too, but Whataburger must have a secret deal with them to keep supplying it. Don't jinx it."

He stuck his tongue out at her, and she giggled even harder. "And your,"—he brought up his hands to make air quotes—"'veggie burger' was good?"

"Of course."

"I don't think exchanging the meat patty with four hash brown sticks makes it any healthier."

"I know, but it sure is yummy."

"Yummy? I don't remember the last time I heard anyone use that word," Hollywood told her, loving how carefree she seemed with him.

"I don't care. It *was* yummy, and I'll say yummy if I want. Yummy, yummy, yummy. Have you ever noticed if you say a word fast and long enough it starts to sound really weird? Like toe. Try it. Toetoetoetoetoetoe." She said the words quickly so they'd all run together. "See? It's weird."

That was it. Not caring about his green tongue, or hers, Hollywood stood and swooped down. He caught Kassie's lips with his own and pulled her against him as he devoured her. He put both hands at her waist and held her tightly.

Her arms immediately wrapped around his neck. Hollywood pulled back just enough to order, "Legs up," before claiming her mouth again.

She hitched one leg up, and he immediately caught her knee with his hand. She brought the other up and Hollywood took hold of that as well. Then he turned and headed for his couch. He wanted to bring her to his room, but had decided before she'd even arrived the day before that he wasn't going to fuck her that weekend. It was too soon.

His dick didn't think it was, but Hollywood ignored the demands of his body and instead held Kassie to him as he walked. His hand moved to her ass and he ground her down on him, loving the moan that escaped her mouth as she wiggled against him.

His first thought was to take her to her back and settle on top of her, but at the last minute, his sanity kicked in and he turned, dropping to his ass and using both hands to keep her glued against him.

Her weight landing on him as he sat made him huff out a breath, and she took the opportunity to pull back a fraction and look at him. She balanced on her knees on either side of his thighs, and their crotches were pressed together so tightly he swore he could feel her heat against him.

"What are we doing?" Kassie asked with dilated eyes and a look of wanting so clear on her face, Hollywood wanted to rip her clothes off right then and there.

Instead he grinned lazily and said, "Making out a bit. We have some time to kill before we need to head over to Fletch's."

She shifted, rubbing against his hard cock. "You call this making out?" she asked breathlessly.

"Yeah. Rules. Clothes stay on. We can touch anywhere and everywhere, but only on top of our clothes. No fingers sneaking under elastic or touching skin."

She grinned at him. "Is this a high school game you played?"

He immediately shook his head. "Nope. Never played sexual games. Took what I wanted and was offered, and never looked back."

The playful look in her eyes dimmed. "Oh."

"Everything with you is new, sweetheart. Believe me, you're one hundred percent sexier to me, just like this, than I've ever had before."

She rallied and gamely smiled at him. "Okay. No skin-on-skin contact. We can still kiss though, right?"

"Face only. No kissing below the neck," Hollywood said immediately.

"So we're in high school on a date. But my parents are upstairs and have an annoying habit of peeking down to the basement where we're watching a movie. We want each other. But we know we can't make love with my mom and dad checking in on us."

"Fuck," Hollywood groaned, loving that she was as into this as he was. "Yeah. You've been teasing me a lot lately. Dropping your books in the hall and leaning over to flash your cleavage at me. I'm horny as hell and want you bad."

Kassie shifted her body away from his until there was around six inches between her pussy and his dick. "We shouldn't. My mom'll be checking on us in a few minutes." Her voice was high pitched and she whined the words.

Getting into the game, Hollywood cajoled, "Just a little bit, baby. Let me make you feel good."

"Okay, but only on top of my clothes. I want to save myself for marriage."

He knew her words were a part of the role playing, but somehow they still went straight to his cock. It jerked and he felt his boxers dampen with the precome that escaped the head of his dick. *Fuckin' A.* Hollywood

213

moved his hands from her waist upward, over her shirt, and up her sides. "Only on top of your clothes, sweetheart. Promise. I love that you're so pure and innocent."

He could tell his words threw her, but to her credit, she stayed in her role. Her own hands roamed down his chest, then back up, caressing as she went. It felt good, but he knew without a doubt when they finally were skin to skin, he'd never feel anything as wonderful ever again.

Deciding now was as good a time as ever to start to make her see herself as the beautiful woman she was, Hollywood praised her. "You feel so good. Soft under my hands. It's such a turn on. I don't know why women want to be all hard angles and skin and bones. I love your curves." He moved his hands to her chest. Laying them flat and running them down her torso. Kassie arched into his touch, pressing her tits into his hands as they passed over the full globes.

He didn't stop to caress them though, Hollywood kept moving downward until he reached her legs. He rubbed up and down her thighs, letting his fingertips brush against her core with every pass. Then he slowly ran his palms back up her sides, and started from the top again. He did this slowly, over and over, all the while watching as a flush of arousal bloomed on her skin.

"You're so responsive. One day when your parents

trust us enough to leave us alone for the night, I'm going to fuck you right here on this couch." Hollywood struggled to stay in the role. It got harder when Kassie leaned backwards, resting her hands on his knees. She arched her back and her hips moved closer to him, once again pressing against his cock.

"You like this," he stated.

"Mmmm."

"I can see your nipples poking through your bra," he told her, not able to take his eyes away from the evidence of her arousal. "I can't wait to touch them. To feel them in my hands. You've teased me for so long now; you know you want my hands on you."

"Graham," Kassie moaned.

Hollywood closed his eyes at the sound of his real name crossing her lips. He had no idea if she knew she'd done it, but it didn't matter. He'd hear his name said in that half moan, half plea for the rest of his life.

"Touch me," she pleaded.

"I am touching you," he told her. "But your parents are going to be checking on us any moment now. I can't do anything more."

"Fuck," she swore. And it was cute. More because Hollywood knew exactly how frustrated she felt. But he'd started this game, and was determined to stick to the rules. He took her tits in his hands, weighing them, molding them to his palms. He alternated between squeezing them tightly, and pressing them flat against her chest as he rubbed his palms up and down the front of her body.

Kassie sat up straight then and grabbed both his wrists, trying to halt his actions.

"I hear your mom coming, Kass. Stay really still. She can't see you, only the back of my head. But if you make any noise, she'll know what we're doing. Don't move and don't make a sound."

Kassie was breathing hard now, her lips parted as she panted with arousal on top of him. Keeping one hand at her chest, Hollywood moved the other down her belly, between her legs. She shifted her knees out, giving him room, but more importantly, giving him permission to continue.

"Don't move," Hollywood whispered, as if there really was someone spying on them from behind. "Stay still, sweetheart." He used the heel of his hand to press hard against her clit. He hadn't really planned this when he'd started the game. He'd honestly just wanted to make out a bit and relax her. But now that he had, he couldn't stop. He wanted Kassie to come. Right here. Right now.

Knowing she'd need a hard caress, especially since he was working her with both her jeans and panties between them, Hollywood squeezed a breast at the same time he pressed against the damp seam between her legs.

"So fucking beautiful, Kassie. That's it. Let go. Let me have this. Let yourself have this."

She was squirming in his lap now, and Hollywood had to move his hand from her breast to the small of her back to make sure she didn't fall off and hurt herself. No longer playing the game, he ordered, "Let me hear you, Kass. You like this?"

"Oh my God, Graham...yesssssss," she hissed.

"You're so hot. I can feel how wet you are through your jeans, sweetheart. You want more?"

"Don't stop. I'm close."

"Good." Hollywood used his whole hand. His fingers touched her belly button as he continued to grind against her with the heel of his palm. He wasn't afraid he was being too rough, as a constant stream of "yes, yes, yes" was coming from Kassie's mouth now.

"Come for me, Kass. Show me how beautiful you are when you come under my hand."

At his words she arched her back, and ground herself down on him. And came. She shook in his lap as it washed over her. Hollywood kept the pressure on her clit until she stilled and her hips moved away from him a fraction of an inch, letting him know his touch was becoming more painful than pleasurable, even through her clothes.

Flattening his hand against her wet jeans, Hollywood used his other at her ass to jerk her into him. Her hands dropped to his waist, where they gripped his T-shirt as if her life depended on it. Her torso flattened against his and he felt her quick breaths against his chest. Her head dropped to the space between his shoulder and neck and goosebumps rose on his arm when warm puffs from her nose landed on his skin.

After several moments, she murmured, "Good Lord. It's a good thing my parents *weren't* checking on us. We totally would've been busted."

He chuckled. "But my hands never went under your clothes. How could they get mad at that?"

"You're lethal no matter where your hands are, Hollywood," she told him with a small smile.

Strangely mourning the loss of her saying his real name, but conversely loving the fact that it came out only when she was in the throes of a sexual release, Hollywood grinned and took the compliment.

"You want me to return the favor?" she asked, pulling back to put a bit of room between them. Her shift allowed his fingers more freedom of movement, and he rubbed her crotch gently.

"You already did," he informed her.

She shook her head. "No, I mean, it's not fair that you gave that to me but didn't get it in return."

Hollywood stared at her. She honestly had no idea. Reaching around to grab one of her hands which still gripped his shirt, Hollywood brought it between them and held it to the front of his jeans.

He rubbed her fingers up and down the fly to make sure his point was made as he said, "I got it in return, sweetheart."

She stared down at her hand, which was now damp, then brought her eyes up to his. "You came?"

"Yeah."

"But I didn't even touch you."

"I realize this. I have a feeling that doesn't bode well for me in the future," Hollywood joked, only half kidding.

"You came," she repeated, except this time it wasn't a question.

"Yeah, sweetheart. I couldn't help it. You were so fucking sexy. Writhing against my hand, begging me to move faster. You're what wet dreams are made of, Kass. *My* wet dreams."

She blushed then. A bright red sheen that moved from her neck up her cheeks. She threw herself back down on his lap and buried her face into his neck again.

"You cannot be embarrassed about this," Hollywood told her, wrapping his arms around her and holding her close.

"I am."

"Why?"

"I don't know."

"Well, don't be. Own it. You're a sexy woman who

turns me on so much I can't control myself around you. We're gonna be explosive together, Kass. I can't fucking wait."

"Aren't you embarrassed?"

"Nope."

"Why?" she asked again, still hiding.

"Because I feel great. Mellow. Relaxed. I've got my woman satisfied and heavy in my arms and I get to hang out with my favorite people on the planet tonight. The fact that you're so sexy you can get me off without a touch is just icing on the cake."

They sat like that for several minutes before Hollywood asked, "You asleep?"

"Mmmm," she mumbled.

"Come on," Hollywood said, easily standing with her in his arms.

"I don't want to go anywhere," Kassie complained.

"You aren't going far," he told her. Hollywood carried Kassie into his bedroom where he placed her on his mattress. She immediately rolled onto her side. He pulled the sheet up and over her.

Her drowsy eyes watched him as he leaned into her and kissed her temple. "Take a nap, sweetheart."

"You aren't going to lie down with me?"

"If I get into that bed, we'll both end up naked and neither of us will get to the barbeque later."

"And?"

Hollywood clenched his teeth together, but managed a smile for her. "You'll be naked in my bed, Kass, but for now...sleep. I'll wake you up in about an hour. Yeah?"

"Okay."

"Okay."

"Hollywood?"

"Yeah, Kass?" He stood at the doorway of his bedroom looking down at the woman who had somehow managed to change his entire life in a short two weeks.

"Thanks for making me feel safe from Dean."

Hollywood's fists clenched at the reminder of the threat that still loomed over her. Keeping his voice calm, he merely said, "You're welcome. It's my pleasure, sweetheart."

Her eyes closed and he watched for several more moments as her breaths eased and she fell asleep in his bed.

Hollywood stepped back into the room and grabbed a clean pair of jeans and boxers before leaving and closing the door almost all the way. He wanted to hear if Kassie woke up and for some reason needed him.

After he'd washed up and changed, Hollywood spent the next three-quarters of an hour strategizing and plotting. The plan the team had thought up today was good, but as they'd learned, Plan A didn't always go as expected. So a Plan B, C and probably D was always necessary.

Jacks was done fucking with the Deltas. And he and his fucking friend were done screwing with Kassie and her sister. In two weeks, one way or another, this would end.

And once it did, Kassie would be his. From the tips of her toes to the top of her head, she'd belong to him, body and soul.

Chapter Fourteen

"**C**AN I ASK you something?" Kassie asked as they drove toward Fletch's house later that afternoon.

"Think I told you before you can always ask me whatever you want," Hollywood said, still feeling extremely mellow.

"I don't understand why you don't want to be at the refuge when Dean and whoever else he's roped into this stupid scheme shows up. You should be there."

It wasn't exactly a question, but Hollywood knew what she was asking. "You're my number one priority, Kass. I have no doubt whatsoever that the others can take care of Dean."

"But if you don't think I'll be in danger, what's the point of you staying with me?"

Hollywood risked a look over at Kassie before concentrating on the road again as he answered her. "For the record, I mostly *don't* think you're in danger, but because I'm not one hundred percent convinced Dean won't send others to the refuge to do Jacks's dirty work and stay behind to do something stupid, I refuse to leave you vulnerable."

He felt Kassie's eyes on him, but didn't interrupt whatever was going on in her head. But when he heard her sniff, his eyes immediately swung to her.

She'd shifted in her seat until she was facing him, as much as her seat belt would allow. Her eyes were filled with tears and she was biting her lip, obviously trying to control her emotions.

"Shit, Kass. I didn't mean to make you cry," Hollywood said, his brow crinkled in concern.

"I know. But, Hollywood, how can you feel that way about me so fast? I could be an awful person. I might kick puppies in my spare time. Laugh at grannies who come into my store and buy godawful clothes simply because they're on sale. Shortchange customers."

"Kass," Hollywood told her, gently smiling at her ridiculousness, "I'm thirty-two years old. I've seen a lot in my life. Things no human should ever have to. I've also witnessed three of the best men I know fall in love, and they have never been happier. They're nicer to be around, and work harder *and* smarter than they used to as a result. I've never felt about another woman the way I feel about you. I'm not willing to chance, even if it's only a one percent possibility, that Dean will decide when all of us are supposedly at that training exercise it's one more opportunity to fuck with you."

"I like you, but I'm not sure we're on the same page

as far as our relationship goes," Kassie said softly. "You're talking forever, at least that's what it seems like to me, but you have no idea what will happen next week, month, or year. I don't understand how you can be so sure that you want me in your life for the foreseeable future."

"I know you're not in the same place I am yet. That's why I'm not pushing to have you in my bed so soon. It would kill me to have you, get a glimpse of paradise, then you decide you don't want the same thing I do. But I'm patient, and I know to the depths of my soul that there's no way I can feel as if you were put on this earth for me to love and not have you feel the same…eventually."

"I'm not used to this," Kassie told him. "Being protected. Being someone else's soul mate."

"I know. But you need to *get* used to it. As you've told me often enough, I'm bossy and pigheaded, so I'm going to do whatever it takes to keep you safe, even if that means keeping watch over you myself. And when I can't do it in person, you better believe I'll make other arrangements for someone I trust to do it for me. But in two weeks, I can be with you when the shit goes down with Dean. So I will."

She didn't respond, so Hollywood asked softly, "You okay with that?"

"I'm definitely okay with that," Kassie said, wiping

the tears off of her face. "But I sorta feel like you're babysitting me. And I'm *not* okay with that."

Hollywood turned down Fletch's driveway and thought about how he wanted to answer Kassie. He didn't want to give her a flippant response. He wanted her to truly understand that she was it for him. He wasn't a fortune teller, had no idea what would happen in the future, but he knew he was going to give a relationship between the two of them the best shot he had of continuing forever.

He pulled his car up near the stairs to the guest apartment and stopped the engine. He undid his seat belt, pushed his seat back as far as it would go, then reached over and clicked open hers. "Come 'ere, Kass," he said softly, encouraging her to climb over the emergency brake and straddle his thighs.

She came without a word, settling on top of him in the small space, much as she had earlier that day. Her hands rested at his sides and she tilted her head, waiting for him to speak.

"First, I am absolutely *not* babysitting you. Believe me, I know the difference. My team has had to babysit dignitaries and political figures who didn't think twice about their own safety, never mind the men guarding them. They didn't care about anyone around them, only about their own selfish needs.

"You, sweetheart, put everyone else first. I don't

think you've really thought about yourself in a long time. I know you're scared, but instead of focusing on that, you've told me how worried you are for Karina and your parents. I know what you went through with Jacks was bad. I got that from your reactions at the ball and the bullshit he tried to make you believe about the Army. I love your compassion for others and hope that never changes. But while you'll be looking out for those around you, I'll have your back. I'll make sure no one comes up behind you and tries to figuratively stab you in the back. I'll stand by your side and keep people from sneaking in sideways to try to throw you off.

"I haven't been blowing smoke up your ass, Kassie. I'm not eliminating Jacks and Dean from your life to get into your bed. I'm doing it because you're you. Because you couldn't help but come clean about the circumstances behind us meeting after only a few hours together. You don't have a devious bone in your body, and I'm going to protect that with everything I have."

Hollywood brought his hands up to both sides of her face, looked into her eyes and held her still as he said softly, "Besides, I'd much rather spend my time with you in a nice climate-controlled apartment than out in some hot-as-hell refuge scratching bug bites. You'll be doing me a favor if you let me hang with you the weekend after next."

She grinned at him then, and grasped his wrists with

her cold fingers. "Nobody's ever wanted to protect me like that before."

"That's their loss, and my gain. It's truly no hardship," Hollywood told her immediately. "Kiss me?"

Without a word, Kassie leaned forward. Neither let go of the other and their lips met in a long, lazy kiss.

After a few moments, movement out of the corner of his eye distracted him and Hollywood reluctantly released Kassie's lips and turned his head—and burst out laughing.

Annie's face and hands were plastered against the window of the car inches away from where they'd been making out. Her nose and lips were scrunched up against the glass and she looked like something out of a horror movie. She was grinning like a lunatic and watching them with avid eyes. As soon as she saw Hollywood looking at her, she backed away and waved frantically.

"Hi!" she called out in a loud voice, easily heard from inside the car. "Are you done kissin'? 'Cause Daddy sent me out here to tell you to hurry up. I'm hungry and we can't start the hot dogs until everyone's here. And you're the last ones."

"Busted," Hollywood told Kassie with a grin.

She smiled back at him. "Emily told me she and Fletch are trying to conceive and that he sends Annie away as much as he can in order to get some alone time with her. What's the chance they're inside making out right now?"

Hollywood guffawed and pulled her against him.

"Come on, guys. I'm hungry!" Annie complained from outside the car. She banged on the glass with her little fist to make her point.

"I'll give you five bucks if you give us another five minutes," Hollywood yelled to the little girl.

"Make it ten and you've got a deal!" she yelled back.

"Jesus, that's highway robbery," Hollywood complained. But when Kassie shifted her hands down from where they were resting between them to the waistband of his jeans and shoved her fingers down his ass as far as they could go, he immediately called out, "Twelve minutes. Ten bucks."

"Okay," Annie yelled back happily. "I'll just go play over here by the garage with my racetrack. I'll be back in twelve minutes on the dot."

"Can she tell time?" Kassie asked.

"Unfortunately, yes," Hollywood said.

"Then we better not waste another second." And with that, Kassie leaned in again and kissed him.

Exactly twelve minutes later, Hollywood opened his car door and helped Kassie climb off him and stand. He got out and pulled her into his arms once more and looked down at her. "I'll keep you safe, Kass," he said seriously.

"I know you will."

"Good. You ready to relax for a few hours?"

"Yeah. I'm looking forward to getting to know everyone."

"They'll love you."

Annie came up to them then and held out her hand. "Ten bucks, Hollywood. You promised."

"So I did, pipsqueak," he told her with a smile, reaching behind him for his wallet. He peeled a ten-dollar bill out and held it down to her. When she grabbed it, Hollywood held on for a moment and said, "This is between us, yeah?"

"It's in the vault," Annie said, pantomiming zipping her lips together. She pulled on the money and smiled when Hollywood let go. She stuffed the bill into her pocket and grabbed Kassie's hand. "Let's go."

As the trio began walking toward the house, Kassie asked Annie, "You going to do anything special with all that money?"

She nodded, but didn't slow her pace. "I'm saving for a tank."

"A tank?" Kassie asked, taken aback.

"Yup. I saw one in a magazine and I'm gonna get it."

Hollywood leaned into Kassie and whispered, "It's a miniature motorized version. Costs over five grand. Fletch doesn't think she'll ever get there, but me and the guys give her money every chance we get. I can't wait to see the little speed demon mowing over everything in her path."

Kassie choked back a laugh and nodded.

They circled the house and arrived at the backyard. Kassie tried not to be jealous of the beautiful landscaped lawn. There was a covered back patio with three tables to accommodate everyone, a huge built-in grill and what looked like acres of green Texas sweet grass. Off to the side was a firepit with benches strategically placed around a hole in the ground. It was a cozy place where the inhabitants, and their friends, could leave their worries behind. She loved it.

"It's beautiful," she breathed.

Hollywood squeezed the hand he'd latched onto as soon as they'd stopped. "You should've seen it when Fletch first moved in. It was all weeds back here. But he didn't want to lose Annie in the grass, so he finally hired a lawn service."

She smiled up at him.

Annie raced toward Fletch. "Daddy! I went and gotted them. They were kissin' in Hollywood's car. But here they are. Can you start the dogs now? Please?"

The adults all laughed, and Hollywood smirked at the blush that crawled up Kassie's neck.

"Okay, squirt. Now that everyone is here, I'll start the grill. Why don't you run inside and get the tongs for me."

"Yay! Hot dog time!" Annie yelled, spinning on her small feet and racing for the sliding glass door that led into the house.

"She makes me tired just watching her," a woman who Kassie didn't recognize said. She had extremely short hair which looked awesome on her.

"Oh my God, me too," Rayne agreed wholeheartedly.

Hollywood led Kassie over to where the two women were sitting. "You know Rayne. But I don't think you've met Mary. Mary, this is Kassie. Kassie, Mary."

"Hi," Kassie said, somewhat shyly.

"Hey. It's good to meet you. I've heard a lot about you from Rayne."

"Oh. It's good to meet you too. Do you belong to any of these guys?" Kassie asked, obviously confused.

"Oh Lord, no," Mary said swiftly. "And I can tell that you've been hanging around with them. I'll never 'belong to' any man."

"I didn't mean—" Kassie began, but Hollywood interrupted her.

"Leave her alone, Mare. Just because you can't see what's in front of your face doesn't mean other women don't. I think you're forgetting that if you belong to a man, that man belongs to you right back. And never say never, you don't know what'll happen in the future,"

Hollywood teased.

"Oh shut up," Mary retorted, but grinned at him nevertheless.

He held up his hands in capitulation and chuckled. "You doin' okay?"

"I'm good," Mary said quickly, almost too quickly.

Hollywood didn't think she looked good, but didn't want to embarrass her, and he wasn't sure what she'd told her best friend. The last thing he wanted to do was say something out of line in front of Rayne. After the ball and talking with Truck about her continued chemo treatments, he wasn't even sure she should be out and about like she was. She was seriously one of the toughest women he'd ever met. She was prickly, yes, but if that gave her the strength to get through not one, but two bouts with cancer, she could be as brash as she wanted. He'd have her back every day and twice on Sunday. Going on with her daily activities as if she wasn't getting poison injected into her body on a weekly basis simply proved his point about how strong she was.

"You need anything, don't hesitate to ask, yeah?" he told her, making sure to look her in the eyes as he said it.

"Thanks, Hollywood. I'm good," Mary responded quietly.

"Besides, I'm here if she needs anything," Rayne said brightly. "Why would she go to you when she's got her best friend?" With that, Rayne threw her arm around Mary's shoulders and beamed up at them.

Mary winced. It was quick, but noticeable nevertheless.

"I'm gonna take Kassie around," Hollywood told the women.

"Bring her back so she can eat with us," Rayne demanded. "I have about a million questions for her about you."

"I'm sorry. I've signed a nondisclosure agreement," Kassie told Rayne seriously. "All I'm allowed to tell you is my name, age, and that I have a sister named Karina. Oh, and that Hollywood is the most amazing man I've ever met."

The looks on Rayne and Mary's faces were priceless, and Hollywood tried to keep a straight face, but failed.

Kassie immediately put them out of their misery and smiled broadly at the women. "Kidding. I'd love to sit with you and tell you all of Hollywood's secrets. Did you know he doesn't even have a bed? He's just got a mattress on the floor. It's pathetic really." She grinned up at Hollywood to let him know she was teasing.

"Oh my God, seriously? Girl...you are totally sitting with us. I gotta know more," Rayne enthused.

"Come on, Kass," Hollywood urged with a hand on the small of her back. "Let's go say hi to everyone else before you tell *all* my secrets."

Hollywood accompanied Kassie around to all the groups. She already knew the men, but seemed happy to say hello to them again. She was a little reticent with Emily; Hollywood figured she still had some feelings of guilt about what Jacks had done to her. He'd keep working to make sure she put that behind her. He knew without a doubt no one held her responsible for anything that asshole had done.

They ate dinner; Kassie sat with Rayne and Mary and the three giggled and laughed throughout the meal. Emily and Harley sat at another table with Annie and their men. The rest of the guys sat at the third, devouring the food as if they hadn't eaten in days. Hollywood loved looking over to the other table and seeing the happiness on Kassie's face as she relaxed with his friends. Her life hadn't been a walk in the park and his aim was to make things much easier for her from this point on.

After everyone had eaten, they all went to sit and relax around the fire pit. Hollywood and some of the other men dragged a few of the plastic chairs from the deck over to the cleared area around the blaze. He settled into one of them and pulled Kassie onto his lap. She squeaked at his move, but settled against him with no protests.

Ghost did the same with Rayne, and Fletch and Emily sat next to each other on one of the benches near the fire. Truck led Mary to another of the chairs and helped her to sit. He took a seat on the end of a bench next to her. The other men took places on either a bench or chair around the fire. The mood was mellow and relaxed.

"So, Kassie," Harley said when they were all seated. "I hear you need the services of a lawyer."

"Oh, well, I—"

"Jacks has a friend who has been making her life hell," Hollywood told Harley, and the entire group, baldly.

"Well, jeez, don't hold back," Kassie grumbled, ducking her chin to her chest in embarrassment.

"Don't feel ashamed about something someone else is doing," Harley told her. "He doesn't have the right to make you nervous, and he definitely doesn't get to follow you around or threaten you."

"I know, it's just...serving him with a protective order seems like it'll only piss him off more."

"It might," Harley said and shrugged. "But that doesn't mean you shouldn't do it."

"Told you," Hollywood whispered. Then said louder, "If you can give your sister a head's up that Kassie'll be calling, we'd appreciate it."

"Of course. And for the record, you'll get the friends and family discount," Harley told both Kassie and Hollywood. "Which means she won't charge you. So don't even ask."

"I don't—"

"I said, don't even ask," Harley repeated, not even letting Kassie get the protest out.

"Thank you," Hollywood told the other woman. "Appreciate it."

"Anytime. And that goes for everyone, in case you didn't know it. Montesa told me to tell all of you if you ever need a lawyer's services, she's here for you. Call it a thank you for doing everything in your power to help find me when I had that accident."

"Oh jeez, don't tell everyone that," Mary joked. "She'll be bailing us all out left and right."

Everyone chuckled at that and individual conversations started back up around the fire.

Fletch helped Annie make s'mores and didn't even care that she had more chocolate on her fingers and clothes than it seemed she put in her mouth. After an hour of running around, burning marshmallows for anyone who wanted one, and generally making the adults laugh at her antics, Annie finally curled up in her mom's lap.

"Have a good time tonight, Annie?" Emily asked.

"Yeah. I like when everyone gets together."

"Me too."

"Mommy?"

"Yes, baby?"

"I want a brother." Annie's words were loud in the

quiet Texas night.

Hollywood choked back a laugh as Emily tried to respond to her daughter's statement.

"Having a child is a big responsibility for parents," she told her daughter.

"Yeah, I know. But Daddy said he wanted to see you round with his baby and that with his super swimmers you'd be preggo sooner rather than later. I don't understand what him being fast in the pool has to do with you being pregnant though."

Fletch coughed and almost spat out the sip of beer he'd just taken and looked over at his daughter with big eyes.

The men around the fire burst out laughing, and Hollywood was suddenly glad he wasn't in Emily's shoes right then.

"Fletch, you want to explain to your daughter?" Emily passed the buck to her husband.

Fletch put his beer down on the grass and plucked Annie from Emily's lap. She wrapped her arms around his neck and snuggled into him.

"I want a baby very badly, squirt. And I'm hoping in a few months we'll be able to tell you that your baby brother or sister is on the way."

Mumbling into her dad's neck, Annie asked, "I want a brother. But Daddy?"

"Yeah?"

"You'll still love me if you have your own real kid…right?"

"Look at me, squirt," Fletch demanded.

Annie lifted her head.

Fletch took her little face between his large hands and said in a deadly serious tone, "You *are* my real kid, Annie. You might not share my blood, but you're as much a part of my heart as if I knew you from the second you were born. Me and your mom having a child together will never change that. You're my oldest daughter. Period. Okay?"

"Okay." She paused a moment, then asked, "Daddy?"

"Yes, baby?"

"I love you."

"I love you too."

And with that, Annie snuggled back into the only father she'd ever known and closed her eyes.

Hollywood looked over at Kassie and saw her gazing into the fire pensively. He leaned over. "You okay?"

She nodded quickly.

Hollywood put his finger under her chin and turned her face to his. "What is it?"

"It's silly."

"It's not if it's upsetting you."

"I just didn't think I'd ever have kids," Kassie said in a whisper.

Hollywood heard his friends talking and laughing around him, but he had eyes only for Kassie. "What do you mean? Why not?"

"I thought Richard was my one chance."

"Kass, you're only thirty," Hollywood told her, confused.

"I know, but you have no idea what the last couple of years have been like. Some days Richard was great, but others he was crazy. I thought we could work things out for a while, but when he started getting paranoid and having Dean follow me around, it got bad. He'd question every single man I said two words to. I'd resigned myself to never being able to have a normal life. I wasn't going to be able to date anyone, never mind get close enough to someone to be able to have a kid. And I wasn't going to consider having a baby while Richard was still around. I wouldn't put a helpless baby in danger. No way."

"You're going to have your babies, Kass," he told her with conviction. "Little boys and girls with your brown hair and hazel eyes."

"It wasn't until just now that I thought I had any hope that it could happen," Kassie told him, emotion heavy in her voice and shining out of her eyes.

Hollywood closed his eyes for a moment, then wrapped his arm around her, resting it right under her breasts, and pulled her back until she was boneless against him once more. "We need to stop talking about babies," he whispered in her ear.

"Why?"

"Because talking about you having babies makes me think about how they're made. And thinking about how babies are made makes me want to take off all your clothes, plant my cock deep inside you and get started on giving you that family you've always wanted."

"Graham," Kassie moaned, shifting on his lap.

Hollywood smiled at the use of his real name and buried his nose in her hair while he clamped a hand around her hip, holding her still. "Relax, Kassie. Enjoy the evening."

"You're evil," she complained good-naturedly.

"So, I guess that whole, 'keep your friends close but your enemies closer' thing worked out for you, huh?" Blade teased from out of the blue from across the circle.

Kassie stiffened in Hollywood's lap, and he scowled at his friend and teammate. Fuck, Blade had the worst timing. But before he could say anything, Fish smacked Blade in the back of his head with his good hand and said fiercely, "Why would you say that? You're an asshole."

"Hey...what'd I do?" Blade asked, rubbing the place where Fish had hit him.

"You insinuated that Hollywood is with Kassie to keep his eye on her rather than because he loves her,"

Fish told him without an ounce of pity.

"I—" Blade turned to the couple in question and paused, obviously seeing how much his words had upset Kassie. "I was teasing, man. You guys were talking about babies and shit and I was making a joke. I didn't mean it in a bad way. I mean, right after the ball we talked about how Hollywood should talk to you to find out what Jacks is up to, but it's obvious that you're meant for each other."

"Just shut up," Fish told him. "You're making it worse."

"I'm a little tired. I think I'll leave you guys to shoot the shit and go up to bed," Kassie said softly.

"Kass, he didn't mean it the way it sounded," Beatle put in, trying to fix Blade's faux pas.

"It's cool. I understand. Let me up, Hollywood," Kassie ordered as she tried to get up and off his lap.

Without a word, Hollywood immediately stood with Kassie in his arms and strode away from his friends. He headed for the apartment over the garage.

"I'll keep Annie home tomorrow," Emily called out. "Breakfast'll be served at nine! But if you're *not* there, I'm siccing Annie on you!"

Hollywood didn't bother responding. He wasn't sure if Em was talking to Kassie, or to both of them, but it didn't matter. He could feel how upset Kassie was by the way she held herself stiff in his arms.

They'd gone from talking about her getting pregnant with his babies to him needing to get back in her good graces in a split second. He'd be the first to admit that he loved how passionate Kassie was, but it sucked when it was going toward pushing him away.

"Hollywood, put me down, I—"

"Shut it, Kass," he bit out.

"What? No, seriously—"

"Yes, seriously, Kass. Wait until we're upstairs."

"I'm tired. You need to go. I'll see you tomorrow."

"Fuck no. You're pissed at Blade, rightly so, and maybe a little at me simply for being friends with him. You're probably hurt too, and that kills me. I need to explain. You need to forgive me, then we need to get back to talkin' about you having my babies."

"Hollywood, no. You're right. I *am* pissed...and hurt. I need some time."

"No, you don't," he countered as he started up the stairs on the side of the garage toward the door of the apartment. "We need to talk this out. I don't mind you being upset, but if I leave you alone tonight, you'll think about all the reasons you think this won't work. You'll decide we're moving too fast, that you need to concentrate on keeping Karina safe, and you'll get in your car and go home." As soon as he finished speaking, Hollywood dropped her legs and held her tightly against him as she got her balance.

"Give me the key, sweetheart."

Without a word, she belligerently pulled the key to the apartment out of her pocket and smacked it into his open hand. Hollywood unlocked the door and deadbolt and held the door open for her. She stomped in ahead of him and went straight to the refrigerator.

Hollywood closed and locked the door behind them and put the key on the small table just inside the apartment. He was upset at Blade's inconsiderate words, but a part of him was weirdly pleased with Kassie's reaction.

He wasn't happy she was upset, but the fact that she *was* pissed at him meant that she cared. He could make her understand that the conversation he'd had with his friends had happened when he was still working through what she'd told him at the ball. Not once since he'd decided he wanted Kassie in his life for a fuck of a long time had he thought about being with her simply to keep tabs on Jacks.

He kept the solemn look on his face as he stalked after Kassie, but inside he was smiling. They'd get past this and she'd realize once and for all how serious he was about her.

She might as well learn now that he never intended for them to go to bed upset with each other. And he had every intention of going to bed with her tonight. His vow to not make love to her this weekend was still intact, but she *would* be sleeping in his arms.

Chapter Fifteen

KASSIE SNATCHED A bottle of water out of the fridge and wrenched it open. She was angry, embarrassed, and heartsick all at the same time. She knew this relationship with Hollywood had moved too fast. She'd been so desperate to feel safe and loved that she'd blocked out all the reasons why she should be careful to keep her heart safe. Stupid.

She guzzled the water but stopped when Hollywood took hold of the plastic bottle and eased it down and away from her mouth. "That's enough, sweetheart."

"Oh, so now you get to tell me what to drink too? Next you'll be telling me I'm too fat and what I can eat," she bit out bitterly. She knew she was being unreasonable…it wasn't as if Hollywood hadn't told her over and over how much he liked and wanted to be with her, but Blade's words had cut deep and she was having a hard time being fair.

"You are *not* fat," Hollywood told her, placing the water bottle on the counter next to the refrigerator. "And if you're saying that because that's what your asshole ex did to you, you have to know everything out of his mouth was bullshit. You're beautiful." He put his hands on her hips and turned her to face him. "Every curve. Every inch. It's all fucking beautiful."

Kassie's heart turned over at his words. He sounded firm and unyielding in his opinion. Never in her life had any man told her she was pretty. Never mind beautiful. "Hollywood," she began, "this isn't going to work."

"It's *already* working," Hollywood countered immediately. "Come on. Let's sit. We'll hash this out."

Kassie let him tug her along behind him until they were both sitting on the couch a few feet away. He looked her in the eye and said, "I know you're upset. Talk to me."

Kassie took a deep breath then sagged into the cushions. Luckily Hollywood had realized she needed a little space. He hadn't hauled her up next to him or taken her in his arms. Instead he'd let her settle on one side of the couch while he stayed on the other.

She couldn't look at him and have this conversation. "I'm not pissed," she told him.

"Kass, I know—"

She interrupted him, "Okay, I'm a little pissed. Mostly at the situation, not necessarily you."

"Then why are you all the way over there when I'm over here?" he asked gently.

"Because I'm hurt," Kassie told him, pressing her

lips together. "I get it. I do. What I did was horrible. Awful. Unforgivable. But after we apologized, I thought we were good."

"We *are* good, Kass," Hollywood said firmly.

"But we aren't," she countered in exasperation. "Your friends, your teammates, haven't moved past it. And that's okay, I can deal with them not liking me because of what I did, but you still need to work with them. You need them to have your back just as they need you to have theirs. I can see what's in front of my face, Hollywood. They love Emily, Rayne, Harley, and even Mary. It's easy to see."

"Kassie—" Hollywood tried again to speak, but she was on a roll.

"Blade bringing it up was just his way of letting me know that they haven't forgotten. And he's right. I don't blame you for coming to find me after I told you why I'd messaged you. I'd want to keep tabs on Richard after what he did too. But I let my guard down. The last two weeks have been amazing. I let myself forget how we started." She closed her eyes to try to control the tears she'd been holding back.

She felt the cushion next to her dip but Hollywood didn't touch her.

Kassie opened her eyes and turned her head to see him sitting next to her. Right next to her. He was as close as he could be and not touch her. The warmth from his body began to seep into her own. "You done?" he whispered.

Kassie was. She nodded. Then thought of something else and shook her head.

"Go on then. Get it all out."

She rolled her eyes. "Thanks for your permission," she said with a hint of her old self. "I like your friends. All of them. Fish with his haunted eyes. The way Ghost looks at Rayne as if he can't believe she's sitting next to him. How Fletch and Emily are with Annie. How Coach can't keep his hands off Harley, even though she blushes every time he touches her. How Beatle and Blade are as close as brothers. And I especially like how Truck takes care of Mary without her even realizing it. I saw how he made sure her water glass was constantly full and when she didn't eat much, he encouraged her to at least try to finish the vegetables. For just a while tonight, I forgot that I was the outsider."

"You're done," Hollywood told her in no uncertain terms.

Apparently so was he.

He brought his hands up and framed her face, forcing her to look him in the eyes as he spoke. "You are *not* the enemy."

"Blade said—"

"No, it's my turn now," Hollywood scolded, then continued, "The morning after the ball, I called a meeting with my team to talk to them about what had happened. You know I was upset. But again, this bears repeating, sweetheart. I was upset because I already cared about you so much. Someone, I forget who now, said something to the same effect of what Blade said tonight. It made sense, but the only reason why it did is because it gave me an excuse to come after you right then. You think we couldn't have kept tabs on Jacks without you?" He scoffed.

"Sweetheart, you'd probably be scared at the kinds of connections we have. We didn't need you to tell us what Jacks was up to. Yeah, having you talk to Dean, who will report back to Jacks, will help neutralize the threat of Jacks faster, but it's absolutely not why you're here right now."

Kassie licked her lips nervously. "Why am I here?"

Without hesitation, Hollywood laid it out. "You're here because you asked me why men send dick pics to women they don't know. You're here because when you smile, I feel it not only in my cock, but in my heart. You're here because you agreed to meet me at an Army function when that shit scared you to death. You're here because I'm head over heels for you, Kass. No matter how many times I need to say it. No matter how many times you forget and I need to remind you, I will."

He paused, then when she didn't say anything, asked, "No comeback?"

Kassie shook her head, not sure she could talk at the moment if her life depended on it.

Hollywood continued, "I hate that Blade's words hurt you. But I can tell you with one hundred percent accuracy, every single person who was here tonight already sees you as a part of the group. Fish has already called dibs on watching over you and Karina when I can't be down in Austin. The girls each pulled me aside at some point tonight and gave me their seal of approval. Harley even told me she's building a character in her new game who looks just like you. You know how Annie feels about you, she's claimed you. And the guys?" Hollywood shook his head. "Blade and Beatle would steal you right out from under me if they thought they had a chance. You already figured out that Truck's taken, even if Mary hasn't admitted it yet. So there's absolutely no reason to be hurt. None."

Kassie closed her eyes to protect herself from the intensity in Hollywood's.

"I get that this is new for you. It is for me too. I'm sure we'll have shit we need to work through in the future just like this. But I'm not going to let you get away with hiding from me. If you're pissed, tell me why. If you're hurt, I wanna know that too so I can fix it for you. Sad, happy, irritated, PMSing...I don't care what it is, if you're feeling it, I wanna know."

Kassie's eyes opened. "Does it go both ways?"

"What, honey?"

"Sharing feelings?"

"Of course."

"Okay, but I have to tell you…I don't deal very well with anger. I know it's not fair, I've been mad at you before, but Richard used to get pissed at every little thing and he'd call me or come over to yell about it. His groceries being bagged wrong, someone cutting him off on his way down to Austin, me embarrassing him in front of his friends…he never hesitated to let me know how angry he was."

"Noted," Hollywood said immediately. "I'll keep that in check, sweetheart."

"I don't mean—"

"I'll keep it in check," he repeated firmly.

"Okay," Kassie whispered.

"We good?"

"I think so."

Hollywood moved, pulling Kassie into his arms for the first time since they'd sat down. "What aren't you sure about?"

Kassie melted into Hollywood's chest. She was sitting sideways over him, her legs resting on the cushion next to him, her ass in his lap. His hands had circled her, and were resting at her hip, and she stuffed one of hers behind him, warming it against his upper back, the other resting on his stomach. She laid her head on his shoulder and inhaled deeply. God, she loved how he smelled.

"Kass?"

"Hmmmm?"

"What else?"

"Oh…it's just that…I'm worried about my family liking you."

He didn't even tense under her. "Why?"

"Well, after I told them about what Richard was like and what he'd been doing to me…and was currently doing through Dean…they weren't happy. My dad threatened to get his shotgun out and kill Dean if he ever saw him lurking around the house watching Karina. My mom cried. And if you think I'm passionate, you should see Karina. She was scared, but also pissed."

Hollywood laughed. "I like them already."

"Seriously, Hollywood, they weren't kidding. They know I went to the Army Ball with you, but they probably thought it was a one-time thing. I'm not sure they're gonna like the fact that I'm actually dating you."

"Call them."

"What?"

"Right now. Call them."

Kassie looked at the clock over the television. "It's late. It's probably not a good idea to call them this late."

"Then call Karina. We'll start with her. She's a teen-ager. I know she's not asleep."

"She's probably out with her new boyfriend."

"Call her, Kass. Let me take at least one worry off your plate," Hollywood ordered.

"This bossiness is gonna get old," Kassie grumbled, but reached for her phone which was still in her back pocket. She unlocked it and clicked on Karina's number, hoping she wasn't going to be interrupting anything major.

"Hello?"

"Hey, sis," Kassie said, trying to sound perky.

"Kass! What's up?" Karina asked.

"You got a second?"

"For you, of course," her little sister said immediately.

"You still on your date?"

"Yeah. The movie just ended. Blake just went to get the car. What's up?"

"Things are still going well with Blake?"

"Yes." Karina's voice lowered to a whisper. "I really like him. He's extremely gentlemanly. Wouldn't let me pay for the popcorn or anything. And now he told me to wait while he went and got the car. Oh, and when he got a phone call in the middle of the movie, he even got up and took it outside so he didn't disturb anyone."

"Why would he take a phone call when he was watching a movie?" Kassie asked. "That doesn't sound gentlemanly to me."

"Don't be a buzz kill," Karina ordered. "Now, what's up?"

"Okay, so you know I went up to Temple this weekend," Kassie said quickly, wanting to get this over with.

"Yeah…although you didn't say why."

"Right. So that guy I went to the ball with…I'm dating him. Seriously."

"That's good…right? I mean, as long as he's not an ass like Richard was."

"He's not an ass."

"Seriously, sis, you deserve so much better. It would kill me if you went back to the way you were when you were dating Richard there at the end. You weren't you…this guy better not do that to you."

"Go to FaceTime," Hollywood said softly.

"What?"

"FaceTime her."

"I'm not sure—"

"Trust me, Kass. Do it," Hollywood said again.

Kassie sighed and told Karina, "FaceTime with me."

"Okay, cool."

They both clicked the icon on their phone to bring up the cameras.

Kassie held the phone out and looked into her sister's dark eyes. She looked pretty. She'd put in the extra effort on her makeup for her date and Kassie recognized, from what she could see of the neckline of the outfit she had on, she'd worn her favorite dress.

"You look nice."

"Don't try to butter me up with compliments, Kassie," her sister said, blushing, her brows furrowed and a stubborn glint in her eye. "So you really did hit it off with him at the ball, huh? Is he good in bed—"

Her words abruptly broke off when Hollywood took the phone from Kassie's hand and held it out farther, putting his head next to hers so Karina could clearly see them both.

"Oh shit," Karina whispered. "I didn't know he was there."

Hollywood grinned. "Hey, Karina. I'm Graham Caverly. And yeah, me and your sister hit it off at the ball."

"Err…good to meet you," the teenager said, then bit her lip. "I guess I should say sorry about the good-in-bed thing. That was rude."

Hollywood chuckled outright now. "I haven't slept with your sister," he told her flat out without seeming embarrassed about it at all. "I respect her too much for that."

"Is that code for you aren't attracted to her and just want to be friends and want to let her down easy?"

"Karina," Kassie protested. "Give me the phone, Hollywood," she insisted, trying to grab it out of his hand, but because his arms were longer than hers, she couldn't reach it.

"Hush," Hollywood ordered gently. "No," he told Karina, "I'm attracted to Kassie. *Really* attracted to her. But I want to take my time getting to know who she is as a person. It's easy to have sex, but when there's more than lust involved between the parties, it's a hundred times better."

"Damn, Kass," Karina breathed, looking from Hollywood to Kassie. "You certainly moved up."

Kassie grinned. "Yeah. Karina, this is Hollywood, it's a nickname. Hollywood, this is my sister, Karina."

"It's good to meet you, Karina. I've heard nothing but wonderful things about you from Kassie."

"Uh, yeah, from what little she told me before the ball…me too. Heard good things about you, that is."

"I want you to know, I appreciate you looking out for your sister," Hollywood told Karina. "I know all about Richard Jacks and I want to reassure you that the situation is being looked into as we speak."

"And Dean? What about him? You gonna make him stop harassing Kass too?"

"Absolutely. And not only her, but you too. You know where you want to go to college?"

At the abrupt change in subject, Karina faltered, but quickly rallied. "Maybe here at the University of Texas. I've also applied to A&M, Baylor, and Southern Methodist."

"All good schools," Hollywood commented.

"Yeah."

"Who you talkin' to, babe?" a male voice asked. Then his face appeared next to Karina's on the screen.

"My sister. Kassie, this is Blake. Blake, this is my sister...and her...uh...boyfriend, Graham."

"Yo!" the boy greeted.

Kassie's eyes narrowed as she saw her sister's new boyfriend on her small phone screen. He was good looking, as Karina had said. He had the boy-next-door kind of looks that she wasn't surprised her sister had fallen for. He was tall enough to easily be able to put an arm around Karina's shoulders and pull her into his side. His light brown hair fell artfully around his shoulders and the blue of his eyes was unusual enough to be almost pretty.

But what bothered her was that Karina had said he looked older...but he *really* looked older.

Hollywood must've felt the same way, because instead of saying hello, he asked, "How old are you?"

"Good to meet you too," Blake said with a bit of the snark typical of a teenager. "I'm twenty. I dropped out of high school, but realized what a bonehead move that was and came back to finish up the last credits I needed to graduate."

"You could've gotten a GED," Hollywood retorted.

"I know, but a lot of businesses look down on GEDs versus actual diplomas. It's cool, man."

"You know Karina is underage, right?" Kassie asked, squeezing Hollywood's leg to shut him up. This was *her* sister, she'd deal with this.

"Yes, ma'am," Blake said quickly. "I like Karina, but we aren't doing anything illegal."

"You'd better not be," Kassie told him, narrowing her eyes again.

Karina stepped away from Blake and told him, looking off camera, "Give me a second, Blake, okay?"

"Sure, babe," he responded.

Karina's eyes came back to Kassie's. "Okay, now that you've embarrassed me, was there anything else?" Her tone held a bit of sass, but also some of the same hurt Kassie knew had been in *her* tone when she'd been talking to Hollywood earlier.

"No. I just wanted to introduce you to Hollywood and let you know that he and his friends are doing what they can to track down Dean and make sure his harassment of me, and you, ends."

"Good." The one word answer got her irritation across loud and clear.

"He looks a lot older than you, Kar," Kassie whispered, not knowing how far away Blake had gone.

"He's not," Karina said.

"I worry about you."

Her face softened then. "I know. Just like I worry about you." Her eyes went to Hollywood. "If you hurt a hair on her head, you'll regret it. I might look little, but I'll still find a way to kick your ass. The last thing Kassie needs is someone else fucking with her head."

"You want, I'll *teach* you how to kick someone's ass," Hollywood offered. "Then I'll let you use everything you've learned on me if I ever hurt your sister."

"Fine," Karina told him. "I gotta go."

"Oh, and one more thing," Hollywood interjected quickly before Karina hung up.

"What?"

"You should go to Baylor. It's closer to Fort Hood and you'd be able to see your sister more."

"Why?" Karina asked suspiciously.

"Because if this relationship goes the way I want it to, Kassie'll be moving up here to Temple. After a few months of us dating, I'll ask her to move in with me. A few months after that, I'll ask her to marry me, with you and your parents' permission of course. As soon as she says yes, I'm going to do what I can to give her the kids she's been wanting her entire life. So yeah, Baylor is closer, and I know you're going to want to be near your nieces and nephews to spoil rotten, right?"

"Hollywood!" Kassie exclaimed, smacking him on the shoulder. "You can't tell her that!"

"Why not?" he asked calmly. "It's true."

"Holy cow. He's serious," Karina said.

"Dead serious," Hollywood told her. "And, Karina, don't let anyone ever pressure you to do anything you don't want to do."

Kassie smiled and copied her sister's roll of the eyes. She leaned toward the phone so all her sister could see was her face on the screen. "He's kinda bossy." She informed Karina of something her sister could obviously see for herself.

"You like him?" Karina asked.

Kassie nodded.

"Then I'll reserve judgement until I get to meet him myself."

"I'd appreciate that."

"You gonna tell Mom and Dad?"

"When I get home. Will you wait and let me talk to them?"

Karina nodded. "Yeah, but if you don't soon, I'm gonna spill the beans," she mock-threatened.

Kassie knew her sister was full of shit, but said, "I'll tell them."

"Good."

"Be careful," Kassie told her sister, settling back against Hollywood. He gave the phone back to her, and wrapped his arms around her hips.

"It's fine, Kass. Stop worrying."

"I'll never stop worrying about you," she told her

sister.

"Whatever. You comin' over to see my dress for the dance soon?"

"I'm not sure what time I'm leaving tomorrow, but I'll stop by the house and talk to Mom and Dad and see your dress. That work?"

"Yeah. Drive safe. I'll see you tomorrow night. Expect more questions," Karina warned.

"Of course. I'd expect nothing less. Love you."

"Love you too. Bye."

"Bye."

Kassie clicked off the phone and lay back against Hollywood as if she were boneless. "I'm exhausted."

Hollywood chuckled. "I think that went well," he told her.

"Believe it or not…it did. She was surprised, but she would've protested a lot more if she truly didn't get good vibes from you."

"She's got a good head on her shoulders," Hollywood commented.

"She does. Although I'm not thrilled with Blake."

"Hmmmm. Yeah, to be honest, me neither. I'll get my friend Tex to see what he can find out about him. It'll be easy enough to check out his story. You'll get me his last name?"

Kassie nodded. "Definitely. I can't believe you told her you were going to ask me to marry you and then get me pregnant."

Hollywood smirked. "I didn't tell her anything that wasn't true, sweetheart."

"You're insane, Hollywood. You don't know what'll happen between us."

"I know what I *want* to happen between us, and I'm gonna act like what I want is what will be. You know, the power of wishful thinking and all that."

Kassie didn't respond, merely closed her eyes and inhaled his amazing scent once more, letting it relax her.

"You good?" Hollywood asked for the second time that night.

"I think so. As good as I can be right now."

"I'll take that," he said. "Wanna watch something on TV?"

"Is there anything good on?"

"No clue. But I'll find something if you want."

"Aren't you tired? Don't you need to get back over to your place?" Kassie asked.

"Nope and nope. I'm staying here tonight. No, don't tense up on me. Nothing's gonna happen. I just don't want to leave you. We only have tonight, then tomorrow you're goin' back to Austin. I'll see you next week, but I can't spend the night. So this is the last time in a while I'll have to hold you in my arms. I just want to be close to you, Kass."

"I can give you that," Kassie said softly. "I'd like it

too. It's weird, but I already miss you and I'm not even gone yet."

Hollywood kissed her forehead and shifted until they were lying down. He tucked her into his side, her back to the cushions, her head on his shoulder.

"Put your hand under my arm," he told her quietly.

"Why?"

"Your fingers are cold. I hate that. Let me warm them with my body heat."

Kassie tried not to melt at his thoughtfulness, but failed. She tucked her hand against his body and he pressed his bicep against it. Her other hand, she curled under her cheek on his chest.

"It's been a weird day," she said sleepily.

Hollywood chuckled. "It kinda has. But I wouldn't change one second of it since it ended with you here in my arms."

"Flatterer," Kassie protested weakly.

He chuckled, but didn't say anything more.

The last thing Kassie remembered was thinking how safe she felt in his arms. Nothing was settled with Dean and Richard, and she still had to give Dean the fake information about the training exercise, but somehow it all didn't matter. Hollywood would keep her safe. She believed that down to her soul.

Chapter Sixteen

"I 'M NOT SURE I approve of you," Jim Anderson told Hollywood as he leaned back in his chair. They'd just finished dinner and were sitting around the dining table chatting.

"Daaaad," Kassie moaned. Her dad had been giving Hollywood the stink eye all evening. She wasn't surprised he'd actually said what he had, just that it had taken so long. Seriously, who said that to someone *after* they'd eaten a meal together? Her freaked-out, overprotective father, that's who.

Hollywood put his hand on her leg to try to reassure her then looked her father in the eye as he said, "I'm okay with that...for now. You just met me tonight and your daughter recently told you that her ex treated her like crap. I hope, though, that you'll give me a chance. Let me show you that not all Army guys are like that jerk."

Kassie appreciated that Hollywood was curbing his swearing in front of her family. She put her hand over his on her leg under the table and squeezed, letting him know how much she appreciated him.

"I'm just not sure she should be dating when all this other stuff is going on," her dad said, obviously still not convinced.

"He's helping me with that," Kassie protested.

"Not sure what he can do when Richard is in jail up in Kansas and that friend of his is following my baby around."

"One of my friends was injured over in the Middle East and just finished rehab. His nickname is Fish. He's medically retired and has watched Karina as she's gone to school the last two days," Hollywood informed her family.

Kassie turned to stare at Hollywood. "He has?"

"I haven't seen anyone following me," Karina piped up.

"And you won't," Hollywood told her with a smile. "He's good at what he does." He winked at Karina, then turned back to Kassie's dad. "I swear to you that I am doing everything in my power to make sure both your daughters are safe."

"It's a start," Jim replied, not completely mollified, but at least thawing a little.

"And I also want you to know that I'm going to do everything I can to show Kassie how she *should* be treated by a man. I get that Jacks changed after the explosion, but that's no excuse. If given the chance, I'll treasure Kassie. I want to show her that just because she can take care of herself, doesn't mean she should *have* to all the time."

Kassie swallowed hard. Man, he was making it really hard to keep an emotional distance from him. She liked him. A lot. But she had decided to take a step back from their relationship until the thing with Richard and Dean was finished. He'd made that hard when he'd driven down to see her Monday night, and then again tonight just to have dinner with her family.

"I've been telling her for years not to settle," her mom said. "I want her to have what Jim and I have." Donna Anderson looked over at her husband with love and respect easy to see in her eyes.

"May I be excused?" Karina asked politely, but followed that up with a teasing, "I'm about to choke on all the lovey-dovey crap in the air."

The adults all laughed and Donna shooed her youngest daughter away. "Go on then."

Karina grinned and pushed back from the table.

"But no texting until you get your homework done," Jim warned.

"Daaaaaad."

"Nope. You know the rules. Blake'll be there when you're done."

"Fine," Karina moped. "I don't have much anyway."

"See ya later," Kassie called out to her sister.

"Later," Karina yelled back as she ran up the stairs to her room.

When the teenager had disappeared and they heard music start up in her room, Hollywood leaned forward and put both elbows on the table in front of him. "You met Blake?" he asked Jim.

He shook his head. "Not yet. He's supposed to pick her up for the dance next Saturday. Why?"

"Hollywood, I don't think—"

"He's older than her," Hollywood said, ignoring Kassie's warning.

"She told us. Should we be worried?" her dad asked, cutting to the chase.

"I don't know," Hollywood said honestly.

"Kassie? What do you think?" her mom asked with concern.

She shrugged. "Like Hollywood said, I don't know. I knew she was dating the new guy in school and that he was older, but I didn't really think about it much. But me and Karina FaceTimed this weekend when she was at the movies with him and I have to admit, he looks too old to be in high school."

"She said that he was twenty. That he'd dropped out and made the decision to come back and finish up," Jim said.

"That's what she told us too, but...is that even legal?" Kassie asked. "I mean, can someone in their twenties even go back to high school?"

"I looked that up," Hollywood told them. "In Texas, anyone who is twenty-six or younger can be admitted to a high school, but if he, or she, hasn't been in attendance at school in the last three years, they can't be put into a classroom setting with anyone under the age of eighteen."

"I think Karina said that he was only out for two years," Kassie mused.

"Then I think it's legal," Hollywood said. "I can have Harley's sister, she's a lawyer, look into it, but I'm not sure there's anything we can do about it in the next week and a half."

"Should we tell her she can't go to the dance?" Donna fretted.

"Mom, you can't do that," Kassie told her. "She's been looking forward to it for the last month. She's so excited."

"But if we don't know about this Blake guy, I'm not comfortable with her attending," she protested.

"Why don't you invite him to dinner like you did Hollywood? You can intimidate him and let him know that Karina isn't an easy mark."

"We do not intimidate people," Donna said in a huff.

"I'd feel better if my attempt at intimidation actually had even a smidgen of effect on your boyfriend," Jim stated matter-of-factly.

Kassie stared at her dad for a moment, then turned to look at Hollywood to see his reaction to her dad's admission that he'd been trying to intimidate him. He was smiling. *Smiling*!

"This isn't funny," Kassie informed Hollywood.

"It's a little funny," he countered.

Kassie rolled her eyes and looked back at her dad. "Anyway, invite him over. See for yourself."

"You'll come too?"

Kassie shook her head. "I can't. I traded shifts with a girl at work. In exchange for me getting this past Saturday and Sunday off, I agreed to take her late shifts. I work twelve to nine for the next seven days straight."

"Good Lord," Hollywood exclaimed. "You have to work the crap shift for a week straight for taking two days off?"

Kassie shrugged. "Not usually, no. But you asked, and it was important to talk about Richard and Dean. So I bit the bullet and made the deal."

Hollywood put his hand on her face and turned her to look at him. "You did that for me," he said softly. It wasn't a question.

Kassie nodded anyway. "Yeah." She knew he wanted to kiss her because she *totally* wanted to kiss him. But even though she was thirty years old, certainly old enough to kiss her boyfriend in front of her parents, she still felt shy doing it.

As if he could read her mind, he pulled her toward him and kissed her forehead gently. Then he whispered, "Thank you."

"You're welcome."

As soon as the words left her mouth, her cell rang. It was sitting on the kitchen counter and Kassie ignored it. Her mom had a thing about having electronics at the dinner table. The ringing stopped, but started up immediately afterwards.

Kassie looked nervously at Hollywood.

"What?" he asked, reading her unease.

"When Dean wants to get ahold of me, he usually calls, then hangs up if I don't answer. Then he calls back. He keeps doing it until I answer."

"Excuse us," Hollywood told her parents, scooting back and standing.

"If this is something to do with my daughters, I want to hear it," Jim demanded as he also stood.

Hollywood held up a hand. "I don't blame you one bit. But if this really is Dean, then you need to give Kassie some space so she can talk to him without worrying what her overprotective, angry father is going to say or do."

The two men stared at each other for a long moment while the phone continued to ring.

"I swear I've got this under control," Hollywood

told the older man. "We have a plan. But Kassie needs to concentrate on the information she gives to Dean, and she can't do that if she's worried about her mom and dad and what they're thinking when she's executing that plan."

Jim's shoulders dropped and he sat back down next to his wife. Donna immediately reached out and grabbed his hand.

"We'll stay put," her dad agreed. "But I want a brief before you both leave."

"Done," Hollywood said immediately, towing Kassie behind him toward the kitchen counter and her phone. Glancing at the screen, and seeing it was indeed Dean, Hollywood asked, "Is there a room we can go to talk to him?"

Kassie nodded. "Dad's office."

"Lead the way."

Without another word, Kassie spun and headed for the other side of the house. They went through the living room and down a hallway. She opened the door at the end and led them into a dark, masculine office. There were bookshelves along two walls, a large window along the third, and a desk against the fourth.

The phone had stopped ringing, but as soon as Hollywood shut the door behind them, it started up again.

"You remember what to say, right?" Hollywood asked as he handed the cell to her.

Kassie nodded.

"Okay. Hang on a sec." He kissed her forehead, then pulled out his own phone and clicked on a contact. "Hey, Ghost. It's Hollywood. Dean's calling. You ready? Right. Standby.

"Okay, sweetheart. You're on. Put it on speaker so Ghost can hear too. He's recording it so we can get everyone on the same page. You got this."

Kassie nodded, more nervous than she'd been in the past when she'd had to deal with Dean.

"Hello?"

"It's about fucking time you picked up, bitch," Dean greeted. "Where the fuck are you?"

Kassie's eyes went to Hollywood's and he nodded at her. "I'm at my parents' house. We had dinner."

"You must not care about your sister because I've been trying to get ahold of you for days," Dean snarled.

Kassie shook her head at Hollywood to let him know that Dean was lying. Hollywood's response was to put his hand on the nape of her neck and lean his forehead against the side of her head. She could smell his wonderful scent. It calmed her somewhat, at least enough that she could think about what she needed to say to Dean. Hollywood's nearness gave her the strength to continue.

"I'm sorry. You got me now. What do you want?" she asked Dean.

"I want to know what information you have for me. You *do* remember the reason you went to that fucking ball the other weekend, right? Did you suck his cock like I told you to? He'd tell you anything you wanted to know if your lips were around his dick."

Kassie stiffened and shut her eyes. She hated that Hollywood was hearing this. But instead of getting pissed, she felt Hollywood's lips against her temple. He kissed her with a feather-light touch, then squeezed her neck gently.

"I'm still not sure what kind of information you wanted me to get from him, Dean."

"Are he and his buddies going out of town anytime soon? If so, where and for how long? Has he bitched about any training exercises coming up? Those assholes are always training...fuckers. What about sick family members? We want any information about those assholes you can get. And we're getting pretty damn sick of waiting."

It didn't escape her notice that he'd used the word "we" instead of "I."

"What did they ever do to you and Richard?" Kassie asked softly, feeling a bit nauseous that they wanted to know if any of the wonderful women, or Annie, were sick. What did they think they were going to do? Blackmail them so they couldn't get the medicine they needed? Her mind spun. That wasn't even possible…was it? She didn't even want to think about what Dean and his friends could do to a sick woman or child.

"You don't have to worry about what they did, bitch. Who you *should* be worried about is your sister. You wouldn't want her to disappear without a trace, would you?"

"If you touch her, I swear to God I'll go straight to the cops. You won't get away with it."

"You do and I guarantee I'll have an iron-clad alibi," Dean retorted immediately. "And all you'll do is assure your little sister will end up flat on her back for some rich foreign sexual deviant. Now, what the fuck information do you have? And it better be good or you'll never see Karina again."

"Okay, okay, okay, let me think," Kassie pleaded, panicked now. Before, Dean had been vague in his threats against Karina, but this…telling her he could make her disappear was something different altogether. She couldn't bear the thought of Karina vanishing into the mysterious sex trafficking underground.

"Breathe, sweetheart," Hollywood said in a toneless whisper into her ear. "You can do this. Tell him about the wildlife refuge."

"They have a training thing coming up soon," Kassie blurted.

"Where? When?" Dean ordered.

"Um…next weekend. Hollywood was talking about

it with some of his friends at the ball. They were saying how much they weren't looking forward to it."

"Who is it with?"

"Uh…I'm not sure. I think they were laughing about how easy it would be because it was a small thing. Like their unit against another."

"So it's not a huge division thing?"

Kassie looked to Hollywood, not understanding the Army term he'd used. Hollywood shook his head quickly, letting her know the answer.

"No. Just them against another small group of men."

"On post?"

"No. One of the guys was bitching about how even though they'd be near the beach, they wouldn't get to spend any time checking out the chicks in bikinis." Kassie was ad libbing, but it seemed to be working. Dean was more interested in hearing the details than threatening her sister.

"Where? Jesus Christ, just answer the fucking question."

"I'm trying, Dean! Give me a second to think."

"You've had two fucking weeks. Where. The. Fuck. Is. It?"

Shivering at the hate in his words, she blurted, "They talked about a wildlife refuge near Galveston."

She heard Dean typing on a keyboard, probably

pulling a map up online. She hated the sick feeling she had inside. Even knowing she was telling Dean exactly what Hollywood and his friends wanted her to, she still somehow felt as if she was betraying them.

"The Brazoria National Wildlife Refuge?" Dean asked. "Why the fuck would they go there for an exercise?"

Ad libbing more now—Hollywood's friends hadn't told her what to say if he asked why—Kassie said, "I don't know, but they said something about their boss wanting them to get some wetland training instead of always doing desert stuff."

"Yeah, yeah, that makes sense," Dean said, more to himself than her.

"Good job," Hollywood whispered before wrapping his arms around her, holding her sideways against his chest.

"Is that good info?" Kassie asked, her voice genuinely quivering. She didn't need to fake her fear.

"For now. But if this intel is false, Karina will pay," Dean threatened.

"It's not!" Kassie said quickly. "I heard them talking about it. I swear. Stay away from my sister. I gave you the information you wanted."

"You're a good little spy," Dean sneered. "If you want to keep your sister safe, I'd nurture the relationship with that fucking loser. We're gonna want more info."

"No! You said the ball was it. You said I wouldn't have to do anything else," Kassie practically shouted.

"I lied. Kiss your sister good night for me. Later."

"No! Dean! Dean? Are you still there?"

Hollywood took the phone out of her hand and clicked it off. He brought his own, which had been in his hand throughout the entire conversation, to his mouth. "You get all that, Ghost?"

"Affirmative. Am I on speaker?"

"Yeah."

"Good job, Kassie," Ghost told her. "You did exactly what you were supposed to."

Ignoring Ghost, Kassie looked up at Hollywood. "I can't live with myself if something happens to Karina."

"Nothing's gonna happen to your sister," Ghost said, thinking she was talking to him. "We got this. It was more than obvious he took the bait. We'll be ready for him next weekend. Have no doubt. Hollywood? I'll see you tomorrow?"

"I'll be there," he told his teammate.

"Later."

"Later," Hollywood responded and clicked off his phone.

He immediately turned Kassie so they were chest to chest and he hugged her tightly without saying a word.

Feeling as if an hour had passed, but knowing it had only been a couple minutes, Kassie murmured, "We should go out and tell my dad what's going on."

"There's no hurry," Hollywood told her, not moving an inch.

"Uh, you were out there when he lost his shit when he found out Dean was calling me, right?"

He chuckled. "Yeah, Kass. I was there. But we aren't moving an inch until I'm sure you're okay and you know what a fucking fantastic job you did."

"I was scared."

"I know. That makes what you just did even more impressive."

"He's going to do something to Karina," Kassie said sadly.

Hollywood shifted her away from him and Kassie knew he was staring down, waiting for her to look up.

So she did.

"I wish I could guarantee that he won't, but I can't. And I promised I'd never lie to you. But I swear to God, if he manages to slip by Fish, and he grabs her, nothing will stop me until I've found her and brought her home."

The tears she'd managed to hold back finally leaked through. "P-promise?" she choked out.

"Swear to fucking God."

That made her smile. "I don't think you're supposed to use the Lord's name in vain when you're promising something as important as this, Hollywood. Or anytime, really."

"Sorry. I swear that I'm going to make your family safe, Kass. You know why?"

She shook her head.

"Because they're *your* family. Because I want a future with you. A long one. Filled with laughter, fights, passion, and children. And in order to have that, I need to take care of what's most important to you."

"I want that too," Kassie admitted out loud for the first time.

"Then we'll have it."

Kassie closed her eyes, took a deep breath, then looked at him once more. "It's late. You should probably get going."

"Yeah," he agreed, but didn't move.

Dropping her head to his chest, Kassie sighed. "I don't want you to go."

"I know."

"There's not going to be a point to come down in the next week since I'm working until late," she told him.

"Unfortunately, I know that too."

"We can talk on the phone. And text."

"It's not the same."

The four words struck Kassie hard. It *wasn't* the same. It absolutely wasn't. But she had to work, and so did Hollywood.

"Fish'll be here and he'll check in with you to make sure Dean is keeping his distance. But if you need something, like you're at work and see that asshole lurking around, you call Fish first, then me. It'll take me at least an hour to get here, but Fish is in the area, he'll get to you quicker."

"Okay, Hollywood."

"Same goes with Karina. You'll have a talk with her? Program our numbers into her phone?"

"Yeah."

"In a couple of weeks this'll be over, one way or another," Hollywood told her.

"Will it? What will happen to Dean and whoever he's recruited to help when you guys catch them at the training thing? How is that going to keep Richard and Dean from messing with me? You're not going to *shoot* them, are you?"

Hollywood chuckled. "No, sweetheart. We aren't going to shoot them. That's kinda frowned upon."

She looked up at him. "Then what?"

"My team'll convince Dean that he doesn't want to continue on this path of destruction he's on. If he resists this convincing, the commanding officer received permission to drag him to Fort Hood to sit in the brig there."

"But he's not in the Army," Kassie said.

"You're right, but interfering with a government

training exercise isn't exactly legal. He and the Army lawyers will come up with a dozen different laws he's broken and they'll be able to keep him locked up for a long time."

Kassie shook her head. "He and Richard have been tormenting me for a while now, Hollywood. I just don't see how this'll make them stop." Looking up at him with huge eyes filled with tears, she whispered, "They won't stop until they're dead. Are you sure you can't shoot them?"

Hating the despair he saw in her eyes, Hollywood still couldn't keep the lip twitch back at her words. "We can't shoot them."

"Darn," she replied.

"This will end after next weekend," Hollywood repeated firmly.

"I hope so."

"It *will*," he insisted. Then he strangely said, "You know there's a JCPenney in the Temple Mall."

"What?" Kassie asked, keeping her eyes locked on his brown ones.

"There's a JCPenney in the Temple Mall," he repeated. "This goes the way we want it, Fletch said you could rent the apartment over his garage for as long as you need. You could see about a transfer at work."

As stupid as it sounded, Kassie hadn't even thought about what would happen with their relationship after the thing with Dean and Richard was done. Yes, she wanted to be with Hollywood, but the logistics of where she'd live and her job hadn't even occurred to her yet. The fact that he was more than aware of both those things, and had talked with Fletch about the apartment, proved how serious he was about a long-term relationship with her.

At what must've been the shocked look on her face, Hollywood grinned and said, "What part of me telling your sister she should go to Baylor so she could be near you to see her future nieces and nephews didn't you understand, sweetheart?"

"I just…it's…I hadn't thought about that stuff."

"Well, now you can. You wanna live somewhere else or do somethin' else, I'm cool with it. As long as you're doing it where we can eventually sleep in the same bed every night."

"You really need to go tonight?" Kassie asked, knowing he did, but asking anyway, making sure he knew how much she wanted him to stay.

"Yeah. Now that Dean has called, I have to brief the guys and we need to finalize the details on this fuckin' fake exercise they're goin' on."

Kassie giggled. He sounded extremely put out.

"I'd much rather hold you all night and wake up with you in my arms like I did Sunday morning."

"Me too."

They stared at each other for a long moment, then Hollywood ordered, "Kiss me."

So Kassie stood on her tiptoes, wrapped her arms around him, and kissed him.

Ten minutes later, they reluctantly left the office hand in hand to talk to her parents.

Hollywood talked, letting Kassie interject here and there with any details he left out. By the time they were done, Jim's face was red with anger, and Donna looked shell-shocked.

"I can't believe the nice young man we knew would end up like this," Kassie's mom said, sniffing.

"Anything you need from us, you got it," Jim told Hollywood, all signs of disapproval gone from his face and tone.

"Get my number from Kassie. And all of my teammates' as well. I'll tell you what I told Kassie, if you sense anything is off, call Fish...err...Dane Munroe. He's here in Austin and can get to you immediately."

Jim held out his hand and he and Hollywood shook. "I'm sorry if I came across like an asshole earlier," he said.

Hollywood immediately shook his head. "No, don't apologize. You're just a dad looking after his daughters. If I'm lucky enough to be blessed with a daughter, you better believe I'll be just as protective as you are. Probably more."

He looked down at Kassie then, and she blushed. He continued, "Unfortunately, I need to head out. Got to get back up to Temple. Oh-four-hundred comes early."

Jim nodded approvingly. "That is does."

Kassie gathered her purse and they all meandered to the front door.

"I appreciate all you're doing for my girls. Thank you for taking the time to come to dinner and get to know us. And for making sure Kassie is protected."

"It was my pleasure," Hollywood told the older man. "Not only did I get to see Kassie again, but I got to eat the best meatloaf I've ever had. But don't tell my mother. She thinks hers is the world's best."

Donna blushed, but rolled her eyes and shook her head. "Thank you for the compliment, but my meatloaf is only passable, and I know it. But if you tell me my *lasagna* is the best you've ever eaten, *that* I'll believe."

Kassie hugged her mom but told her, "You're so full of crap," when she did. Her mom was an excellent cook and they all knew it. She shifted to her dad and gave him a bear hug. "Love you, Dad."

"Love you too, Kass. You take care, hear?"

"Yes, sir."

Hollywood wrapped his arm around her waist and led her to their cars, which were sitting in the driveway. He'd met her at her parents' house since he'd come up from Temple that evening. They stood by his car and Kassie sighed heavily.

"What was that for?" he asked, once more pulling her against him.

"I want to make out with you, but don't think it's exactly appropriate in my parents' driveway. The neighbors are all probably spying on us. Not to mention Karina, and with my luck, Dean too since I told him I was here."

"Normally, I wouldn't give a shit," Hollywood told her with a grin. "But because I'm still trying to impress your dad, and don't want him to come out of the house with a shotgun, I'm gonna play it safe tonight." His smile died then. "You'll call when you get home from work every night?"

"I'll call," she reassured him.

"Tell me you have next Saturday off," he demanded.

"I have next Saturday off," Kassie reassured him. "I'm supposed to come over here and help Karina get ready for the dance. Do you think that's still okay?"

"Yeah. It'll be fine."

"And you're still coming to my place?" Kassie tentatively asked. He'd said he would be with her rather than at the refuge with his team, but she wasn't sure.

"Absolutely," he said with conviction. "There's no other place I'd be."

"Okay. Then I'll see you next weekend."

He nodded, then leaned down and kissed her. It wasn't a peck on the lips, but it also wasn't anything that would have her dad storming out of the house threatening his life, either. When he pulled back, he said, "One of the best sexual memories I have is when I made you come without even touching your bare skin. I dream about the orgasm I had that afternoon. I want to make love to you so badly, I ache."

When he paused, Kassie tentatively asked, "But?" as it seemed like there was a big one there.

"But I'd like to wait until you're free of Jacks. And Dean. When you know that we're together because we want to be, not because I'm keeping you safe. Not because you were blackmailed into getting to know me. When we're two regular people dating and moving forward with meshing our lives together, that's when I'll make you mine, and you'll make me yours."

"You're awfully sure of yourself," Kassie teased.

"Actually, I'm not. I'm absolutely terrified, sweetheart," Hollywood told her in a soft voice.

"Of what?" she asked, blown away.

"That you'll come to your senses and wonder what the fuck you're doing with a Special Forces soldier who gets called away on missions sometimes without any warning. That you'll decide my OCD when it comes to keeping my apartment clean is something you can't deal with. That you'll stop thinking me not having a proper bed is cute. That once this is over, you'll realize that you don't need anyone to protect you because you've been doing a hell of a job of it all by yourself for a fuck of a long time."

"Hollywood, I'm not going to think that. You don't need to be afraid."

"I've never had a real relationship. Not one where I want it to continue forever. I'm afraid I'm going to screw it up."

"The last relationship I had I thought was going to be forever, and the man forced me to drink foul-tasting punch, French kiss his friends, and is now threatening to do something horrible to my sister. I don't think you can screw this relationship up that badly. I think you're good."

Kassie was relieved when Hollywood smiled down at her. She didn't like to think of him as scared. He seemed invincible to her. He was her strength when she didn't have it and stood like a wall between her and anything that might hurt her.

"Go home, Graham," she whispered. "Dream of me, just as I do of you every night. I touch myself wishing it was your hands on my body, and I hold out hope that we'll get there sooner rather than later. I kind of like the thought of waiting until all this is over though. I don't want to think of anything other than you when we make love."

His hands pressed against her back until they were touching from knees to chest. "You get yourself off thinking about me?" he asked with his eyes narrowed.

"Uh...did I say that out loud?" she asked rhetorically.

"Yeah, you did. Fuck," he swore, then put his head back and stared up at the stars. "I'm never gonna get to sleep now that I've got *that* image in my head."

Kassie giggled and stood on tiptoes to kiss the underside of his jaw. His head came down and he caught her lips once more with his. Stepping away long before she was ready, he said, "If I don't leave now, I won't be able to."

Putting him out of his misery because she knew he really did need to leave, Kassie said, "Drive safe. Let me know when you get home."

"I will. You too."

"Okay."

"I liked meeting your parents," Hollywood said as he opened his car door. "They seem like good people."

"They are."

He leaned over once more and grabbed her chin, then kissed her briefly before letting go and getting in.

Kassie stood back and let him shut the door. He rolled down the window and said, "I'll talk to you soon. Stay safe, sweetheart."

"I will. Bye."

"Bye."

The words "I love you" were on the tip of her tongue, but Kassie held them back...barely. It was insane that she loved Hollywood after only a few weeks, but there it was.

Kassie gazed up at the same stars Hollywood had just been looking at. A shooting star careened across the sky right as she looked up.

Kassie hadn't wished upon a star in a long time, but tonight the plea came without thought. "Please let this work out in the end," she whispered.

Chapter Seventeen

KASSIE SAT ON her couch, sipping a glass of red wine, watching Hollywood cooking in her kitchen. She'd tried to help, but he'd shooed her away, telling her to go sit and relax. It was Friday night and it'd been a long, stressful ten days. Dean had called half a dozen times, fishing for additional details about the exercise. She hadn't been able to give him any more information than she already had, simply because she had no idea what Hollywood and his friends had planned.

Work had sucked. She hated working the night shift, and she'd had seven straight days of it. Even though she'd talked to Hollywood every day, it wasn't the same. They'd both been tired by the time she called when she got home and while she still loved talking to him, it was obvious the stress of the situation was getting to both of them.

So when she'd gotten home from work tonight and he'd been waiting, Kassie was more than excited. She'd thrown herself into his arms and finally felt her mood lift. She'd been walking around as if she was in a fog for the last week and a half, but Hollywood being in her space made her feel safe.

She couldn't remember a time when she felt that way.

"So you're going over around eleven to help your sister, right?" Hollywood asked from the other room.

"Yup. I'm going to the hair salon with her then we'll go back to the house and get her makeup done. Blake is coming over around four so Mom and Dad can take pictures. They'll go to eat, then head over to the hotel for the dance."

"How is your dad handling the fact that he couldn't get Blake over for dinner to properly intimidate before the dance?"

"Not well," Kassie admitted. "He was pretty put out Blake had one excuse after another for why he couldn't come over."

"At least he's coming to the house to pick Karina up," Hollywood said.

"Yeah. Did your friend do the background check on him?" Hollywood had told her earlier that week he had a guy in Pennsylvania who would see what he could find out about Blake to try to put her mind at ease.

"He's been really busy with some other stuff, but said he ran a preliminary check and nothing alarming came up. Blake Watson dropped out of high school when he was eighteen, he started a year late because of a fall birthday. He worked at a few dead-end jobs before re-enrolling at your sister's high school."

"Well, that's something," Kassie said. "What are you going to do tomorrow when I'm with Karina?"

"Me 'n Fish are going to hang out."

"He seems nice," Kassie observed.

"He is."

"And he's moving to Idaho, did I hear that right?" Kassie asked.

"Yup. He signed the paperwork this week."

"Why Idaho?"

"Because it's out of the way and has lots of space. He doesn't do well with crowds. I think it's gotten worse as time goes on. He's seen a psychologist about it, but doesn't think it's doing much good. He's stubborn and determined to work through his issues on his own."

"That sucks," Kassie said, looking down into her wine glass. "I hate that for him."

"Me too," Hollywood agreed. "You ready to eat?"

"Absolutely," Kassie told him, standing up and wandering over to the small kitchen. "It smells awesome."

Hollywood had apparently stopped at the grocery store before he'd arrived because he'd had all the ingredients to make stuffed green peppers with him. Kassie sat down at her small kitchen table and stared down at the dinner Hollywood had made.

"I'm impressed," she told him honestly.

He shrugged. "It's actually pretty easy to make. Brown the meat, season it, mix in some tomato sauce and some half-cooked rice. Core the peppers, stuff them with the meat mixture. Cover with more tomato sauce and cheese. Then bake."

"Somehow, I don't think it was that easy," Kassie told him with a smile.

"It was my pleasure, sweetheart. I don't think you've had a nice sit-down meal since last week with your parents."

"No, but I'm guessing you haven't either."

"It's no fun to cook for yourself," he said.

Kassie swallowed. "No, it's not," she agreed.

Hollywood sat down next to her and put his hand on the table, palm up, obviously wanting her to put her hand in his.

Without thought she did, wanting to feel his skin against hers.

Hollywood closed his hand around hers and shook his head. "I can't believe how cold your fingers always are."

"It doesn't even faze me anymore."

Bringing his other hand up to cover hers, Hollywood said, "Well, it bothers me." He chafed her fingers for a moment before saying, "It's good to be here with you, Kass. Cooking. Talking. It seems so normal and right."

"Yeah, it does."

Hollywood picked up her hand and kissed the back of it before saying, "Dig in. You'll have to let me know what you think."

"It's wonderful," she said as she picked up her fork.

Hollywood laughed. "You haven't even tried it."

"I don't have to. If it tastes half as good as it smells, it's going to knock my socks off."

And she was right. It was awesome.

AT TEN-THIRTY THE next morning, Hollywood kissed Kassie as they stood in the entryway in her apartment. He held her loosely in his embrace when he forced himself to release her.

"You'll call when you get there?"

She nodded. "When is the training thing supposed to start?"

They'd talked about it a bit last night before they'd put a movie in, but Kassie had been jumpy and nervous, so Hollywood had wanted to make her relax and not think about what was happening at the refuge.

"It's already happening. Ghost and the others are down there now. Got there yesterday afternoon and set up. The other Delta team is also there, acting as the 'bad guys.'"

"And you've worked with them before? They know what's going on?"

"Yes, Kass. We train with them all the time and they know what's going on."

She closed her eyes and took a deep breath, obviously trying to get ahold of her emotions. "Do they have funny nicknames like you and your friends do?"

Hollywood smiled at her. "Our nicks aren't funny."

"Uh, yeah, they are," Kassie informed him. "Truck? Beatle? Hollywood? Totally funny."

"Trigger, Lefty, Oz, Grover, Lucky, Brain, and Doc," Hollywood said.

"What?"

"Their nicks. Trigger, Lefty, Oz, Grover, Lucky, Brain, and Doc," he repeated patiently.

Kassie giggled and shook her head. "Okay, I won't say your names are funny again because theirs are hysterical."

Glad he could make her smile, Hollywood leaned in and rested his forehead against her own. "I loved waking up with you in my arms, Kass." He felt her melt against him.

"Yeah. Me too."

"Want that. Every morning."

"It'd be nice," Kassie responded. "I'm sorry about your...err...problem this morning."

Hollywood pulled back and teased, "You mean my rock-hard cock?"

"Hollywood!" Kassie protested, her eyes wide as she blushed.

He grinned. "I can't believe you're flustered about me saying the word cock after what we did last night."

If possible she turned even redder. "It's morning. I'm not out of my mind with lust, and you're staring at me," she defended herself.

"I like these games we're playing." Hollywood informed her of something she undoubtedly already knew. "Making you come with only my hands and mouth on your tits is something I wasn't sure I could do, but thankfully you proved me wrong."

"You're just too good looking," Kassie grumbled, wrinkling her nose. "It's physically impossible for me *not* to come with you touching and kissing me."

His smile grew. "You keep flattering me, I might get a big head."

"You've already got a big...head," Kassie told him, smirking.

Hollywood laughed and palmed the back of her head as he held her to him with an arm around her waist. "You're amazing, Kassie Anderson. I can't wait until this is all behind us and you give me all of you."

"Me too, Hollywood. But..." Her eyes skittered away from his.

"Eyes on me, sweetheart. What? I want you to always feel free to say anything to me."

She looked up at him and ran her hands up and down his sides as she said, "If this somehow doesn't end today and Dean doesn't show up and he still wants me to get information to feed to him...do we still need to wait? I want you, Hollywood."

"I've been trying not to rush you. I don't want to push you into anything you're not ready for. If you're truly okay with us, then no, we're not waiting. I might be bossy, but I'm not calling the shots in our relationship like a dictator, Kass."

She smiled then. "Good. Because I've been going slowly for your sake, but I'm about done with that."

Hollywood chuckled again. "Slowly, huh?"

"Yup, totally."

Hollywood put pressure on her head and drew her into him. Her hands went to his back and she clutched his shirt as he kissed her. Kassie gave as good as she got, tilting her head to get a better angle. Her tongue dueled with his and by the time they pulled back, they were both breathing hard.

"Have fun with Karina today, sweetheart. Call when you're on your way home."

"I will. And you'll let me know if you hear anything from the guys?"

"Of course. I want this done just as much as you

do," Hollywood told her. "Now go, before I haul you back to bed and you don't get to spend the afternoon with your sister."

"Thanks for being here," Kassie said as she gathered her purse and opened her door.

"No place I'd rather be," Hollywood told her.

"Later."

"Later, sweetheart."

Hollywood watched from the doorway until Kassie disappeared around the corner. Then he shut the door and put his head against it and closed his eyes. "Come on, Ghost. Call," he murmured, then straightened and headed into Kassie's apartment.

"HOLLYWOOD?" KASSIE CALLED after she opened her apartment door. It was five-thirty and she was ready to hang out on the couch and not deal with people for a while.

"Hey," Hollywood said as he came around the corner of the hallway. He came straight to her and gave her a hug. He briefly kissed her lips and said, "You look beat."

Ignoring his appropriate observation, Kassie asked, "You hear anything?"

"No."

"Does that mean something went wrong?" she fretted.

"No. It just means nothing's happened yet. Ghost called about two hours ago. He said they were going through different scenarios with the other Deltas like they would if they were really doing an exercise. They have scouts around the area and satellite surveillance shows a group of men about three miles away from their base camp. They're there, and they'll fall into the trap. We just have to give them time to do it. Okay?"

"I just want this to be done," Kassie told him, aware of the whine in her tone and hating it.

"It will be," Hollywood said resolutely.

"What smells so good?" Kassie asked, changing the subject.

"A roast. I found your slow cooker and put it in early this afternoon. I asked Fish to stop by the store and pick it up for me."

"You're always feeding me," she told him.

"You complaining?" he retorted.

"No. Absolutely not. Feel free to feed me whenever you want."

"I will." Hollywood took her purse off her shoulder and placed it on the table near the door. Then he grabbed her hand and led her to the kitchen. "Sit. You want wine?"

"Yes, please."

As he was pouring her a glass, Kassie asked, "How's Fish? Ready to go to Idaho?"

"More than. Now that the house is his, he's itching to leave."

"I'm not holding him back, am I?" Kassie asked, worried she was keeping the man from doing what he wanted to.

"No. Don't even go there. Fish doesn't do anything he doesn't want to. He's excited about his new house, but wouldn't even think about leaving before this is done. He wouldn't do that to you, and he definitely wouldn't to me and the team."

"I really like him."

"Me too. Now, how about you stop telling me how much you like my friend and talk about how beautiful your sister looked instead. You got pictures?"

"Do I have pictures?" Kassie asked, her eyes lighting up. "I got pictures," she told him. "And I hope you don't mind spending three hours looking at them with me."

He smiled, but it died with his next words. "And Blake? How were your parents with him?"

Kassie shrugged. "Okay. Not great, not awful. They were taken aback at how old he looked, but he laughing- ly showed them his driver's license. He said he'd take care of Karina and treat her the way she deserved. By the end of the million and one pictures they'd taken, I think they'd thawed toward him."

"Good," Hollywood said, putting a plate on the table in front of her. It was piled high with tender beef on a hoagie roll. "Fish left about an hour ago and he's tailing them to dinner then to the dance. Once she gets inside, he'll hang out, keeping his eyes on the parking lot for Dean, just in case."

Kassie nodded. "Karina said she'd shoot me a text when she got home."

"Good." The gleam was back in his eye when he said, "You wanna play spin the bottle tonight? Or seven minutes in heaven?"

She bit her lip and said, "I'll do anything you wanna do, Hollywood."

He didn't reply, but merely smiled and dug into his dinner.

For the hundredth time, Kassie marveled that he was sitting at her table, eating food he'd cooked for her, and that she was the one who'd fall asleep held tight in his arms. She wasn't exactly a troll, but knew she wasn't in Hollywood's league either. His nickname was Hollywood, for goodness sake. He was as good looking as any leading man she'd ever drooled over in the movies. And he was hers. It was about time good fortune came her way for once.

Kassie blinked.

She wasn't sleeping well, even though Hollywood had done his best to help her relax. He knew she was too keyed up and anxious to play any games, so they'd simply lain together on her couch watching television while they'd waited to hear from Karina.

Finally, around twelve, he decided to move them into her bedroom. She'd gotten ready for bed, putting on an oversized T-shirt and sleep shorts, and Hollywood had stripped down to his boxers and a tight white T-shirt.

Every other time he'd slept in her bed, he'd worn a pair of sweats. This was the first time she'd seen so much of him and he was absolutely beautiful. She could see his six-pack under his shirt and the muscles in his thighs rippled as he climbed under the covers. He took her in his arms and his familiar scent worked its magic. Even though she hadn't heard from Karina, she fell asleep, feeling safe and loved.

But something had woken her up. It took a moment for Kassie to remember the night before, but when she realized she'd fallen asleep without hearing from her sister, she turned her head to look at the nightstand.

She could see the faint glow from her phone letting her know she had a text. Kassie's eyes went to her clock. It was four-thirty in the morning. She was going to kick Karina's ass for worrying her so badly.

Sometime in the last couple of hours, Kassie had shifted away from Hollywood. He was lying on his back with one arm resting over his head. He was breathing heavily, obviously exhausted from whatever he'd been doing in the last week to keep watch over her and Karina.

Turning on her side slowly so as to not wake up Hollywood, Kassie grabbed her phone and pressed the button with her thumb to unlock it. She clicked on her text messages and the smile faded from her face as she saw the picture that had been sent from Karina's phone.

It was her sister. She was sitting on the ground with a blindfold around her head. It was dark, but because of the flash used for the picture, Kassie could see her sister's beautiful dress was ripped and filthy. She had dirt on her face and her hands were tied behind her back. There were a few scrub bushes to the right and left of her, but otherwise Kassie couldn't make out any other details that would tell her where Karina was.

Her heartbeat immediately picked up as adrenaline shot through her body. Her first thought was to wake up Hollywood and have him take care of this for her, but as she turned, another text came in.

Karina: *If u wnt 2 c her again, come now to the dizzy rooster on Sixth. Alone.*

Kassie's fingers flew across the screen as she replied.

Kassie: I want to talk to Karina.

Karina: No. She's an hour away from being carried across the Mexico border. U don't show, she'll be gone forever. I'm sure she'll love being fucked by banditos all day and night.

Kassie: No!

Karina: Then get your ass to the dizzy rooster. You got 20 min. if you bring your boyfriend, you'll make your sister a whore.

Kassie: I'll be there.

Kassie: Don't hurt her.

Kassie: Hello?

"Fuck," Kassie whispered. She slowly sat up and eased her legs off the side of the mattress. She knew she was doing the wrong thing, but couldn't take the chance that whoever was texting her on Karina's phone would do what he threatened. It certainly looked like Karina wasn't around Austin. With the sand/dirt she was sitting on and the scrub bushes around her, she probably wasn't in the immediate area.

It had been hours since she'd left for the dance. Time enough for someone to drive her south to the border.

Kassie's hands shook as she grabbed a pair of jeans from the floor and carried them to the door of her room. She looked back once and hesitated. Hollywood was right where she'd last seen him. Dead to the world, sleeping peacefully.

She should wake him up.

She should ask him to deal with this for her.

He could help her.

But if she woke him, she'd essentially sign her sister's death warrant.

She closed her eyes. She was being too stupid to live. She knew she was. Hollywood was a badass Special Forces soldier. He could take care of this for her. But she couldn't get the words on her phone out of her head.

If you bring your boyfriend, you'll make your sister a whore.

Taking a deep breath and ignoring the tear that fell down her cheek, she swallowed hard. She'd text Hollywood when she got to Sixth Street. She was an idiot, but she wasn't a complete one…okay, she was, but time was ticking. She had to leave. *Now.*

Her shoulders sagging as if the weight of the world was on them, Kassie turned away from Hollywood and snuck out of her bedroom.

HOLLYWOOD JERKED AWAKE at the sound of the vibration of his cell phone against the wooden tabletop next to him. He reached for Kassie, but his hand met with nothing but cold sheets. He turned his head and saw in the faint morning light coming through the window that she wasn't lying next to him.

He sat up and rubbed his face. He'd slept like a log. He'd been awoken by a phone call from Ghost around two. Kassie hadn't stirred as he'd had a short conversation.

The op was done. Dean had shown up with six other men who were playing at being soldiers. They'd been surrounded by both Delta teams and everyone immediately surrendered, except for Dean. When his friends had dropped their guns, he'd turned on them, screaming at them for being weak and calling them traitors and losers. He'd trained his weapon on his friends and began to shoot, the nonlethal rounds from the Deltas' weapons not seeming to faze him. One of Dean's friends turned his own pistol on him and brought the out-of-control situation to a halt.

Dean was dead. Killed by one of the men he'd recruited to "play" his war game with him.

As was required by the commander, none of the Deltas had any live rounds in their weapons. There would be no blowback from the Army about Dean's death. Kassie was free from Dean's threats once and for all.

Hollywood hadn't had the heart to wake Kassie. Deciding to let her sleep and tell her the good news in the morning, he'd said goodbye to Ghost and gone back to sleep, satisfied for the first time in over a month that Kassie and her sister really were safe.

Leaning over, Hollywood grabbed his phone to see who was contacting him this early. There was a text from Fish.

Fish: *Get your ass up! Karina's in the wind and Kassie is on the hunt.*

At reading the words, all mellow feelings of being relieved Kassie was safe were wiped away. Hollywood punched in Fish's name and brought the phone up to his ear.

"About time," Fish said as a greeting.

"Talk to me," Hollywood ordered even as he was pulling on a pair of jeans.

"Thirty minutes ago I got a text from Kassie. She said someone had kidnapped her sister, sent her a picture of Karina tied up, sitting in the dirt, and told her she had to come alone to The Dizzy Rooster down on Sixth Street."

"Fuck!" Hollywood roared. "Dean's dead, so it wasn't him. Who the fuck texted her?"

"No clue," Fish told him. "I tried to call but she didn't pick up. Texted her and got no response."

"Where are you?" Hollywood asked.

"Outside The fucking Dizzy Rooster. It's deserted. The only life around here are a couple businesses down the street near the Voodoo Doughnut place. Asked, and no one there saw a fucking thing."

"So she's just gone?" Hollywood asked disbelievingly.

"Looks like it."

"Fuck, fuck, fuck," Hollywood chanted as he paced Kassie's bedroom. "Why didn't she wake me up? What was she thinking?"

"Hollywood, don't blame her—" Fish started, but Hollywood interrupted him.

"I don't fucking blame her. I know she was scared out of her mind. Asshole probably told her if she said anything to anyone he'd kill her sister or some such shit. She's extremely protective of Karina and there's no way she'd do anything at this point to put her in danger." Hollywood sighed. "She doesn't know about Dean," he told Fish.

"I guessed. But it doesn't really matter one way or another. If Dean's dead and Jacks is in jail...who took Karina and texted Kassie?"

The answer became clear to Hollywood in a flash. "Fucking Blake. It has to be. There's no one else."

"The new boyfriend?" Fish asked.

"One and the same," Hollywood responded, on the move to the living room.

"Damn. I fucked up," Fish told him quietly. "Once they got to the dance, I sat in the parking lot for a couple of hours and when Ghost sent me the text saying Dean was at the training exercise, that they'd gotten visual confirmation, I figured she was good. Left her."

"This is not your fault," Hollywood returned immediately. "I had Tex do a background check, but he told me flat out it was only a surface one. He was busy with some SEAL team stuff. I didn't push for more. I should've. Knew that fucker seemed off."

"No sense beating ourselves up now. We gotta figure out where he took them and what his plans are."

"You think he's been in touch with Jacks?"

"Maybe," Fish said. "I've been putting off neutralizing that fucker until after this thing with Dean was over, but I'll make some calls. See what I can find out."

"Don't get yourself in trouble," Hollywood warned. As much as he wanted to find Kassie and her sister, he didn't want his friend going down as a result.

"I might not be Tex, but I know some people. Ones who owe me. I'm calling in my markers."

Fuck. A Delta calling in a marker was a big deal. They met many kinds of people in their line of work. People the government wouldn't be happy their super soldiers were consorting with. And Fish using those markers to help him and Kassie was huge. Fish might've lost his teammates over in the desert all those months ago, but until now, Hollywood hadn't been sure Fish was really all that fired up to make those kinds of connections again.

"Any information you can find would be great, Fish," Hollywood told him.

"Call the others. They're probably on their way back to post. They're probably closer to Austin by now than they were a few hours ago."

"On it," Hollywood told him. "But first I'm calling Beth."

"Beth?"

"Long story, but she's a hacker down in San Antonio who's been working with Tex. I'd prefer his expertise, but if he's knee deep in an op, I won't put my fellow SF guys in danger."

"Keep me informed," was all Fish said, not even questioning if Beth could get the job done.

"Thanks for the call."

"Anything for a Delta," Fish responded, then hung up.

Hollywood yanked the shirt he'd grabbed on the way out of the bedroom over his head and dialed Beth's number.

"'Lo?" she answered sleepily.

"Need you to track a phone," Hollywood barked impatiently.

"Who is this?" Beth asked.

"Hollywood."

"Shit. Okay, okay, I'm up. Give me a sec." Her

voice got muffled then, and Hollywood knew she was talking to Cade "Sledge" Turner, her boyfriend. "Go back to sleep, hon. It's work."

He couldn't hear Cade's response, and Beth came back on the line. "What's up?"

"My girlfriend and her sister are missing. The sister disappeared probably sometime after nine last night. Kassie got a text with a picture of her sister, tied up. She was told to meet someone at The Dizzy Rooster here in downtown Austin. She texted one of my teammates."

"They both have their phones on them?" Beth asked.

Hollywood could hear her typing in the background and said, "No clue. But it's a place to start."

"Give me their numbers," Beth ordered.

Hollywood did and listened as the other woman did her thing in the background. Visions of Kassie lying dead somewhere, if only for Jacks's satisfaction, and Karina being sold to some depraved fucker as a sex slave ran on rewind through his brain as he waited impatiently for Beth to find out something that would help him find them.

"Yeah, okay," Beth said more to herself than Hollywood. "I can see why Kassie would run off without saying anything to you."

"What? Why?"

"I'm looking at the picture and text conversation she

had with whoever sent her the picture. I'm not saying it was the right decision, but I can understand why she did it."

"Fuck," Hollywood swore. It was the only word he could think of that would sum up what he was feeling at the moment. "I can't believe you got it already."

"Hey," Beth said, sounding offended, "you called me for a reason. I'm good at this shit. Now don't piss me off while I'm trying to help you."

Normally, Hollywood would've found her funny, but at the moment he couldn't find anything humorous. "What did it say?"

"Oh, the usual shit assholes like this say to get their target to sneak out of their house and not tell their badass boyfriend who could easily wipe the floor with them where they're going. It's the picture that most likely got to her."

"For God's sake, Beth, what—"

"Check your phone. I just sent it," Beth told him.

Hollywood put the conversation on speaker and clicked the screen to open his email. He had to wait a second for the picture to download, but when it did, he sucked in a breath.

"Jesus," he said.

"Exactly. I'm trying to pinpoint the GPS location on where the photo was taken, but it's taking a bit. Looks to me that it's somewhere south of Austin. How far south, I'm not sure. But it's not in the Hill Country, that's for sure."

Hollywood only half heard Beth's continued mutterings. He'd only met Kassie's sister that one time when he'd gone over to her house for dinner, but he'd liked her. She was a younger version of Kassie for sure. Sassy and funny, but also respectful to her parents, and it was obvious to see the love the entire family had for each other. Their family reminded him a lot of his own in many ways.

So the look of absolute terror on Karina's face in the photo hit him like a ten-ton truck and took his breath away. Her eyes were covered by a piece of cloth and her hands were bound together behind her back, but he could still see how scared she was by looking at her face and body.

Lips tight, shoulders hunched forward as if they could protect her from whoever was taking the picture. Her makeup was smeared and she had black tracks running down her cheeks, obviously from her mascara running when she'd cried. Her legs were drawn up in front of her and Hollywood could see scrapes and bruises on her legs through the ripped material of her fancy dress.

He hated that Kassie had snuck out of the room and hadn't turned to him, but as Beth had said, he understood.

"Got you, you little fucker," Beth exclaimed excitedly. "Okay, I was right. The picture of Karina was taken almost at the border. Right outside of Laredo. It takes about three and a half hours to drive to Laredo from Austin. So whoever took her could've driven her down there, then come back and texted Kassie and met her downtown."

"Or he could be working with someone," Hollywood said.

"True. But I don't think so."

"Why not?" Hollywood asked, impatient now.

"Because I've got locations of both phones on my screen right now."

"And?"

"And they're currently about to enter the outskirts of San Antonio. From the pings, it looks like whoever has the phones is driving south on I-35."

"Dammit," Hollywood said. "I'll never catch up."

"You won't," Beth agreed. "But I happen to know some people right here in San Antonio who wouldn't mind kicking some ass this morning."

Hollywood immediately thought of TJ Rockwell, known as Rock when he was a member of his Delta team. "Call TJ first," he ordered. "Then anyone else you can think of who can help. I'll see if I can't get a chopper from Fort Hood. Gotta pick up my team, but we can be in the air within the hour."

"So you want a watch-and-wait strategy?" Beth asked.

That was the million-dollar question. It seemed to him that if it was Blake who had kidnapped Karina and come back for Kassie, he was on his way south to wherever he'd stashed Karina. But if he was wrong, and if Kassie was hurt, waiting could cost her life. If she died because he'd made the wrong decision, Hollywood wouldn't be able to live with himself.

On the other hand, if they waited and got Blake out in the open in the middle of the desert, they could more easily take him down.

"Yeah," Hollywood told her, making the decision. "Have TJ follow them, but do not intercept. We'll find him from the air."

"Who should I look up to find out details on what you're dealing with?" Beth asked.

Hollywood was impressed with her no-nonsense demeanor and smart questions. "Blake Watson. Said he was twenty, but fucker looks years older. I knew it, but didn't push."

"Got it."

"I'll call her parents. Get the make and model of his car. They have to be freaking out that she's not home yet. Of course Blake could've used her phone to text them some bullshit story, but if it was my daughter, I'd be panicking."

"Good call. I'll call back with any other pertinent info I find that you'll need to know when you catch up with him," Beth said.

"Thanks." It was obvious Beth had learned a lot from working with Tex. She stuck to the facts and knew exactly what was needed when the shit was about to hit the fan. Not to mention she was excellent at working under pressure.

"I owe ya," Hollywood told her.

"No you don't," Beth returned immediately. "Taking fuckers like this off the street I do for free. Later." She clicked off without giving Hollywood a chance to reply.

Not caring about the niceties, Hollywood's only thought was to get to Kassie, he pressed a button to call the Andersons. The most important mission of his life was about to unfold. He couldn't fail now.

Chapter Eighteen

KASSIE TRIED NOT to panic. She'd gone to the closed bar on Sixth Street as she'd been instructed, but at the last minute had sent a text to Fish telling him what had happened. Why she didn't text Hollywood she didn't know... Actually, yes she did. She was scared.

Afraid he'd yell at her. Or tell her she was an idiot. Which she was. So she'd texted Fish, then gotten out of her car. She remembered a man coming at her wearing a hoodie, and knew it was whoever had taken Karina and who she was supposed to meet, but had panicked and turned to run anyway. But obviously she hadn't gotten far before he'd hit her so hard she'd blacked out.

She'd woken up in the backseat of a moving car...and to Blake Watson. She should've known.

He'd tried to treat her like she was a guest in his car instead of a kidnapping victim. He'd invited her to climb over the seat. She'd refused until he half turned in his seat and pointed a knife at her. He gave her a drink of water and two aspirin for her throbbing head. He'd even supplied her with a washcloth so she could clean the blood off her face. What a gentleman. Not.

But when she'd asked where they were going, he didn't reply. When she'd asked where Karina was, he didn't reply. When she'd demanded to speak with her sister, he'd merely laughed and told her she'd see her soon enough.

She'd watched San Antonio go by in silence. She'd tried to catch people's eyes as they passed them, but Blake had seen her and said in a chillingly cold voice, "If you do anything to make me get pulled over, your sister is going to die."

"What?"

"I'm the only one in the world who knows where Karina is. And if you prevent us from getting to her, she's going to die. Alone. A slow, painful death. You ever been so thirsty you swallowed sand by the handful because it was better than nothing?"

Kassie had shaken her head.

"It's not a nice way to die. So sit there. Keep your thoughts to yourself. And you'll get to see your sister again."

That had been thirty minutes ago. Kassie couldn't keep quiet any longer. "Why are you doing this? What have I or my sister ever done to you?"

"To me? Nothing." He didn't elaborate.

"Then to who?" she insisted.

"My brother."

"And who is that?" Kassie almost screamed, so sick of the game he was playing.

"You don't know?"

"Obviously not."

"Dean Jennings."

"Oh my God, you're Dean's brother?" Kassie breathed in disbelief. "You look nothing like him."

"That's because we have the same slut of a mother but different fathers. I didn't grow up with him and we have different last names, but he tracked me down recently. We clicked. He told me all about you and how you disrespected his homie, Richard."

Kassie shook her head. "No, it's not like that, we—"

His nice-guy persona cracked as he took his hand off the steering wheel and punched her. Luckily she moved quickly enough that it hit her shoulder instead of her face. But it hurt a lot.

"I know all about what it's like. You led him on. Promised him the world. But when he got hurt, you turned hot and cold. Making him beg for your snatch. Refusing to move with him to his duty stations. Making eyes at all his friends. Oh yeah, Dean told me how you were so hot for him, you were almost gagging for it. But what you didn't know is that he told Richard all about you and your actions while he was gone." Blake shook his head in mock sadness. "Why is it so hard to find a woman who will suck and fuck on command? Huh?"

"How old are you?" Kassie asked instead of answering what to her seemed like a rhetorical question. A disgusting one with awful implications at that.

"Twenty-nine," he said immediately. "And I have to say, I hadn't been interested in teen pussy before this gig, but now that I've had it, I've changed my mind. Teenagers are so easy to manipulate and fuck with their minds. It's awesome."

She wanted to ask, yet she definitely *didn't* want to. But she didn't have to.

"And in case you're wondering, no, I haven't fucked your sister. The buyer wanted a virgin, so I couldn't touch her. Although with the way she lit up for me when we kissed and how she sucked my cock, I regret that."

Kassie felt the bile move up her throat, but resolutely swallowed it down. She really, really hoped Blake was telling the truth and he was taking her to her sister. She'd do whatever it took to make sure she escaped this hell. She'd trade places with Karina if it came to that. Kassie wasn't a virgin, but whatever...

"What are you going to do with us?" she asked meekly, trying to get as much information from Blake as she could to come up with some sort of plan. She knew she'd texted Fish, but at this point she had no idea what he could do. She wasn't even in Austin anymore. She was on her own.

"Sell you," Blake said without pause. "Richard made friends with some guys up there in his fancy prison. They know people who know people who buy and sell pussy. He decided he was done with you, and arranged with Dean to get rid of you once and for all."

"Why drag Karina into all this?" Kassie asked, sick to her stomach.

"Why not?" he replied. "You love her, and Richard wanted you to suffer. It was easy enough for Dean to pay a guy to alter my records and get me new identification saying I was twenty. I didn't think anyone would buy it, but apparently people are stupid and go along with whatever they're told, even if it's obviously a fuckin' lie."

"I'll pay you whatever you want if you let us go," Kassie said in desperation.

"I don't want your money, cunt," Blake said, the disdain clear in his voice. "I'm doing this for my brother. For Richard. For men everywhere who get fucked over by women."

"I'm sorry your dad got fucked over by your mom," Kassie said softly, trying to get on his good side...if he had one.

"Shut the fuck up!" he ordered. "You don't know anything about what I went through or about my mother. She's a cunt. Just like you. Just like your sister. Just like your fucking mother. Weak. All women are *weak*. This world would be a better place if we could keep all women locked up. Their only purpose to breed. The boys would be taken away and raised to become strong men. The girls only kept alive if they were pretty and could be used to birth more boys."

Kassie huddled against the door in shock. How in the hell had everyone missed the fact that Blake was absolutely insane?

"Fucking women. Good for one thing and one thing only," Blake said under his breath.

Kassie didn't ask him anything else after that. She sat in the seat, her head resting on the window, watching the Texas countryside go by. She thought about Hollywood, and how he'd probably woken up wondering where she was. She hadn't even left him a note. He had to be worried by now.

Actually, he was probably out of his mind. Fish had to have contacted him about the text she'd sent. They were both trying to figure out where she was. Kassie had no idea if the rest of the team was still down at the refuge trying to deal with Dean and whatever he had planned for them.

Allowing herself a moment of self-pity, Kassie didn't even bother to wipe away the tear that fell out of her eye. But as soon as it escaped, she scrunched her eyes shut as hard as she could, forcing the rest back. She couldn't give in to despair. By the time the day was up, she'd either be the new fuck toy of a man south of the border or she'd be dead. But whatever happened, she would not sit back and merely take it.

A month ago, she might've. But Hollywood had changed all that. And learning about what Rayne, Emily, and Harley had been through. They hadn't sat back and given up. No, they'd fought like hell. She might've let Richard and Dean mess with her for most of her life, but that was done.

Once she'd gotten control over her emotions, Kassie began to plot, thinking through different scenarios and what she could do to rescue her sister. She hadn't seen anyone else with Blake as of yet, and if it was only him, then maybe she and Karina had a chance. Two against one was always a good thing, wasn't it? Even if Blake was bat-shit crazy, they might be able to overpower him.

As they continued south, Kassie prayed that Dean was busy over in Galveston. That Blake didn't have any other half-brothers out there in the world that he'd roped into this insane scheme. And that whoever was planning on buying her and her sister wouldn't be showing up until later. When they were hopefully long gone.

She closed her eyes and pretended to be asleep as Blake continued to mutter about useless women, and she thought about Hollywood. What would he do in a situation like this? He'd wait until the perfect moment, then he'd make his move. So that's exactly what she would do too.

Chapter Nineteen

"**B**ETH, IT'S HOLLYWOOD. Any updates on the coordinates?"

"No. They're the same as they were thirty minutes ago," she told him. "You guys there?"

"Just landed. We're a couple miles away, should be there in ten minutes or less," he told her.

"Be careful," Beth cautioned.

"Always," Hollywood returned, then clicked off the phone.

He turned to his team. As it turned out, Ghost and the guys were close to Austin. They were *in* Austin, as a matter of fact. They'd driven up from the refuge and gotten a hotel room before heading home. Even though it was only another hour drive, something had made them all agree to stop there for the night and go home Sunday, showered and refreshed, rather than pushing through.

Thank God they had.

Even their commander was in Austin, and he'd quickly taken over and received permission for the chopper, which had been on standby at the refuge, to fly to Austin, pick up the team, and head to Laredo.

The way the commander had explained it to his superior officer was that it was an extension of the exercise. Because it was the Delta Force team, not many questions were asked, and they'd been able to meet at the airport and head south within an hour.

Coach had been in communication off and on with Beth, reporting back to the team what she'd learned about Blake Watson.

Turned out Dean was his half-brother. Unfortunately for them, their mother had an extreme mental illness and had committed suicide several years ago. It looked like both her sons had inherited that mental instability.

Blake was twenty-nine, close to Dean's age, and had grown up in a small town down near Laredo. He'd been in trouble with the law since he was in his teens. He'd dropped out of high school, but he'd done it when he was fifteen. Dean had tracked him down and they'd apparently gotten close, with Blake going all-in on Dean and Richard's schemes.

Beth seemed to think Blake was a loner and most likely was working by himself, but she wasn't sure.

So now the team, Ghost, Fletch, Coach, Beatle, Blade, Truck, and Hollywood, were making their way through the desert toward where both Kassie and Karina's phones were pinging. They hadn't been turned off nor destroyed. Blake either didn't know enough about electronics to realize he was broadcasting his location to anyone who knew how to look for it, or he was setting them up.

Regardless, the team had to check it out. If the sisters weren't there, they could hopefully get their hands on Blake and make him confess what he'd done with them. The thought that Kassie might be dead was something Hollywood refused to consider. He couldn't if he was going to still function.

No, she was fine. Maybe hurt, probably scared, but he could work with those. He couldn't fix her if she was dead.

The team prowled silently through the hot morning desert, communicating through a series of clicks in their headphones, and hand gestures when they were close enough to see each other.

In ten minutes they gathered to discuss their approach of the small shack, which Beth had described from looking at satellite photos.

Kneeling down in the sand and dirt behind scrubby trees and tumbleweeds, they planned.

"Ghost, you and Blade go around this way," Hollywood ordered, drawing a picture in the sand as he spoke. "Fletch, you and Beatle approach from the other direction. "Coach, you go around to the back and cover any exits that way. Truck and I will move in from the front. We'll listen to make sure no one else is there but the women and Watson. Beatle and Fletch, one of you guys throw a flash-bang in through the window on the side. It'll fuck with all of them, but it'll give me and Truck time to get in through the front door and take Watson down. Questions?"

The men all shook their heads. They'd done this often enough that Hollywood really didn't even need to spell it out for them. They knew what they were doing. But they also knew their teammate needed to feel in control in this out-of-control situation. No one suggested he take watch on the back of the cabin. No one tried to convince him he'd be better off letting someone else take point. It was his woman in danger, and he'd be the one to face that danger head-on.

The men fanned out, ever alert for anything that would change the dynamics of the plan and make them switch to plan B, C, or D. One way or another, this would be done in minutes. They could then figure out if they had to sneak into Mexico to rescue Kassie and Karina from the sex-slave trade or if they could head home, with both women safe.

AFTER TRAVELING WHAT seemed like forever, Blake stopped the car along the side of some road and forced her out. They walked across the dry and dusty landscape for quite a while until they reached a hut. Without a word, he opened the door and shoved her inside.

Kassie landed on her knees right next to her sister. Without waiting for permission, she ripped off the blindfold and started working on freeing Karina's hands. Through it all, Blake stood with his back against the door, grinning at them.

"Aw…how cute. The sisters are reunited."

Ignoring him, Kassie hugged Karina hard, then pulled back and asked, "Are you okay?"

The younger woman nodded, but looked a little shell-shocked.

Kassie turned to Blake. "Do you have any water? She needs to drink something."

"Why in the fuck would I waste any water I *do* have on either of you?" he sneered.

"Because you don't want to deliver us to whoever is coming half dead on our feet. You think someone wants to carry us out of here?"

"They wouldn't carry either of you, sweetheart," Blake told them. "They'd drag your asses instead."

Kassie heard the small whimper come from Karina's lips, and she turned to her sister. She gave her a fierce look. "Ignore him. He's nothing. Understand? We got this."

"What do you mean I'm nothing?" Blake asked,

pushing off the door and stalking toward them.

Kassie pushed Karina behind her and held her arms out as if she could prevent the pissed-off man stomping toward them from getting behind her.

"I just meant that we have bigger things to worry about than water." She tried to placate Blake. But he wasn't having it.

Kassie saw it coming, but stood her ground, knowing if she ducked, her sister would be vulnerable. The back of Blake's hand hit her cheek and Kassie almost fell over. She caught herself with a hand on the floor. She kept her head down, but resumed her place in front of Karina. Blake could hit her all he wanted, she wasn't moving. It was obvious from the bruises already forming on Karina's face that he'd hit her, but he wouldn't do it again if she could prevent it.

When he bunched his hand into a fist and drew it back, Kassie whirled around and grabbed Karina. She tackled her to the ground and they huddled together on the floor.

Kassie waited for the blow to fall, but apparently her sudden movement surprised him enough that he pulled his punch. Instead he kicked her. Hard. Kassie grunted with the force of his foot on her back. It hurt. A lot. But she didn't move. She curled farther over her sister, who cooperated by tucking herself into as small a ball as she could and huddling in her arms.

As Blake worked himself into a frenzy above them and took great delight in kicking Kassie everywhere he could reach, Kassie whispered into Karina's ear.

"There's a window above us." She grunted with the pain of Blake's foot hitting her thigh. "I'm going to distract him. There's a—" She cried out as his foot landed on her ass. "A board right behind you. Use it to break the window and dive out. It's gonna hurt, but," she barely held back the whimper that tried to force its way up her throat when Blake cackled as if he was about to do something really horrific, but pushed on without looking back at her tormentor, "it doesn't matter. Get out and run, Karina. Don't s-stop no matter what you hear. Understand?"

Kassie felt her nod under her at the same time Blake reached down and wrenched her away from her sister. His arm went around her throat and he yanked her upward.

Kassie fought with everything she had. She had to keep him busy while Karina broke the window and escaped.

"Now, Kar! Now!" Kassie yelled as she reached back and grabbed ahold of Blake's penis. She squeezed as hard as she could, thrilled when he screamed a high-pitched, painful sound that actually hurt her ears.

Kassie heard the sound of glass breaking and twisted her hand, wishing she had the strength to rip Blake's dick right off. He let go of her neck and Kassie breathed a sigh of relief, but it immediately turned to a scream when he punched her as hard as he could.

The blow landed on the side of her head and Kassie went flying. Knowing she couldn't lose consciousness now, she sprang upward and in the direction she thought Blake was. She couldn't see with blood dripping in one of her eyes and black spots in front of the other, but she managed to grab hold of his arm.

"What are you doing, bitch? No, get back here!"

Blake lunged in the direction of Karina and the window, and Kassie used all her strength to punch him in the side, right over where she hoped his kidney was. It worked, sort of. Blake doubled over in pain, but didn't go down.

Kassie looked up and saw her sister's legs kicking in the air as she tried to get leverage to lift herself the rest of the way up and out the window. Throwing herself toward Karina, Kassie grabbed her legs and shoved.

She heard a roar from Blake and gave her sister one last thrust when she felt a pain like she never had before in her back. She screamed and threw herself sideways to try to get away from whatever it was. But Blake followed her down. She felt another horrific, sharp pain in her upper back and immediately gasped for air. It felt like she was suffocating.

"She'll never get away," Blake said above her.

"You've only postponed the inevitable. She's still gonna get sold, but now I'm gonna go get her and fuck her in every hole right in front of you before the buyer gets here. And *you* did that to her, cunt. I was gonna let her go with her buyer nice and easy like, but because of your interference, she's gonna wish she was dead before he gets his hands on her and *really* makes her life hell."

Kassie couldn't get any air in her lungs, and whatever Blake had hurt her with was excruciating, but she couldn't give up. Couldn't let him get his hands on her baby sister.

With the last bit of strength she had, which Kassie knew came from adrenaline and not from anywhere else, she screamed once more and threw herself up toward Blake, twisting her body to face him as she moved. She saw his smirking face above hers for a second and she aimed right for it.

Just as she was thrusting her index finger toward his eye, an explosion rang through the small hut.

HOLLYWOOD MADE HIS way toward the hut as fast as he dared. He could hear voices from inside, but not what they were saying. He glanced over at Truck who nodded and held two fingers up then pointed to the right and left.

Hollywood nodded. It was almost time.

He knew he needed to wait for his team to be ready, but everything in him wanted to rush the hut.

Truck put a hand on his arm. "Ten seconds and they'll be in place and ready to go," he told him urgently.

Coach's voice came over the headset as he said, "Someone's coming out the back window. It's the sister."

Hollywood held his breath as time literally seemed to stand still. He saw the ramshackle hut as if he was standing at one end of a really long tunnel and the building was at the other. All his focus was centered on the front door, his entire being straining toward it.

"She's out," Coach informed them. "Fuck, she's running."

Out of the corner of his eye, Hollywood saw a small figure running full out away from the cabin. He saw Coach quickly catch up to her and take her to the ground, making sure he took the brunt of the fall.

"We need to get in there," Hollywood told his team through the headset.

"Karina's good," Coach informed them. "Banged up, but otherwise good."

Hollywood was relieved, but it didn't lessen his anxiety one iota.

Neither did the loud, terrified, pissed-off scream

from Kassie that came from inside.

"Now!" Ghost ordered, and almost simultaneously, the flash-bang grenade went off inside the shack. It had been thrown into the building from the window on one side of the hut.

Hollywood was moving even as Ghost ordered the grenade to be thrown. Used to the noise and light from the devices meant to incapacitate rather than kill or maim, he kicked the flimsy door open and stepped inside.

Blake was on the ground, one hand over his face and the other covering one of his ears. Even as Hollywood watched, he dropped the hand by his ear and reached for the knife he'd obviously dropped when the grenade went off.

Hollywood pulled the trigger on his weapon at the same time Truck did. Both bullets hit their intended marks. Truck's went into Blake's hand, forcing him to drop the knife once again, and Hollywood's into his temple.

Not caring that he'd just killed another human being, or that he'd purposely been aiming to kill, Hollywood holstered his weapon and went straight to Kassie, who lay unmoving on the ground. He went to gather her into his arms, but Truck stopped him with a firm hand.

"She could have a spinal injury, moving could paralyze her," he warned.

Hollywood grit his teeth in frustration. He landed in the dirt at her side and his hands hovered over her.

A commotion took his attention away from Kassie, and he had only a second to compute what it was and take action. Karina had tried to throw herself at her sister as she wailed in despair. Hollywood caught her and whirled her around so she didn't hurt Kassie more than she already was.

He vaguely heard Fletch calling for the chopper to move in and to put the hospital on standby. Coach was then speaking, telling Ghost and the others that Karina had said a buyer for both of them was supposed to be on his way and they needed to stay vigilant.

Beatle and Blade appeared in the small hut and knelt down next to Kassie. They began to assess her injuries. Hollywood wanted to be the one caring for her, but at the moment, Karina needed him.

He pulled back and took a quick look at Karina. She had some cuts on her arms, and a few on her legs, most likely from diving out the window, but they were superficial. He hugged her again, and she snuggled into him as if she'd known him her entire life.

"Shhhh. We're here. You're okay," he told her, keeping his eyes on his teammates and the woman who meant the world to him.

"She told me to," Karina said between sobs. "She

put herself between me and him. He was kicking and hurting her and she still was only thinking about me."

"Are you surprised?" Hollywood asked. "She loves you. So much."

Karina didn't respond, except to sob harder.

"I'm sorry, man," Blade said softly, looking at Hollywood. "It doesn't look good."

"What?" Hollywood asked, not understanding what his friend was saying.

"She's lost a lot of blood. Too much. She has a pulse but it's weak, and her hands are ice cold."

Hollywood turned to Coach and practically shoved Karina at him. He was gentle about it, but he needed to get to Kassie. There was no way she was dying. She couldn't. He couldn't have been too late.

Without waiting to make sure Karina was okay, Hollywood turned to Kassie. He picked up her hand and found that Blade wasn't lying. He was sweating with the heat in the small hut, but Kassie's hands were like ice.

Blocking out the murmurings from Blade saying how sorry he was, Hollywood reached out a shaking hand and put it to Kassie's neck. He had to swallow back the bile lodged at the back of his throat before he could speak. "She's okay," he told Blade.

"Hollywood, I know you want to believe that but—"

"Her hands are *always* cold, Blade," Hollywood told

him. "Always. I don't know why. Maybe bad circulation or something, but that's normal for her." He turned his head and looked Blade in the eyes. "Her pulse might be weak, but she's going to be okay. I know it."

As Hollywood put both hands around one of Kassie's cold ones, Blade picked up her free hand and tried to warm it, just as Hollywood was doing with the other. "Sorry man," he said. "I just couldn't imagine why else she was so cold when it's absolutely *not* chilly in here in the least."

"It's okay," Hollywood assured him quietly. "You can get her a pair of gloves for Christmas."

"It's on my list," Blade told his friend with a smile. But it quickly faded when he said, "But she *is* bleeding way too fucking much. We need to turn her over and see what that asshole did to her."

Hollywood nodded, and helped Blade turn Kassie to her side as Beatle held her neck still. Both men swore at the gaping holes in Kassie's T-shirt and the amount of blood pooled under her.

"Is she okay?" Karina asked from across the room.

Without taking his eyes from the woman he loved more than anything in the world, Hollywood said firmly, "She's going to be fine, Karina."

"But there's so much blood," the other woman insisted.

"She's strong. There's no way she went through

what she did to give in now. Right, Kass?"

After they'd turned Kassie so she was lying on her stomach, Hollywood leaned down and spoke directly in her ear as Blade took out one of his ever-present knives and sliced up the back of Kassie's T-shirt so they could see what they were dealing with.

"You kicked his ass, didn't you?" he asked, keeping one of her hands in his own while his other lay lightly on the back of her neck. "You did what you had to do, got Karina out of here while you stayed back to make sure that asshole wouldn't be a threat ever again."

He glanced over at Blake who was lying motionless feet away, and noticed the blood coming from his eye. Trying to avoid looking at her back, Hollywood leaned in once more and said, "You nailed him in the eye, didn't you? Good job. I'm proud of you, sweetheart. I—"

"Chopper's sixty seconds out," Ghost informed them all through the headphones. "Hollywood, you and Karina with Blade and Kassie. The rest of us'll stay here. We'll wait and see if anyone shows up for a meet, and take out that garbage as well."

Hollywood nodded, not taking his eyes from Kassie's face. He wanted to see some sign that she was in there. That she was fighting to come back to him.

"Two stab wounds. One looks like it punched a hole in her lung. The other looks too high to have hit anything vital, but I can't be sure," Blade informed them all.

Hollywood heard Ghost relaying the information to the medics in the chopper, but couldn't take his eyes away from the obscene tears in Kassie's flesh.

He'd promised to keep her safe, and look at her. He closed his eyes and took a deep breath. He had to get his emotions under control. He wouldn't do Kassie any good right now if he lost it.

"It'll be easier to just bundle her up and let the guys in the chopper deal with this," Blade said, even as he began to pull Kassie's T-shirt back up and over her wounds.

Hollywood felt like he was once again in a long tunnel. Everything around him was muted and he only partially heard them. All his focus was on Kassie. He stepped back, letting Blade, Beatle, and Truck pick her up, wincing when she moaned at the movement. He kept his hand on the back of her head as they walked out of the hut toward the chopper, which had landed a short distance away.

The dust was thick but Hollywood didn't even bother to try to protect his mouth. He walked crouched over, doing whatever he could to protect Kassie instead. He climbed into the helicopter and helped his teammates ease Kassie inside. The two medics in the chopper took over then, and Hollywood moved to Kassie's head once again. Blade helped Karina up and into the space and followed behind her. The teenager crab-walked over to Hollywood and her sister and snuggled into his side.

Hollywood put one arm around Karina and laid the other on the back of Kassie's head as the medics did their thing. He felt the chopper rise into the air and vaguely noted Truck asking Beatle through the headset if he thought Kassie was going to make it.

His answer made Hollywood smile for the first time in hours.

"Fuck yeah, she's going to make it. She's one of us. Made of fucking steel."

Chapter Twenty

HOLLYWOOD SAT WITH one arm around Karina in the waiting room at a hospital in San Antonio. He had no idea which hospital, but it didn't matter. Kassie was in surgery. Blade had been right. One of the knife wounds had punctured a lung, and the other, while ugly, hadn't hit any vital organs. Blake had missed her heart by merely an inch. It tore through some muscle and would be painful, but wasn't life threatening.

Hollywood had asked the doctors to check to see if Kassie had been raped as well. Karina had insisted that Blake hadn't touched her, but Kassie had been with him for a long time as he'd driven down to Laredo. He could've stopped and assaulted her along the way. Hollywood wanted the doctors to do their exam while she was unconscious and wouldn't remember it. There was no way he wanted to add more trauma to Kassie's plate if he could help it.

The doctors said as soon as they had the rest of her injuries under control, they'd do a thorough physical exam to make sure she didn't have any other issues to worry about...including determining if she'd been sexually assaulted.

At first it'd only been the three of them in the waiting room, Hollywood, Blade, and Karina. Then Rock had arrived with two other men. Then slowly but steadily, more and more people filled the room. The staff had finally relented and shown the growing group into a small conference room.

Before he knew it, there were almost two dozen people waiting to see how Kassie was doing.

"Who are all these people?" Karina whispered to Hollywood at one point after they'd said hello to everyone in subdued tones. They'd come over to say a few words to them and let them know they were praying for Kassie, but Hollywood didn't know who most of them were.

Rock overheard her question and answered, "These are some of the finest people I've ever known. Over there," he indicated to one side of the room with his chin, "are my friends from law enforcement. Daxton, Quint, Cruz, Wes, Hayden, Conor, and Calder. The redheaded female is a cop, Hayden, but the other women are girlfriends."

He turned to indicate the other side of the room. "And these are also my friends. They're firefighters. Sledge, Crash, Chief, Squirrel, Taco, Driftwood, Moose, and Tiger. Sledge's girlfriend isn't here, but Crash's is…the woman with the dog is Adeline."

"Beth's not here?" Hollywood asked. "Why? Is something else going on?"

Rock quickly shook his head. "No. She's agoraphobic…well, she was. She's working on it, but from what Sledge told me, she felt more comfortable sticking near her laptop and following the action from there, and relaying information to Tex."

Hollywood felt Karina sag against him and tightened his hold on her. "You doing okay?" he asked, even though he knew the answer. He had a hunch she was feeling much the same as he was. Overwhelmed, tired, impatient—and terrified that the doctor would enter the room and tell them Kassie hadn't made it.

He didn't know how much time had passed since she'd been taken to surgery, but it seemed like forever.

Just when Hollywood didn't think the room could get any more crowded, the door opened and Karina's parents entered, followed by Fish.

Karina leaped from the chair she'd been sitting on and ran to her mom and dad. They huddled in the doorway for a long moment before Fish took hold of Donna's elbow and steered the group to a set of chairs nearby.

Hollywood got up and went over to talk to them. He shook Fish's hand. "Thanks for bringing them down."

"I'm sorry," Fish said, not quite meeting Holly-wood's eyes.

Hollywood gripped the other man's hand hard, not letting him drop it. He waited until Fish looked at him. "Nothin' to be sorry about, Fish."

"I should'a stayed and made sure Karina got home all right."

"No. You had no reason to suspect anything. Dean was neutralized and we thought the threat was over."

"Still—"

"Fish, no," Hollywood told him fiercely. "This is not your fault."

The two men looked at each other for a long mo-ment before Fish finally nodded. Hollywood dropped his hand and looked to Kassie's parents. "She's still in surgery. We don't know a lot, but I have no doubt she's going to be fine. She's a fighter."

"You shoulda seen her, Dad," Karina said in a wob-bly voice. "From the second she entered the hut where Blake had stashed me, she took charge. S-she didn't waste any time in getting me untied and finding a w-way for me to get out."

Jim Anderson ran his hand over his daughter's hair and kissed her temple. "I bet she was a sight to see."

Karina nodded and laid her head back on her dad's shoulder.

"Thanks for calling us, son," Jim Anderson told

Hollywood. "We got the text that was supposed to be from Karina, but could both tell something was up. First, she wouldn't stay out all night, no way, and second, it didn't even sound like her. On one hand, your call didn't stop us from worrying, but on the other, at least we knew we weren't crazy and that you were doing all you could to find her. Have you heard anything new about Kassie's condition?"

Hollywood opened his mouth to tell the man who was still holding his youngest daughter tightly what he knew, but they were interrupted by a doctor standing in the doorway.

"Kassie Anderson's friends and family, I presume?" At the affirmative responses, the doctor quickly said, "She's going to be fine. The surgery went well. We repaired her punctured lung and stitched up both wounds on her back. She's going to be uncomfortable and she'll need to stay in the hospital for a while to make sure there aren't any complications.

"It looks like she took quite a beating. She's got a bruised kidney, a couple cracked ribs, and several large bruises on her back and thighs." He turned and looked directly at Hollywood, letting him know without coming right out and saying it that she hadn't been raped. "We didn't find any other serious injuries. While she's going to be in pain for several weeks, she's a very lucky woman."

Hollywood closed his eyes in relief. Her injuries were horrific, but at least she didn't have to add the mental anguish of being violated on top of everything else. He had no doubt she'd need to speak with someone about what she'd gone through...being kidnapped and almost dying would do that to a person, but he could help her deal with some of that.

"Can we see her?" Donna asked anxiously.

"She's in ICU right now," the doctor told them. "But I'll authorize two ten-minute visitations. But a maximum of two people at a time," he cautioned. "She's not going to be awake, so the best thing you can all do is go home and get some sleep. If she does well tonight, I'll see about moving her to a regular room tomorrow."

"Thank you," Kassie's mom breathed. "Can we go now?"

Hollywood wanted to protest. Wanted to insist he be the one allowed to see her, but he needed to step back and let her family reassure themselves that their daughter was going to be all right.

"Yes, if you'll follow me," the doctor told her, and turned back to the door.

Surprisingly, Donna touched Hollywood on the arm. "We'll be fast so you can get in there," she said in a soft voice.

Hollywood's eyes met Donna's and saw understanding and empathy for him, alongside the relief that her daughter was going to be fine.

"Thank you," he choked out. He couldn't have said anything else if his life depended on it.

"Stay here with Hollywood," Jim requested of Karina. "We'll be back, and then we'll go find a hotel to crash in for the night."

"Excuse me, sir?" a man said from behind them.

Everyone turned and faced the tall blond man who'd spoken.

"Yes?" Jim replied.

"My name is Conor Paxton. I'm a game warden with Texas Parks and Wildlife. I'm an acquaintance of Hollywood's...and I wanted to extend my hospitality to you and your family. I've got a house not too far from here. You are more than welcome to stay there."

"Oh, but...I don't think we could. It's not right," Donna protested weakly.

"Please," Conor encouraged. "I can take you there tonight, get you settled, and I'll spend the night at my friend TJ's house." He motioned to the former Delta Force soldier standing nearby. "It's not a palace, but I think you'd find it more comfortable than a hotel."

Donna glanced at her husband, and he looked from the man standing in front of him, to the group of people sitting around the room, then back to his wife.

"We'd appreciate that, thank you," Jim told Conor, then shook his hand.

"I'll wait here while you visit with your daughter," Conor told him. He nodded at the family and Hollywood then backed away, giving them space.

Jim reached out a hand to Hollywood, and it seemed as if everyone in the room held their breath. Slowly, Hollywood put his hand in the older man's and they shook.

"Thank you for finding my babies," Jim said softly.

"I shouldn't have let them get in that position in the first place," Hollywood told him honestly.

Jim didn't let go of his hand, and instead gripped it tighter. "Maybe. Maybe not. But what's done is done. We can't change the past, all we can do is go forward. But tell me one thing..."

"Anything," Hollywood responded immediately, knowing Kassie's dad was much more forgiving than *he* probably would be in the same situation.

"Am I going to have to worry about this happening again? Are those men done terrorizing my family?"

He opened his mouth to answer, but Fish got there first. He stepped up next to Hollywood and said firmly, "This, or anything remotely similar, will not happen again, sir. Your daughters are free to live their lives however they want, *with* whoever they want."

Jim finally dropped Hollywood's hand and narrowed his eyes at Fish. "Do I have your word on that?"

"Absolutely," Fish said without hesitation. "Richard

Jacks, Dean Jennings, and Blake Watson, and any of their friends, will *not* be an issue for your family from this day forward."

"Good." And that was that. As if Fish's word was law, the stress in Jim's face disappeared as if wiped away with an eraser. "Thank you for keeping us informed about what was going on and for driving us down here," he told Fish. "We were worried sick. Knowing you and your friends were aware of what was happening, and even where our daughters were, made the entire experience…not good, but at least better. I've always respected the men and women who fight for our country. I'm glad to know Kassie's ex was an exception rather than the norm."

"Yes, sir," Fish said. "There are assholes in every profession, including the US Armed Forces, but there's no one you can trust more than the men and women here in this room."

"If you're ready?" the doctor said from the doorway. "We should go."

Hollywood watched as Kassie's parents followed after the doctor. One of the women came over and convinced Karina to sit down with her and her friends. Hollywood wasn't sure who it was, but was just glad someone else was taking responsibility for her at the moment.

Every fiber of his being wanted to be with Kassie.

To watch her chest move up and down. To see for himself that she really was all right.

"Hey, Kass," Hollywood said softly twenty minutes later. Her parents had come back to the waiting room and had left soon thereafter with Karina and Conor.

He'd thanked everyone who had shown up to show support for Kassie and had followed the nurse up to Kassie's room. The machines around her beeped as they monitored her breathing, heart rate, and even the oxygen levels in her blood.

But he only had eyes for her. There was a large bruise around her temple, and she had a shiner forming under one eye. She was lying on her back with an IV in her arm and oxygen under her nose. It wasn't until Hollywood touched her arm that he breathed out a sigh of relief.

Warm. She was warm.

He shifted until he was holding her hand in both of his. His lips twitched. Cold. He chafed her fingers gently as he spoke. "Your sister is fine. You protected her from that asshole hurting her. She got out and ran like hell. You should've seen her. I didn't think Coach was going to be able to catch up with her."

He paused and pulled his chair as close to the bed as

he could get it. He shifted until he was near Kassie's head. He said the words he knew he'd never say when she was awake and conscious. He hadn't realized exactly how angry he was with her until right this moment. He'd been too concerned about finding her and then getting her the medical help she needed. But seeing her lying in the hospital bed, hurting, had brought it all to the surface.

"I've never been as pissed at anyone in my life when I woke up and realized you'd snuck out. You should've woken me up, sweetheart. You wouldn't be lying here if you had. My team and I are trained in this shit. We could've handled this."

He paused. The moment the words left his mouth, it was as if the anger went with them. "I hate seeing you like this. But you should know, I'm gonna help you through this. I'll be by your side every step of the way. You'll bitch at me, get sick of me babying you, and you'll wanna get back to your routine way before you're ready. But that's okay, because I'll be there to make sure you only do what you can. I love you, Kassie Anderson. I want to marry you. I want to give you as many babies as you can handle, and then a couple more. I don't want to live one more minute of my life without you in it."

She didn't even twitch.

Hollywood smiled. "Sleep, sweetheart. Heal. I'll be back in the morning and we'll get started on our life together."

He carefully tucked her hand next to her side and covered it with the blanket. He did the same to her other arm and hand, making sure not to disturb her IV. When she was tucked in to his satisfaction, Hollywood stood up and put his hand on her cheek. He leaned in and lightly kissed her dry lips. Then he rested his on her forehead and vowed, "Thank God your ex-boyfriend was an ass and blackmailed you into messaging me on that dating website."

He stood, kissed his fingers, laid them over her lips, then turned and left the room with a big smile on his face.

Chapter Twenty-One

Six weeks later

"FOR GOD'S SAKE, Hollywood, go already," Kassie bitched.

"No. You're not ready."

"I'm *fine*," Kassie told him. "It's been a month and a half. My doctor said that I could resume most of my normal activities. I love you, but I don't need you fused to my hip anymore." Her voice softened. "You need to get back to doing your job, hon. How are we going to eat if you don't have a job to earn money to feed us?"

"I don't want to leave you," Hollywood admitted.

They were standing in the kitchen in Fletch's garage apartment. Hollywood had wanted to move Kassie into his, but felt better that Fletch and Emily were only steps away if he needed help with Kassie or she needed anything when he was on the Army post working.

She'd stayed in the hospital in San Antonio for a week, then had asked to be transferred up to one in Austin. She wanted her parents and sister to get back to their normal routine, and living in Conor Paxton's house in San Antonio wasn't normal for them.

She'd spent another week recuperating and having her bandages changed at Austin Memorial. Her parents had wanted her to move in with them while she continued to heal, but Hollywood had convinced her to temporarily move to Temple while she got back to normal.

She was on sick leave from her job, and the thought of continuing to be able to see Hollywood every day was too much to resist. He'd driven down every day to see her while she was in the hospital in Austin, and she'd gotten used to him being there every time she'd woken up.

So she'd let him convince her to stay in the garage apartment, and Hollywood had essentially moved in with her.

They'd had their first fight a month after she'd been hurt when she found out from Rayne that the team was supposed to go on a mission, but Hollywood had flat out refused to leave her. Since he did, the rest of the guys had too. Their commander had not been happy, to say the least; it wasn't as though they could actually say no to orders. But Hollywood had.

Kassie had yelled, cried, and generally worked herself up, telling him he had to go. That she didn't want him to be court-martialed or demoted or whatever would happen if he didn't leave when Uncle Sam told him to go.

But Hollywood refused to budge, saying that she wasn't well enough to stay home by herself for whatever length of time they'd be gone. Luckily, clearer heads prevailed, and Ghost talked to the guy in charge of the other Delta team they'd worked with down at the refuge and they'd arranged to have them complete the mission.

But now it was two weeks later, and Kassie felt good. She wasn't one hundred percent, but she was a lot better than even two weeks ago. She could maneuver the steps leading up to the apartment with no problem, as long as she went slowly. She could even put a bra on by herself, which was a huge accomplishment in her eyes.

She put her hand on Hollywood's arm. "I'm okay. I swear."

He took a huge breath and carefully wrapped his arms around her waist, pulling her into his body. "I've spent the last forty-plus nights with you. I don't want to spend even one without you now."

"I know," she soothed, running her hands up and down his back as she laid her cheek on his chest. "But you have to."

"I don't want to," he said stubbornly.

"I know," Kassie repeated. "But you *have* to."

She felt him nuzzle the hair by her ear then he whispered, "Yeah."

"I'll be fine, Graham," Kassie told him.

"Yes, you will." Hollywood then took a step back and said, "I have something to show you."

"Okay?"

"Go sit on the couch. I'll be right back," Hollywood ordered.

She rolled her eyes, but smiled at him. Without a word, she did as he asked. He'd been especially bossy ever since she came home from the hospital, but since most of the time he ordered her to do things she wanted or needed to anyway, Kassie didn't call him on it.

It was almost as if he knew her body better than she did. He could tell when she'd overdone it and was tired, or hurting, and needed a pain pill. She would've been worried he could read her mind, but it honestly didn't bother her. It felt nice to be so cared for.

She gently eased herself to the cushion on the couch and waited for Hollywood to return.

He came back into the small living room a second later. He'd gone into the bedroom and was now carrying what looked like a letter.

He sat and held it out to her.

"What's this?"

"Read it and see," Hollywood told her. He settled into the corner of the couch and pulled her into the circle of his arms.

Kassie shifted until her back was against him. His arms went around her chest and she relaxed farther into them. They'd spent many a night sitting just like this as they watched television together or simply talked.

It had been uncomfortable for her to lay flat on her back for a long time, and they'd found that this position was the most enjoyable. She could sit up, taking the pressure off her wounds and ribs, but it also allowed her to snuggle, which was more important in her eyes.

The letter had already been opened, so she pulled out the single piece of paper and began to read.

Hollywood,

Hello from beautiful Idaho. It's so quiet sometimes it's almost eerie. I hope you and the rest of the team will come visit and help me break in the grill I bought the other day. Friends are hard to come by up here, as the state motto seems to be "leave me alone." You'd probably hate it because it's impossible to tell the difference between a simple prepper who's paranoid the world is gonna end and an actual terrorist who's planning destruction on a massive scale.

I swear I've been feeling like I've got eyes on me all the time. Not sure if it's just because I'm the newcomer, or if it's something more. Wouldn't it suck if I moved all the way out here for some peace and quiet and found myself in the middle of some underground ISIS terrorist sleeper cell, huh? But no worries, I've got Tex on speed dial and Truck calls me every fucking week to chat like a girl. You know I'll let you guys know if I need backup.

Anyway, please say hello to everyone for me. Tell Annie that I expect her parents to bring her out here to visit. I've got a huge yard and can build the biggest obstacle course she's ever seen.

I hope Kassie is healing all right. She's one tough chick and you're a lucky son of a bitch. I thought the enclosed might speed up the healing process for her. At least a little bit.

~Fish

A newspaper clipping was attached to the short letter with a paperclip. Kassie ran her eyes over it—and gasped in shock. She looked up to Hollywood with wide eyes. "Is this…is it really truly over?"

Hollywood kissed her lightly and nodded. "It's over."

Kassie read through the short article. The gist was that there had been a riot at the Leavenworth federal prison, and an inmate and two guards had been killed. The prison was currently on lock down, and no visitors were allowed in until an investigation was completed. The guards killed were suspected to have been bribed by visitors to smuggle items into and out of the prison. Phone calls had mysteriously not been recorded, as was procedure, and the government was "looking into" increased terrorist activities as a result of information that was passed from prisoners to visitors.

"Holy shit," Kassie said under her breath.

"We don't know the specifics," Hollywood told her softly, "but Fish hinted several times that he had connections with the prison. We don't know who or how, but we suspect this was his doing. He called in a marker or two and took care of it."

"He had Richard killed?" Kassie asked, wanting clarification.

Hollywood nodded.

"So it's really done," Kassie stated.

"It's really done."

She dropped the letter and article on the floor, not caring where they landed, and turned to Hollywood. He held her hips steady as she straddled him and said, "You need to get back to your life. I wish we could live here and not have to worry about jobs or anything. But we can't. We need to eat. I'm going to want to get back to work. I've already talked to my boss at home, and he said he didn't think it would be a problem to transfer me up here. They always need managers, and I'm damn good, if I do say so myself. Stop giving the commander shit and do what you do best."

"Will you be all right if I'm gone?" he asked.

"Yes," Kassie told him without hesitation. "I'll miss you. And I'll worry about you. But I'll be fine. Emily and Annie are here. And I've seen Rayne and Harley almost every other day. I've never had such good friends before. Richard somehow manipulated me into giving up my friends and alienated me from a lot of people who cared about me. It feels really good to have girl-friends again. I've got people here who will watch out for me."

"You have a doctor's appointment coming up. Will you let one of the girls take you?"

"Yes. If it would make you feel better."

"It would," he said immediately.

"Then yes. Hollywood," Kassie said firmly, "I was hurt. It sucked. But you saved me, and then nursed me back to health. I want a relationship between us to work, but in order for that to happen, we need to get back to the way we were before."

"I don't want that," Hollywood told her. He brought a hand up and palmed the side of her face. "I want the *new* us. The us that lives together. Who eat dinner together. The us who hang out with our friends and laugh until we want to puke."

"Me too," Kassie said, tilting her head, giving him her weight.

"I'm glad the other team took the previous mission, but I'll tell the commander I'm in this time," Holly-wood said.

"Good. And you should know, I'm going to ask the doctor about his thoughts on when he thinks I'll be able to have sex."

"You're not ready," Hollywood protested.

"I knew you were going to say that," Kassie said with a laugh. "And I'm not. Not today. But I will be. Soon. I love you, Hollywood. I wasn't even able to *think* about being intimate with you until recently. But I want it. I want you. I want all of you."

Hollywood's fingers tightened on Kassie's hips, but he immediately gentled his hold. "I love you so much, Kass," he said softly. "I didn't know I could care about anything or anyone as much as I do you. Yes, I want to make love to you, but I'm more terrified of hurting you."

"I won't let you."

"You better not," he growled. Then he sighed and said, "We leave tomorrow afternoon."

Kassie flinched, but quickly controlled it. "Good. We can snuggle tonight, then tomorrow you can go and kick some ass."

He smiled, but Kassie could tell it was forced.

"You gotta get back on the horse, Hollywood," she chided. "I probably won't even know you're gone."

They both knew she was lying, but he let it go. "I'm proud of you, Kass. You've been through hell, but you don't let on how much it's taken out of you. I've watched you talk to your sister for hours, then call your mom to let her know what's up with her other daughter so she can keep an eye out. Then immediately welcome Annie up here and listen to her chatter on for hours about nothing. Please…take care of yourself while I'm gone. I won't be here to send Annie home. Or tell you to take a pain pill. Or cut you off when you want to talk to your mom for hours."

"I will. I promise. Do you know how long you'll be gone?"

Hollywood scrunched up his nose and shook his head. "It could be a day, or it could be weeks. It all depends."

"Well, don't *you* get yourself hurt. The last thing we need is both of us injured. It would suck to get the all clear to finally be able to have sex, only to have *you* benched."

Hollywood laughed. "I won't."

"Love you," Kassie told him, folding herself down onto his chest.

He immediately wrapped his arms around her and said, "Love you too, Kass."

She closed her eyes and soaked up the love she could feel emanating from the man under her.

Two weeks later

HOLLYWOOD OPENED THE door to the garage apartment and slipped inside. He'd been gone a hell of a lot longer than he thought he would be, but their missions were sometimes like that. It wasn't as though a terrorist would jump up and say "Here I am!" when they were trying to elude the good guys.

The apartment was quiet as he put his duffle bag down, and Hollywood headed for the bedroom. He needed to hold Kassie in his arms and see for himself that she was all right.

He opened the door to the single bedroom and stared in disbelief. The bed was empty. It was made as if no one had slept there for days.

Just as he began to panic, his phone softly dinged with a text.

Fletch: *She's over here*

Sighing in relief, Hollywood spun and headed back to the front door. He had no idea why Kassie was over in the big house, but it didn't matter. Maybe she was lonely. Maybe she was worried about him and Emily was giving her moral support. Maybe *Emily* was worried and Kass was giving *her* moral support. Whatever. He didn't care. If she was happy and healthy, it didn't matter what bed she slept in, as long as he could be there with her.

Fletch was waiting for him at the front door as he quickly strode across the lawn. As soon as he was inside, Fletch closed it and reset the alarm. He pointed down the hall toward one of the guest rooms. Hollywood gave his friend a chin lift and headed that way.

He cracked open the door and the light from the hall illuminated Kassie, sound asleep in the queen-size bed. Hollywood shut the door silently and took off his T-shirt and jeans. Wearing nothing but his boxers, he slipped under the covers behind Kassie and snuggled up against her. He threw an arm over her waist and gently kissed her shoulder before lying his head down on the pillow next to her.

She didn't wake up, but did shift until her ass was pressed more firmly against him. Hollywood felt his cock stir, but was too tired to get a true hard-on. For the first time in two weeks, he relaxed completely. All was right in his world again.

One month later

KASSIE STOOD BEFORE Hollywood completely naked. Over the last two weeks, they'd slowly begun to introduce intimacy back into their relationship. They'd started with making out on the couch. Then they'd rounded the bases, second, then third. Two days ago they'd showered together, and Hollywood had held her in his arms while he'd used the portable showerhead to make her come harder than she ever had before in her life. Then she'd gone to her knees and showed him her appreciation.

Last night they'd taken a long hot bath together.

When she'd started stroking him, he'd moved them to the bed and eaten her to another out-of-this-world orgasm, then let her give him a hand job until he came.

But tonight she was determined to have Hollywood inside her. She felt great. The doctor had said she could do whatever she wanted, as long as it didn't hurt. Her ribs were healed. The wounds on her back were now ugly scars, but she was alive, so she didn't give a shit about them.

She wanted Hollywood. Bad.

He'd grilled steaks for dinner over at Fletch's and they'd excused themselves after Annie showed them the new moves she'd learned in her Taekwondo class.

She'd barely shut the door when Hollywood had his hands under her shirt and was lifting it over her head. Kassie wanted to shout in glee, but refrained.

Now they were here. She was standing by their bed as he pushed his jeans and underwear down his legs. She inhaled.

"I'll never get over how beautiful you are," she told him, her hands coming up to caress his chest.

He caught her wrists in his and tsked. "If you think I'm going to let you touch me with those ice-cold fingers of yours before I've had a chance to warm them up, you're crazy."

She smiled and shifted closer to him. She moved her hands behind her, and his arms followed as he hadn't let go of her wrists. She brushed her nipples against his slightly furred chest and gasped at the sensation. She closed her eyes and did it again, feeling her nipples bead even tighter.

"You're the beautiful one, Kass," Hollywood said softly. She looked up into his eyes and saw nothing but love.

"Make love to me, Graham."

"With pleasure."

The next hour was spent in the most sexual bliss Kassie had ever experienced. Her entire being was consumed by Hollywood. He took his time, learning every inch of her body. Finding out what she liked and what turned her on. He made her come with his fingers, then did it again with his tongue. Then he let her have a chance to get to know his own body.

Finally, when neither of them could take the teasing, Hollywood rolled on a condom and knelt over Kassie.

Spreading her legs with his own, he propped himself up with one hand by her hip, the other around his cock. He pressed in until just the head was inside her then stopped.

"More, Graham," Kassie pleaded.

"Look at me," Hollywood ordered.

She looked up into his eyes as one hand pressed on his ass, trying to get him closer, and the other gripped the sheet next to her hip.

"I love you," he stated simply.

"I love you too," Kassie returned.

"Tell me you'll marry me and let me give you those babies you've been longing for."

It wasn't a question, but Kassie gave him what he wanted to hear. "Yes. Absolutely."

"At least three."

"What?" Kassie asked, trying to lift her hips to get him to move, but he merely shifted backwards, not giving her what she needed.

"Three kids. I don't care what sex."

"Whatever you want," Kassie breathed.

"Whatever I want?" he asked, and moved in another inch.

Arching her back in ecstasy, Kassie nodded.

"I want you to be happy, Kassie. That's what I want. Three kids, twelve, it doesn't matter. If you want to move to Alaska and live off the land, that's what we'll do. If you want to quit your job and be a full-time mom, that's what you'll do. If you want to keep working, we'll figure that out too. I can live anywhere, do anything, be anything, as long as I know you're content and living the life you've longed to for the last decade."

"Graham," Kassie moaned. "That's sweet. But what I long for right now is for you to fuck me."

He smirked then said, "Your wish is my command," and sank into her until he couldn't go any farther.

Kassie sighed in relief and tilted her hips up. "It's so much better than I dreamed."

"Me too, sweetheart. Me too," Hollywood agreed.

"Now…make me yours, hon," Kassie ordered.

"Now who's bossy?" Hollywood joked, still smiling.

Kassie squeezed her inner muscles as hard as she could and watched as Hollywood's grin faded.

"You're not playing fair," he complained as he pulled out, then pushed back into her.

"Life's not fair," Kassie told him. "Faster. I need more."

Hollywood obviously decided that he was done talking, because he immediately concentrated on making love to Kassie. He started out slow and smooth, making sure she was truly ready for him and he wasn't hurting her. Then he sped up his thrusts, his eyes on Kassie's breasts as they bounced up and down with his rhythmic movements.

When Kassie knew she was close, she looked him in the eye and said, "Hard, Graham. Fuck me hard. You won't hurt me. I've never felt anything so amazing in all my life."

Taking her at her word, Hollywood let loose the control he'd been exerting over himself and pounded into her. The slapping noises as their skin came in contact were loud and almost obscene in the quiet room. Kassie arched her back and moved one hand down to where they were coming together.

She caressed Hollywood's cock as it slid in and out of her, and, using her own juices as lubrication, brought her finger to her clit. She frantically began to rub herself even as her head went back and she moaned.

Kassie felt Hollywood shift her but couldn't focus on what he was doing as she was hurtling over the edge. Her orgasm moved through her and she shuttered and twitched in his grasp.

"Look at me, Kass," Hollywood ordered.

Her eyes went to his and she gasped at what she saw. He was beautiful. Absolutely beautiful. Every muscle in his body was taut and a vein in his forehead was clearly visible as he said between clenched teeth, "Best thing I ever did was respond to your message. I've got the world right here in my bed and I haven't ever been happier."

Then his eyes closed into slits and he thrust once more inside her and stilled as he came.

Kassie trembled in the aftermath of her own orgasm and watched lazily as Hollywood came back to himself. He smiled and closed his eyes for a long moment. Then he moved, turning onto his back and holding Kassie's hips to his own as he did.

Kassie snuggled into him and it took several moments for both their breaths to even out.

"I didn't hurt you, did I?" Hollywood asked softly.

"Not even close," Kassie said firmly.

"Good. Because it seems as if my girl likes it a bit rough."

Kassie tried not to blush, but knew she failed. "I never did before."

"It must be my magic cock," Hollywood told her.

She giggled. "Does it shoot glitter when you come?" she asked.

He chuckled. "Not that I know of."

They lay there for a moment longer. Kassie moved her nose until it ran along the bottom of his jaw. She inhaled and sighed in contentment before asking, "Twelve kids?"

"Or so."

She shook her head. "Let's start with two or three and go from there."

"Deal."

Kassie bit her lip, then tentatively asked, "Hollywood?"

"Yeah, sweetheart?"

"I want kids. And I wouldn't mind having them sooner rather than later, but my parents are kinda old fashioned. The only reason they haven't said anything about you practically living with me is because I was hurt. But—"

"Not going to get you pregnant until you've got my ring on your finger, sweetheart."

"Oh...okay. Good. 'Cause my dad would lose his

ever-loving mind if I told him he was going to be a grandfather before he got to walk me down the aisle."

"My parents have a beach house in North Carolina," he told her weirdly.

"Yeah?" Kassie asked, lifting her head so she could see his face.

"It's beautiful."

"I bet."

"I've always imagined getting married by the ocean. Bare feet. The wind blowing my bride's hair. A simple white dress."

Kassie's eyes filled with tears as she pictured their wedding in her mind.

"I know it's a long way from here, and logistics would be a bitch, but my sister would love to help, as would my mom. We could fly your folks and Karina out and have a simple family affair."

"Don't you want to invite your friends?" Kassie asked. "I'd kinda like for Rayne, Emily and the others to be there."

"If you want them there, I'll absolutely invite them. But don't be surprised if they're all hyper alert the whole time. After the experience at Emily and Fletch's wedding they'll probably be a bit wary."

Kassie heard all about the four armed men who thought it'd be a good idea to rob the wedding reception, having no idea that the guests included some of the deadliest men in the world.

"I can't blame them. Do you think we could have a casual party here afterwards so everyone who can't make it out can get together?"

"Absolutely."

Kassie was quiet for a second, then she asked, "Did we just plan our wedding?"

"Yup."

"Did you even ask me to marry you?"

"Doesn't matter."

"It doesn't matter?" Kassie asked incredulously, pushing up to her elbows, ignoring Hollywood's grimace as they dug into his chest.

Without a word, Hollywood carefully flipped them until Kassie was on her back under him, and he held her hands above her head in his strong grip. "Kassie Anderson, will you make me the happiest man on the planet and marry me? Let me give you babies to spoil and love? Let me make your life easier and keep you safe for as long as we both shall live?"

"Well, since you put it that way…yes."

"I love you," Hollywood whispered as he leaned toward her.

"I love you too," Kassie returned.

Twenty minutes later, they celebrated their engagement with mutual orgasms.

Three months later

"SHE'S BEAUTIFUL," DIANE Caverly told her son as they stood near the makeshift dance floor on the beach.

Kassie was dancing with her father. They were swaying back and forth. Her feet were bare and her calf-length dress swished around her as she moved with her dad. The dress was sleeveless and had a scoop neck in front and back. She'd been concerned that one of the scars on her back was visible because of the neckline, but when she'd called Hollywood to ask if he thought it would be okay, he'd reassured her that he didn't give a shit about her scars, and as far as he was concerned, she could show them both off because they meant that she'd survived the worst life had tried to throw at her, and was standing taller and stronger as a result.

"She is," Hollywood agreed.

"Happy for you," his mom told him.

"I know you are."

"Thank you for giving this to us."

He knew she meant the beach wedding, but what she didn't realize was that he'd done it as much for him and Kassie as for his own family.

"You're welcome," he said simply.

"You look good," she told him. "Happy."

"I *am* happy."

"That's all a mother could ask for," Diane told her son, beaming.

The song changed from a slow and sappy tune, to an upbeat, cheesy eighties song. Emily, Rayne, Harley, and Kassie were hooting, hollering, and dancing like lunatics. Glancing at his friends, Hollywood saw Fletch, Ghost, and Coach lovingly shaking their heads at the spectacle.

Hollywood beamed when he looked at his wife and saw her grinning and crooking her finger at him. He immediately strode toward her, memorizing the feel of the soft sand beneath his feet and the wind blowing through his hair.

Ignoring his friends who had similarly claimed their own women, when he got close, Hollywood grabbed her finger and pulled her into him. Kassie grinned up at him.

"Your hands are cold."

"What are you going to do about it?" she taunted.

He brought them up to his mouth and blew on her fingers, then rubbed them between his own. Then he informed her of what he'd been thinking about since the moment he saw her walk toward him on the beach.

"In about an hour, when it's acceptable for us to leave our own wedding reception, I'm going to carry you across the threshold of our hotel room, eat you to your first orgasm, then fuck you bareback for the first time, filling you to the brim with my come. Then *you're* going to fuck *me* until we both lose our minds."

"I can't wait to get pregnant," Kassie whispered as they danced to the fast beat as if it was their first dance all over again.

"I've never had sex without a condom," Hollywood informed her. "I've never seen my come dripping out of a woman before. I can't wait to experience that with you."

She wrinkled her nose at him. "Uh…hate to break it to you, Romeo, but that's not sexy."

"The fuck it's not," Hollywood retorted. "Every drop of my come that leaks out of you could have been the one carrying the sperm that wiggled its way into your unprotected womb. That's sexy as fuck."

Kassie rolled her eyes at him. "Whatever. If you like it so much, then you can be the one who cleans it up when we have sex."

"Deal," Hollywood said immediately.

"What? No, Hollywood, I was kidding. I—"

"No take backs," he said immediately. "It's now my job to make sure you're clean and happy after we make love. I'll have to inspect you up close and personal every time to make sure I did a good job."

Kassie punched him on the arm. "Stop it. Our parents are here."

Hollywood didn't say anything, but merely grinned down at her.

Finally, she gave up her snit, and melted back into

him.

As the music continued to play around them, and their families chatted and laughed together, Hollywood glanced up at the dark sky and thanked his lucky stars for his life.

Five weeks later

KASSIE SAT ON the bed and drummed her fingers nervously against her thigh.

Hollywood took hold of her hand in his and squeezed gently. "Relax, Kass."

"I can't. How long's it been?"

"About thirty seconds," Hollywood told her with a grin.

"Jeez," Kassie moaned. "This is so stressful."

Hollywood flat-out laughed at that. "I think you'll survive the next two and a half minutes," he replied dryly. "Kass," he said seriously, "look at me."

She brought her eyes up to his.

"Relax. This is not the end of the world."

"I know. But I really, really, really want it to be positive."

"Me too. But if it's not, no big deal."

"Okay."

"Okay."

Kassie tried not to fidget as she waited for the next couple of minutes to go by. Finally, Hollywood said,

"It's time."

She leaped up and ran toward the bathroom. It was stupid to leave the test in there and wait in the other room, but since her mom always used the phrase "A watched pot never boils," she thought it probably applied in this case too.

Knowing Hollywood was right on her heels, she went straight to the sink and looked down. Not sure she was seeing right, she blinked, then her entire body sagged. Every muscle went lax as she stared down at the little stick she'd peed on not five minutes earlier.

"Kass?" Hollywood asked.

She picked up the pregnancy test and held it up so he could see it as she turned and showed it to him.

"Positive," she whispered.

Hollywood grinned. Huge. "Hey, Mamma," he said softly.

"Hey, Daddy," she returned.

Then she was in his arms as they both laughed in absolute delight.

"Those are some pretty awesome swimmers you got there," Kassie teased.

"Nah, it was your fertile womb," he countered.

"I don't think this bodes well for the future," she said when he'd stopped spinning her around.

"In what way?"

"I got pregnant the second you stopped using condoms. If you weren't serious about those twelve kids, we'll need to be careful."

"I was only half kidding," Hollywood told her carefully.

Kassie knew she was grinning like a lunatic, but couldn't stop. All her life she'd wanted to be a mother. Getting to know Annie, and seeing how wonderful the little girl was, just solidified it all the more. Oh, she wasn't an idiot, she knew parenthood wasn't all giggles and hugs, but she couldn't wait to experience it for herself.

"We'll play it by ear," she told her husband.

"Awesome. When can we tell the others?" he asked.

Kassie's smile fell and she scrunched up her nose. "We should wait at least another two months or so. After the baby is twelve weeks old, it has a better chance of making it all the way."

"Then we'll wait," Hollywood said easily.

Kassie tilted her head at him. "*Can* you wait? I'm not sure you can keep a secret from your buddies."

"Me?" he asked, his eyebrows raised in mock affront. "I belong to the most top-secret team of badass soldiers this country has. Of course I can keep a secret!"

"We'll see," she drawled, then hugged him again. "I'm so excited."

"Me too, sweetheart. I think this calls for a celebration."

Kassie smiled as Hollywood led her out of the bathroom and into the master bedroom toward their bed. It was huge, and had a massive headboard and footboard. It had been the first piece of furniture they'd bought together after their wedding and moving into their new house.

As Hollywood showed her how happy he was that she was pregnant with his child, Kassie could only think to herself how thankful she was for her wonderful life.

One week later

IT WAS LATE, as usual. Very late, or early. Dane "Fish" Munroe walked around the grocery store gathering the food he'd need for the week. He wasn't much of a cook, but had a grill and a microwave...he wouldn't starve. He'd begun to shop late in the evening because there were less people around. It wasn't as if Rathdrum was a hopping metropolis anyway, but ever since he'd moved to Idaho, his ability to be around people had diminished.

He hated that he was letting what had happened to him and his team affect him. But it was. Not only that, but he was getting as paranoid as many of the people who lived in the area. He wasn't building a bunker in his backyard yet, but he'd begun to think he was being followed. Fish felt eyes on him all the time, especially here in the grocery store.

Looking around, Fish didn't see anyone, but the feeling didn't go away. He completed his shopping as fast as he could and hurried out to his truck. He hated being paranoid, but he'd never been wrong about the shit hitting the fan when the hairs on the back of his neck stood up.

Watching in his rearview mirror as he pulled out of the parking lot, Dane saw nothing unusual. No one followed him and he didn't see another soul all the way home. Trying to shake off the feeling that his life was about to change, Dane decided as he entered his house that he needed to be extra vigilant. He'd made enemies over the course of his Army career. He knew Truck and his team would have his back if needed, and could get to Idaho in a matter of hours, but he'd have to stay alive so they'd have a chance to get to him.

As he fell asleep that night, Dane wondered for the first time if moving to Idaho was a bad idea. He felt lost with no purpose. After being medically retired, he'd realized that much of who he was had been tied up with being a Delta Force soldier. Protecting others. Now he had no one to protect. He didn't have anyone's back. He was truly alone, in more ways than one. And he hated it.

BACK AT THE grocery store, unknown to Dane, a pair of eyes *had* been watching him. Just as they did every time he came into town. The woman was curious about him. Very curious. She could tell simply by looking at him that he didn't belong there. He was too…large…for this little part of the world. She could tell with one glance that he was someone special. Destined for great things. Yet here he was.

The woman was small. Very small. Short enough that anyone who saw her would dismiss her as any kind of threat, rightly so. And plain. She blended in with the people in the small town, which was her goal. Her brown hair was nothing extraordinary and the clothes she wore were made for comfort and durability rather than drawing attention to herself.

She'd seen him one night, and he'd immediately piqued her interest. She'd started following him. Learning as much as she could…from a distance. The desire to get to know him, to find out everything about him, was eating at her.

Bryn Hartwell was a genius. An honest-to-God one. She'd come to this small town in the middle of nowhere for a reason. She figured the man at the store had too. She'd keep her eye on him. Watch him. Have his back. Maybe eventually she'd get the courage to approach and say hello. Maybe.

She stood by the large glass window of the grocery

store for several minutes after his truck pulled out of the parking lot. Where was he going? Did he have someone waiting for him at home? What was his name?

Shaking her head, Bryn mentally scolded herself. He wouldn't want to get to know a weirdo like her. No one did.

Look for the next book in the *Delta Force Heroes* Series, *Rescuing Bryn*.

To sign up for Susan's Newsletter go to:
http://bit.ly/SusanStokerNewsletter

Or text: STOKER to 24587 for text alerts on your mobile device

Discover other titles by Susan Stoker

<u>Delta Force Heroes</u>

Rescuing Rayne

Assisting Aimee – Loosely related to Delta Force

Rescuing Emily

Rescuing Harley

Marrying Emily

Rescuing Kassie

Rescuing Bryn (Nov 2017)

Rescuing Casey (TBA)

Rescuing Wendy (TBA)

Rescuing Mary (TBA)

<u>Badge of Honor: Texas Heroes</u>

Justice for Mackenzie

Justice for Mickie

Justice for Corrie

Justice for Laine

Shelter for Elizabeth

Justice for Boone

Shelter for Adeline

Shelter for Sophie (Aug 2017)

Justice for Erin (Nov 2017)

Justice for Milena (TBA)

Shelter for Blythe (TBA)

Justice for Hope (TBA)

Shelter for Quinn (TBA)

Shelter for Koren (TBA)
Shelter for Penelope (TBA)

SEAL of Protection
Protecting Caroline
Protecting Alabama
Protecting Fiona
Marrying Caroline
Protecting Summer
Protecting Cheyenne
Protecting Jessyka
Protecting Julie
Protecting Melody
Protecting the Future
Protecting Alabama's Kids
Protecting Kiera (June 2017)
Protecting Dakota (Sept 2017)

Ace Security
Claiming Grace (Mar 2017)
Claiming Alexis (July 2017)
Claiming Bailey (Dec 2017)

Beyond Reality
Outback Hearts
Flaming Hearts
Frozen Hearts

Connect with Susan Online

Susan's Facebook Profile and Page:
www.facebook.com/authorsstoker
www.facebook.com/authorsusanstoker

Follow Susan on Twitter:
www.twitter.com/Susan_Stoker

Find Susan's Books on Goodreads:
www.goodreads.com/SusanStoker

Email: Susan@StokerAces.com

Website: www.StokerAces.com

To sign up for Susan's Newsletter go to:
http://bit.ly/SusanStokerNewsletter

Or text: STOKER to 24587 for text alerts on your
mobile device

About the Author

New York Times, USA Today, and *Wall Street Journal* Bestselling Author Susan Stoker has a heart as big as the state of Texas, where she lives, but this all-American girl has also spent the last fourteen years living in Missouri, California, Colorado, and Indiana. She's married to a retired Army man who now gets to follow *her* around the country.

She debuted her first series in 2014 and quickly followed that up with the SEAL of Protection Series, which solidified her love of writing and creating stories readers can get lost in.

If you enjoyed this book, or any book, please consider leaving a review. It's appreciated by authors more than you'll know.